DARK
METROPOLIS

DARK METROPOLIS

JACLYN DOLAMORE

HYPERION
LOS ANGELES   NEW YORK

First Edition
10 9 8 7 6 5 4 3 2 1
G475-5664-5-14091
Printed in the United States of America

Library of Congress Cataloging-in-Publication Data
Dolamore, Jaclyn.
Dark metropolis/Jaclyn Dolamore.
pages cm
Summary: Sixteen-year-old Thea's mother is sinking deeper into mental illness
since her husband was reported missing, presumed dead, during the war, but it is
the disappearance of Thea's best friend, Nan, that allies her with Freddy, whose
magical abilities are connected with the sinister city's darkest secrets.
ISBN 978 1-4231-6332-9 (hardback)
[1. Magic—Fiction. 2. Mothers and daughters—Fiction. 3. Mental illness—
Fiction. 4. Marriage—Fiction. 5. Revolutionaries—Fiction.] I. Title.
PZ7.D6975Dar 2014
[Fic]—dc23   2013040303

Reinforced binding
Visit www.hyperionteens.com

To Jenn Laughran,
without whose enthusiasm this book might not exist

DARK
METROPOLIS

⊙NE

"I'm glad you girls are all here; by the looks of the crowd outside we'll be busy, even for a Saturday." Mr. Kortig raked his hand through his hair. "Lottie—I'd like you in the front. Nan, the private rooms. Thea, the balcony."

Who would Thea serve tonight? Any night at the Telephone Club held the prospect of a glamorous customer or an unexpectedly generous tip, and the balconies were among the most exclusive real estate in the room.

The hostesses had ushered in the first wave of customers, filling chairs with every sort of notable the city had to offer, from jewelry-bedecked socialites to political radicals. Thea always hoped to see the actresses. She rarely had time to go to the cinema, but she read about their parties and love affairs in the papers. Today a slim, younger man looked down from the left balcony above the Telephone Club's bright stage, where women dressed as planets swung from ropes. His hair glinted in the dim light. The color was odd, almost silver.

It *was* silver, Thea saw when she had climbed the stairs and passed through the curtain. How odd for a boy who looked close to her own age. He was accompanied by the sort of man who would play "Father" in the pictures—friendly eyes balanced by a severe and graying mustache, conservative suit on a tall but somewhat frail build. She smiled at him, but she kept looking at the silver-haired boy, who was still at the railing.

"Hi, boys," she said—older men liked being lumped in with their sons. "Can I get you something?"

The boy glanced at her over his shoulder. "What is going on with this show?"

"Is something wrong?" She stepped beside him. Onstage, a woman in a metallic lunar-themed costume was facing a man representing the sun, his gold lamé suit no less dazzling. Her stocking-clad legs moved furiously, her hands on her hips, eyes challenging, smile plastered on. Not to be outdone, the man came forward, legs like liquid as he kicked this way and that, swinging a cane.

"Are the moon and the sun actually having a dance-off?" the boy asked.

"Of course," Thea said. She saw what he was getting at now. Insulting the show. Thinking it silly. One of those more-intellectual-than-thou types. "They aren't giving a science lesson, anyway." She looked to the older man again, to let him know he was free to step in with a drink request anytime.

"Let me guess," the boy said. "When the moon wins, night comes, and in the morning the tables turn once again."

"That is the idea."

"*Kind of* a science lesson, then."

"Just wait until the spelling portion."

"Hmm." His lips quirked. "And what do you spell?"

4

"T-R-O-U-B-L-E," she said, which was ridiculous: once she left the club, she was the very opposite of trouble, but that was what made the job fun—the nightly illusion that this was her real world, this flirting and joking with wealthy clientele.

He laughed. "Well, I'm F-R-E-D-D-Y," he said. "Freddy Linden. Your parents must have been interesting people to give you a name like Trouble."

"Freddy, is it? More like C-H-E-E-K-Y." She pretended to rap his knuckles, touching him only lightly.

But something happened when her skin brushed his. The lights and the music of the club faded into the distance, while a dreamlike vision filled her head.

Eight years ago, she saw her father for the last time, when he'd been called up to fight in the war and she and her mother had said good-bye at the train station. After that, she'd had only letters. She never saw his body. The very moment he was dying alone, she might have been at school, laughing with her friends, blissfully unaware—until the telegram came. *Missing, presumed dead,* in the bloody Battle of Vonn.

She saw his body now.

He was laid out on a table, wearing his army uniform, which was dark with drying blood, his face pale and slack. At the touch of a slender hand, his eyes opened slowly. He was exactly as she remembered him, only she hadn't realized until now just how young he was when he died. . . .

"Miss?" The older man's voice tore into the vision. "What happened, lad?"

"Nothing, Gerik. She's fine." Freddy drew his hand away from her, but her skin felt electric where they had touched. She shook her fingers and looked toward the row of dancers on the stage.

"Miss?" the older man repeated. "Are you all right?"

"Y-yes," she said, her head fuzzy.

"Looking out over that balcony can be dizzying," Freddy said. He had taken a step back from her. She wondered if he had seen her vision, too.

What had just happened? Why had she seen her father? It might have been a vision of his death, with all the blood, but his eyes had opened.

"Do you need to sit down?" Freddy asked, motioning to the chair.

"No." How embarrassing to have some kind of spell in the middle of lighthearted banter. "I think I'd better bring you a round, already. You might not think the show is silly after a Milky Way Twist."

"What's in it?" Freddy asked, slowly taking the seat he'd tried to offer her.

"I couldn't tell you if I wanted to. Confidential information."

"We'll try it," Gerik said, "and make them strong."

"Make *one* strong," Freddy said, frowning slightly.

"But which one? That'll be the fun," she said, collecting their menus.

"Also some of your knuckle of pork and meatballs with capers, please," Freddy added.

Thea gladly turned away and rushed back down the stairs, cheeks hot. She was fine, surely—she had recovered, and they'd forget all about it with a few drinks. But she couldn't imagine what the vision had meant. It had been so clear in that brief moment—the drying blood, the details of her father's uniform, the clarity of his features.

Mother always insisted he was still alive, but Thea knew that couldn't be.

She wanted to tell Nan, only it wasn't something she could talk about while dashing back and forth at the club. Mother had been so absentminded lately that Thea didn't even dare to have coffee with her best friend after work. Maybe tonight she could spare an hour. . . .

Of course, Nan wasn't the type to mince words. She might simply say what Thea didn't want to consider: *Could you have bound-sickness, too?* Just the thought made her feel dizzy again, so she did her best to chase it from her mind. She put in the food order to the kitchen, came back for the Milky Way Twists, and was up the stairs again, the tray balanced on one hand.

"That girl is a rustic," she heard Freddy say before she brushed back into the balcony.

A rustic. No one said that as a compliment, especially after the war. It suggested dirty peasants, immigrants from Irminau, and even witches. In school, where everyone knew her Irminauer last name, people sneered at her. But the Telephone Club was the kind of place where your origin didn't matter; pretty girls of every stripe worked there, and she was offended that he assumed he knew her background—even if he was right.

"And I like her," Freddy continued. "Didn't you say this was my night?"

"You're right, lad. I'll stay out of your way."

Stay out of his way for what? She didn't go out with boys after work, if that was what he hoped for.

She shoved the curtain aside, trying to look cheerful, but between the embarrassment of her vision and having been called a rustic, it was almost too much. "Here are your drinks."

Freddy didn't reach for the drink when she put it down. His hands were in his lap, well away from hers, and she wondered again if he had seen the strange vision, too. He was certainly strange enough himself. His silver hair reminded her of the color plate of the young sorcerer in her book of fairy tales. Freddy's eyes were gray, with a hint of shadow beneath them. She almost might have thought him a rustic, too, only Gerik was obviously old money. It didn't make sense.

"You've grown awfully quiet, Trouble," Freddy said. "Something on your mind?"

"My thoughts aren't available on tonight's menu." She raised her brows, trying to make a joke of it. "But your food is almost ready. I'll be back in a moment."

Nan crossed paths with her by the kitchens. "I see you're serving Gerik Valkenrath," she said. "We don't see the chancellor's circle in here often."

"Valkenrath?" Thea glanced at the balcony. "I wouldn't recognize him." Nan was much more interested in politics than she was.

"He's been in government even since the imperial days. The revolutionary papers are always talking about all the terrible things he's involved in."

"He's here with a boy. . . ." She hesitated, torn between wanting to mention Freddy and the vision and wanting to pretend it never happened. "I don't think they're related, because he called Gerik by his name, so I'm not sure who he is. His hair is silver."

"How mysterious. Meanwhile, I've got Helene Lapp, and she's awful, asking for drinks I've never heard of, wanting the veal and cream sauce without the cream sauce, then complaining that it tastes dry."

"Helene Lapp the actress?"

"Who else?"

"Did she bring her tiger?" Thea had just read about the pet tiger in the society pages.

"I don't think the club would let a tiger in, even to the private rooms," Nan said. "And she's doing a good job of tearing me to shreds all on her own. I'd better get this to her while it's still hot enough to burn her mouth."

Thea brought Freddy and Gerik their food, but they didn't say much more, and now the rest of the balcony seats were filling up, so she couldn't linger. Anyway, she wasn't sure what else she expected to happen. The vision had come and gone.

Before he left, Freddy said he hoped to see her next time, but that might not mean a thing. The rest of her shift seemed to go on and on, but at least she was kept too busy to worry much over what had happened.

"How did it turn out with Helene Lapp?" she asked Nan at the end of the night.

Nan waved a few bills. "Not bad after all. Before she left, she said she wanted to put me in her pocket and take me home. I guess I should take that as a compliment."

"You probably had a dangerous look in your eyes when she

was complaining about the veal, and it reminded her of her pet tiger."

Nan laughed as she tugged her hat on; it was one of the new styles that bared the forehead.

"That's a lovely new hat," Thea said. "I'm sorry I haven't gone out shopping in so long."

"Don't worry about it; I can fend for myself," Nan said. "Is the color all right? They told me it was dark blue."

"Yes, and it's perfect on you." Some time ago, Nan had confessed that she couldn't actually see colors and asked if Thea might like to help her shop. Thea always felt less guilty leaving Mother for a shopping trip with Nan, telling herself it was for a noble purpose. But it was also fun. Nan made her own clothes—gorgeous dresses with cunning details like cape collars and appliqués. Sometimes she talked of having a dress shop and making Thea the fabric buyer.

Nan handed her one of her bills. "Cheer up and take care of yourself. Buy some bonbons the next time you get groceries."

Thea didn't dare try to give the money back. That never went anywhere with Nan. So she just thanked her and then set off down the dark and lonely streets to get home before her mother woke up.

T⊠⊙

Freddy was used to being woken at the crack of dawn, but not after a night like last night, with drinks and loud music and flirtation—and that touch. He had slept poorly, remembering both the dead man in his military uniform and the look of shock on the waitress's face, as if she'd seen a ghost.

"You look tired, lad," Gerik noted after breakfast, leading Freddy into the workroom, where a single fresh corpse rested on the table. "But you'll be happy to know it's just one today."

"I'm not that tired." Freddy didn't want Gerik to think he couldn't handle a night out. He nodded to the door, dismissing the older man, and pushed up his sleeves as he appraised the body.

She was young, younger than they usually were, eighteen at most. Attractive in a modern way that was more interesting than lovely. Her hair was shingled close to her head, enhancing the lines of her cheekbones. Her lips were narrow and still had lipstick on them. Her body was narrow, too, dressed in a gray wool coat.

There were no marks on her body, so she must have taken poison or pills. Gerik said it was no use wondering about people Freddy would never see again. But he had to wonder anyway.

And he remembered them. He felt he had a connection with each one, like an invisible thread. He never forgot the face of a person he'd revived, even though the bodies were countless by now.

He placed his hands over hers, surrendering to the magic, letting a stream of life flow from his hands and into hers, tingling all the way down to his feet before the sensation passed. It always left him slightly dizzy, and today it seemed especially potent, shuddering through him so that he had to adjust his feet to stay balanced. It worked through him, and with him, but it was greater than him, too. The girl's cold fingers warmed.

He smiled. This moment never failed to satisfy.

Her skin remained pale, but life flowed back into it. He could feel the return of her spirit and, finally, see the flutter of eyelids that had probably been pressed shut by another hand not long ago.

She took a breath and coughed. He tightened his hand on hers and helped her sit up.

"Where am I?" She seemed disoriented, which was normal, and angry, which was also normal enough. "What *is* this place?"

"My workroom."

"Workroom? Are you a doctor?" she said. "You don't look any older than I am."

"Not exactly."

She hunched forward, eyes darting around the room, across

the shelves lined with vials and powders. Her glance was furtive and troubled.

"Who are you?" she asked.

Uncle had said he should never tell anyone who he was or exactly what he could do. *People will do anything for immortality,* he'd said. *They'd tear out your liver and eat it if they thought it would keep them from death. You must keep your secrets.* "I'm here to help you."

Her eyes widened, as if she suddenly remembered something important. "You have to let them go."

"Let who go?" Her intensity gave him pause.

She reached under her coat and released the knot of her necktie with one tug. Her dress was familiar. Too familiar. Dark blue, white collar, slim necktie—the same clothing the Telephone Club waitress had worn the previous night. Then, in one quick motion, she pulled the tie around his neck.

He jerked away from the table, pain jabbing through him as she tightened her grip around his windpipe, and she came with him. Where were the guards? They were supposed to be just outside the door! He reached back and grabbed fistfuls of her coat, and when that failed to break her hold, he stomped his heel on her toes. She gasped, but she didn't let go.

The door burst open; the sound of their struggle must have finally alerted the guards, two tall men in crisp uniforms. They carried guns but didn't need them. In a moment, they had pulled the tie from her grasp and caught her arms behind her back.

Her hazel eyes were subdued now, almost emotionless. "You're the one," she said. "*You're* the one she warned me about."

He stared at her, rubbing his neck. "Who?" he croaked. He wanted to say more, to ask her if she worked at the Telephone Club, but . . . well, she wasn't *his* waitress. If some other troubled girl there had wanted to kill herself . . .

A broad hand clamped over her mouth before she could answer. The guards hauled her from the room.

Although she was the only revival of the day, Freddy lingered in the room a moment. He kept thinking of that spark in her eyes. She had tried to kill him—quickly, purposefully, without explanation. It didn't seem real, and it didn't make sense. It was as if she had suddenly known who he was, and hated him for it.

But she couldn't possibly know. And if she did, she ought to be grateful.

THREE

Thea's mother shuffled into Thea's bedroom; she never took off those old slippers anymore, and Thea hated the constant sound of them. Her mother pushed the curtains open, and Thea blocked the morning light with her palm.

"Mother, please, it's shining right on my face."

Mother stood at the open window, watching the birds.

She liked birds, always had, and when Thea was a little girl, Mother used to take her bird-watching. They would stay with Mother's old friends in the country for two weeks during summer and hike in the woods. "There is a waxwing," she might whisper in Thea's ear while pointing.

Now Thea didn't even like Mother to put an arm around her. Her bound-sickness would bleed out, and Thea would know what her mother was thinking—always, always about Father: *Where is he? I can still feel him. He can't be dead. But why can't I find him?* On and on.

But Father *was* dead. He had to be dead. Surely he would have found them by now if he were alive, even if he had to fight his way out of a foreign prison or overcome amnesia or any of the other scenarios she'd envisioned. The binding spell would have called him home.

Suddenly she wasn't entirely certain.

"It's Sunday," Mother said. "We have to go to church."

Thea wrapped Father's old army blanket around her shoulders and joined her mother at the window. A blackbird pecked at the feeder while a warbler clung to the bars of the fire escape.

She didn't want to go to church. She wanted to sleep. But Mother was insistent, and Thea always wondered if maybe it helped her, if the familiar rituals were a thin but unbroken line to her old memories.

"I made a cake yesterday, so we can have it for breakfast," Mother said, finally removing her gaze from the birds.

Thea hoped for a moment that it would be one of the old cakes, but of course it wasn't. Mother didn't even know how to make a cake right anymore. Years ago, before the war, she used to make buttery pound cakes, and moist apple cakes, and gingerbread. But when Thea opened the pantry, she saw the same old chocolate cake sitting there. It wasn't even a good chocolate cake. Rationing had ended several years ago, but Mother still kept baking without eggs or milk or even very much chocolate. Thea could already imagine the cake's heavy, drab sweetness in her mouth.

Still, she sliced it and got the coffee going. She set the table with plates and cups and pulled Mother away from the window and into a chair.

Mother picked at her cake. "I do like this cake."

"*Please* wait for me to get home before you use the oven.

Maybe tomorrow I'll make apple spice cake." That was Thea's favorite, though it never tasted quite as good as Mother's used to. Her hand wandered to a stack of letters that needed answering, Mother's old friends from Irminau. Thea had to respond to them so they wouldn't worry.

"Maybe Henry will be at church today," Mother said.

"No," Thea said gently. "I don't think so."

"Father Gruneman might know where he is."

"Father Gruneman conducted the service for Father. Do you remember? When we got the telegram that he was dead?" Thea no longer bothered saying "missing, presumed dead," as she once did.

Mother looked confused for a moment. "I'm sure he wouldn't have done that. He must know Henry isn't dead."

Thea just sighed. They were having this conversation every week nowadays.

Only sticky, dark crumbs remained of her cake, and she dumped the plate in the sink with her coffee mug. "Mother, put your good dress on, please."

If Thea's mother were her old self, she would have been the one giving orders, telling Thea not to roll her stockings down quite so low, but now Thea had to be the one to make sure Mother was presentable. The mother who had organized singing groups in the neighborhood and taken food to the poor on holidays was gone. The mother who had told Thea to eat every bite on her plate and make her bed every morning was gone. Thea tried not to think about it, but sometimes her armor cracked and despair leaked in, poison thick as oil sliding through her veins.

They walked to church, Thea in her daytime good-little-sixteen-year-old guise: conservative print frock, lips free of paint and eyes free of kohl, her auburn hair set in neat waves under a cream cloche. Her mother was still beautiful, but she looked fragile in her peach crepe dress. Her eyes were gentle but distant. Thea felt a sudden surge of love and fear, thinking of what it would be like to lose her mother altogether. She took her hand and squeezed it. Her mother smiled at her, but Thea could feel her wondering about Father. What a torment never to think of anything else. She let go of the hand.

The white church was one of the oldest buildings in this modernized district, with broad brown beams exposed at each corner and on the roof frame. A simple steeple with a bell reached toward the sky, but even this tower was shorter than the offices surrounding it. The chapel doors were carved with an angel reaching out to a weary woman holding a baby, and above the entrance were the words COME AND REST IN THE SOLACE OF GOD.

It was the same church she had gone to all her life, but the war had changed it, too. Government regulated religion, and many of the old hymns of Thea's childhood were now banned. All the ones that mentioned adversity or rebellion were gone, and so were any that mentioned magic or even miracles. But other things had relaxed—books that had disappeared for years had slipped back into circulation, although maybe it was just that the government couldn't keep up with regulating them because of the labor shortage after the war's heavy casualties.

Thea and her mother settled into their familiar pew, made from golden wood that was speckled with color from the stained-glass windows. The smell was ancient and comforting.

Today, Father Gruneman spoke of being kind to one's neighbor. Thea always had trouble concentrating on sermons: how could she think of kindness to her neighbors when she had so much to worry about? She kept wondering if she ought to tell Father Gruneman how much worse Mother had become in recent months.

Father Gruneman had been a good friend of her father's. He had given her the book of fairy tales, stories to whisper and drive back the darkness, right after the memorial service for her father.

She was sure he knew Mother was bound-sick, but Thea didn't know if there was anything he could do. And she found it difficult to admit that she waitressed at the Telephone Club at night and slept fitfully all day, worried her mother would wander off somewhere or set something on fire.

When church let out, that was the difficult part, because she had to hurry Mother home without acting too suspiciously. Some of Mother's friends always said hello and whispered to Thea that her mother didn't look well and did she need anything?

Father Gruneman approached her before she could escape and clutched her hand. He was getting old, and his skin felt fragile and dry, but he still had a firm grip. "Thea, dear girl! And Mrs. Holder! How are you? Always in a hurry to leave after my sermons, aren't you?"

"Oh, no." Thea winced even though she knew he was teasing. "It's just— "

He didn't wait for her to come up with an excuse. "It's all right. I just wondered how you were."

"I have a hole in my shoe," Mother said. She spoke matter-of-factly, almost peevishly, like a child. Her voice was too loud.

Thea couldn't hide her horror. She didn't know how to pretend this was appropriate. "Mother, it's all right," she said hurriedly. "We'll go to the cobbler tomorrow." She forced a smile at Father Gruneman. Mother didn't say anything else. She was looking at the ground, fidgeting.

"I've been wanting to speak with you for a while now," Father Gruneman said. Most of the congregation had filed out around them, the children running excitedly after having sat still all morning.

"Oh—have you seen Henry?" Mother asked, as though she'd just remembered that Father Gruneman had known him.

Father Gruneman shook his head grimly. "Thea . . . how long has it been like this?"

"It wasn't always this bad," Thea said. "She gets a little worse every year." *Every month, almost.* She still didn't want to admit the extent of it.

"Your father had told me they were bound. That was before we had ever heard of bound-sickness. And I've noticed lately that she's . . . she's changed. You should have told me."

"There isn't much you could have done," Thea said. "And I try not to talk about it to anyone. I don't want the government to take her away."

"You know I'd be the last person to report her sickness to the authorities! Look at how they 'cured' poor Mrs. Hart. She used to be such a delight, and now she doesn't even smile at my jokes."

"I know you wouldn't report it, but I've gotten used to

keeping to myself. Most people don't understand why my mother ever would have wanted a binding marriage to begin with."

Marriage-binding had already been considered a backwater custom when Thea's parents married. They had chosen binding so each would always know where the other was, so her mother could find her father if he ever got lost hunting or traveling, but city people assumed all bound marriages were arranged and forced. And after the war, the sickness started. Rustic women going mad, insisting their husbands were alive even though they had been reported killed—sometimes even when the wives had seen the bodies.

Father Gruneman's thick white eyebrows furrowed. "I understand, but what a burden it must be. If you ever need some company, you're always free to come for dinner, you know. You and your mother. Borrow some books, if you'd like."

"Thank you," Thea said, feeling guilty. She just didn't read much, the way she had as a little girl. He probably still thought of her that way, Thea with skinned knees and a book under her arm. "I still have that book of fairy tales you gave me when Father died."

"I've always felt fairy tales are as true as anything that really happened."

She smiled. Sometimes he reminded her of a fairy-tale creature himself, a wizard who had crawled out of a magic cave. "You are a dear man," she said.

"I try to do my part in these grim times," he said. "At least there isn't rationing anymore, and you have work. You do still have work, don't you?"

She nodded quickly, hoping he didn't ask about it.

"You know what this nonsense with bound marriages is really about," he said. "The officials want to suppress magic. They shudder at the idea of power in the hands of the poor. But you can't suppress people's magic. It's no better than suppressing art. Of course, they do that, too, don't they? And they say they can cure bound-sickness, but you know what they really do, don't you?"

"No . . ." It made her nervous when Father Gruneman began to speak against the government, as if an official might, in fact, be hiding behind a pew.

"They take their memories away. That's what they did to Mrs. Hart. It's tragic. It's all going to come to something ugly. Your generation is going to have to be very strong. But, Thea, don't be afraid to ask for help. You are never alone, you know."

She nodded. But she certainly felt alone.

FOUR

Gray clouds had moved in, spread across the sky like blankets above Thea's four-story apartment building. Katrin Weis was sitting on the stoop, her arms laced around her bare knees above brown schoolgirl socks. She lived on the first floor, and Thea used to walk to school with her every day. But Thea didn't see much of her anymore.

"Good afternoon, Thea," Katrin said, the way she might greet an adult.

"Hi, Katrin. Are you waiting for someone?"

"Yes." Katrin flushed. "I have a boyfriend. He comes by for lunch on Sundays sometimes."

"Oh. Terrific," Thea said without much enthusiasm. Katrin was fifteen, just a year younger, and yet a much wider gap existed between them, marked on the surface by stockings versus socks, and a purse versus schoolbooks—but by so much more than that underneath.

"How are you, Mrs. Holder?" Katrin asked Thea's mother.

"I have a hole in my shoe."

"She's—she's fine," Thea said. She shrugged one shoulder

toward the stairs. "We'd better start making our lunch."

"Oh, of course! Don't let me keep you." Katrin's eyes moved past Thea, looking ahead toward the boy she was expecting.

Thea felt a stab of pain, imagining herself waiting on the stoop for a boyfriend to come for lunch. But Katrin didn't get to flirt with mysterious silver-haired boys or rub elbows with the rich and famous. And it wasn't like Thea missed going to school.

She hurried up the stairs, stopping impatiently to wait for Mother, who kept looking at her shoe. Once safely locked inside, Thea sliced bread and cheese, spreading butter on one piece of bread and mustard on the other. Mother took more of the cake, too, and Thea was glad it wasn't going to waste, at least.

After lunch, Thea wondered if she could slip out to buy groceries. Maybe even peek into a shop for a new style of hat like Nan's—no, no. She'd better stick to the essentials—the butcher, the baker, and the produce stand. Mother had been acting too strangely today.

"Mother, I'm going out for groceries, all right? Stay here and don't open the door for anyone."

"Unless it's Henry."

"Well, sure, but he'll probably have the key anyway. And don't turn on the oven. Eat the rest of your cake if you get hungry."

"Yes."

When Thea returned, her arms laden with bags, the apartment door was hanging wide open.

Her heart rose into her throat. She dropped the groceries just over the threshold and ran in. "Mother?"

She wasn't in the hall toilet they shared with Miss Mueller—Thea would have noticed when she came in. Obviously, she wasn't in the kitchen. And she wasn't in her bedroom, though the wooden chest that held Mother's most precious possessions had been opened and rummaged through. Thea couldn't tell whether anything was gone.

Oh god. What to do, what to do? She couldn't alert the neighbors. She couldn't tell the police. They would take Mother away. Thea had to find her.

Now she was noticing that all the food from lunch was gone—the rest of the cake, the bread, the cheese. So Mother was probably trying to take food to Father. These moments were the worst, when Mother became confused and thought Father was working at the train station and she needed to take food to him. Thea prayed Mother hadn't gone farther. Once Thea had caught her trying to go down to the subway stop at the end of the street. The stop had been closed off years ago, and Thea had to tell a passing policeman that her mother was just visiting from the country. She always worried about seeing that policeman again.

She had to find Mother among all the Sunday travelers waiting in lines and consulting schedules and standing around with their bags. Mother would be wearing her shabby old coat— she still had the same one from before the war—with a red print scarf over her head. Thea could imagine her so keenly it seemed wrong that she didn't spot her anywhere, even when she stood on a bench to get a better look. She tried calling for Mother, but her voice disappeared among all the other voices echoing in the soaring room. Finally, she was forced to snag one of the porters.

"Excuse me, have you seen my mother?" Thea's voice was shaking, but she managed to keep the tone light. "I seem to have misplaced her. She's a few inches shorter than I am, wearing a red kerchief, carrying a bundle?"

The young man's brow furrowed as she spoke. "I might have. I did see a woman like that. But it's been some thirty minutes, maybe. Did you lose her just now? I could tell the guards to look—"

"Thank you!" Thea said quickly, disappearing through a crowd.

Thirty minutes!

Maybe Mother had come to her senses and gone home.

When Thea rounded the corner and her apartment came into view, so did a cluster of neighbors—Mrs. Weis with her youngest on her hip, old Miss Mueller in a faded housedress, one of the bachelor twin brothers—Fritz or Franz? And there was a sturdy, imposing police car parked on the street.

"There she is!" shouted Miss Mueller.

Thea's heart sped. "What's the matter?"

"A policeman just brought your mother home, dear," Mrs. Weis said. "He's still upstairs with her, and I think . . . she's—"

"No!" Thea said, as if she could stop it.

"She's gathering her things," Mrs. Weis finished. "I knew

your mother took your father's death hard, but I never knew she was bound-sick. Why didn't you say something?"

Thea swallowed hard. Why didn't she *say* something? As if she hadn't told a thousand lies just to keep it secret. She hadn't even wanted Father Gruneman to know, and at least she trusted him not to report her mother to the authorities. It was so easy for Mrs. Weis to say this now, when a policeman was already here. She'd heard people whisper about bound-sickness, shake their heads over it—at church, at the Telephone Club, even waiting in line at the butcher. *I don't know why the rustics ever clung to those horrible rituals. Magic going wrong even after someone dies? So tragic.*

"They could help her, you know," Fritz-or-Franz said in his haughty accent. He'd been rich once but had lost his money right after the war, like a lot of people who'd had extra in the bank. "They have clinics, the government. You don't have to pay a thing."

She worried every day about Mother being taken to one of those clinics. "She—she doesn't want—" No. Why bother explaining to him? If Father Gruneman was right about the officials taking Mother's memories, she couldn't even speak of such a violation. She broke off and ran up the stairs.

The door to the apartment was open, and a policeman was waiting there, offensive in his mere presence, like a gun in a nursery. He stood with arms crossed, his eyes probing and touching Thea's life—the mess in her kitchen, the pile of letters from Mother's friends, and the photographs of Father on the ledge— but they cut to Thea herself as soon as she entered.

"Are you Thea Holder?" the policeman asked.

She nodded.

"I found your mother wandering by the river. Is it true, Miss Holder, that your mother and her husband, Henry Holder, were bound?"

Thea nodded again. *Don't make a scene. He won't care, and all the neighbors are downstairs. . . .*

"I'm sure you are aware that such magic is against the law," the policeman continued. "Moreover, we have cures nowadays. It isn't really fair to your mother, to lose her mind over a spell."

Thea was still nodding. No use saying Mother didn't want to go. No use begging or pleading. Thea steeled herself. They would take her memories away, and maybe—god, maybe it might even be for the best for Mother to be free of those memories. What kind of life did she have now?

Mother walked out of her bedroom just then, dragging along her traveling bag. Her eyes were angry and lucid. In rare moments, the real Mother was there. "He's alive," she said. "I'm sick because he's alive and I can't find him."

"Mrs. Holder, I know you think he is alive. It's only because the crude spell placed upon you at marriage has corrupted. He is deceased, I assure you, and I'd imagine your daughter has suffered because of your madness. I will take you to the doctor, and everything shall be made right."

"He *is* alive. You and your doctors can go to hell!"

"Shh! Shh!" Thea flew to Mother, pulling her back as she took a step closer to the policeman. "Mother, please. She doesn't mean it, sir."

The policeman's eyes narrowed slightly. "Oh, I know she doesn't mean it." He was going to get what he wanted. It wasn't like Thea or her mother could do a damn thing about it.

"Mother, just think, when the spell is broken, it will be like old times with us," Thea said, trying to smile, although she knew it would never be like old times again.

Mother straightened. "Before I go, let us have a moment to say good-bye."

"A moment." The door shut behind the policeman. Thea didn't hear the footsteps creak any farther, and she would have bet money he was listening at the door.

"I know he is alive!" Mother said, too loudly.

"Well, where is he, then? What can I do about it?"

"Nothing." Mother took Thea's hand and squeezed it. "Just know it. Remember it."

If only Mother were right. Thea used to believe her, but as the years passed, the hope fell away. She thought again of her vision at the Telephone Club: Father waking up in his military uniform. It was scary just to think of it, to allow any hope back in. She took a deep breath. "I will."

Mother pulled her into an embrace, and Thea soaked up the feel of her, as if this might be the last time.

The tears were coming now. No. No. She battled them off. *My good little soldier,* she could almost hear her father say. She could almost see him, too, when she held Mother so close. Mother was full of confusion and panic, but also memories—and when Thea let her go, the memories would go with her.

She drew away from the feel of Mother's coat on her cheek, the smell of her perfume and soap, and opened the door.

"How long will it take to remove the spell?" she asked the policeman.

"It can take a year, I've heard, if it is a bad case." He was already heading down the stairs, glancing back sharply every time Thea's mother lagged.

"A year? Where will she be? Can I visit her?"

"She will be at the city asylum for magical disorders. I believe visits are frowned upon. They can disrupt the treatment. I'm sure she will be well cared for." He marched to his car and opened the back door. Thea's mother looked tenderly at Thea one last time. Then she climbed inside. The door slammed shut, and the car drove away.

The neighbors were all gathered around watching. Thea didn't speak to any of them; she just bolted for the stairs.

All the forced smiles and lies to Mother's friends, all the nights she'd rushed home to keep Mother from wandering off or hurting herself . . . and now Mother was going to the asylum anyway.

Thea climbed into Mother's bed and cried. She wished, more fiercely than she had in years, for her father to walk through the door. Occasionally, a creeping tendril of relief would reach her: *I'm free. I can go out with Nan after work. Go to the pictures. See boys if I want.*

But how horrid to be glad, even for a moment, that her mother was gone, just so she had time to try on new hats.

Mother's words haunted her. *I know he is alive!* Suppose

she was right all along. Suppose Father had lived through the battle, and the vision was a sign? If there was any chance at all, she had to find out. She owed it to Mother, who was now trapped behind the asylum walls, losing her precious memories.

FIVE

Thea knew going to work could only help her feel better. Distract her. But it was still hard to drag herself into the world on Monday.

As usual, the floor of the streetcar was scattered with pamphlets. They were underground publications, often written badly and peppered with capital letters and exclamation marks, warnings of doom and gloom. MAGIC MAY BE FORBIDDEN, BUT IT IS NOT WRONG! THE GOVERNMENT IS FEEDING YOU LIES! MAGIC IS THE TOOL OF THE PEOPLE.

An old woman settling onto the car kicked several of the pamphlets under her chair with a look of disgust. She glanced at Thea with disapproval, as if merely being a young person made her complicit, and Thea shook her head. The last thing she wanted was a revolution, when everyone finally had food and coal, and even hats and chocolates and hair curlers and everything else. Had people forgotten standing in breadlines so quickly?

"Good, you're here," Elsa said as Thea walked into the club a few minutes late. "Nan's late, too."

Thea's face fell. She needed a friend right now. "I'm sure she'll be here soon," she said, reassuring herself as much as Elsa. "She's never missed a day."

"I hope she's not sick."

"Nan is never sick." Nan seemed like the type who could repel germs by force of will. But other things could happen. Thea had seen less of Nan in the past couple of months, and Nan talked of politics when she used to not care. People disappeared sometimes, Thea heard, if they read the wrong papers and spent time with the wrong people in the wrong places. But it wasn't like Nan was a revolutionary just because she was more informed than Thea.

All this worry, and probably Nan's streetcar was just late. She'd be here soon, and they could go to Café Tops for coffee after work and have a good, long chat.

Mr. Kortig had Thea handling the private rooms tonight, the only tables without any view of the show. They were as exclusive as the balconies, being few in number, and the best tips often came from these privacy-seeking groups. Right now it hardly seemed to matter. She just had to get through the night. Would she see Freddy and Gerik again? she wondered.

When the first performance ended, she began to lose hope on that account. Last time they had come early. Anyway, it was Monday. They might appear next Saturday. She had a table of military officers who lingered awhile and got quite drunk, and a large, jolly group. They were, at least, very polite and left plenty behind for her. Thea would be glad of the money later, she knew, but money couldn't buy her mother back.

And there was no sign of Nan. Thea kept looking for her,

asking if she'd turned up, but no one had seen her. What if she *was* sick? Thea thought of a classmate who had died from influenza when she was a girl; one day she wasn't at school, and a week later they were burying her. She ought to check on Nan, really, except she didn't know where she lived. Thea had never been able to pay a visit, on account of the need to get home to her mother.

Her night was half over, the second performance of the revue in its opening number, when she approached an older couple in the smallest of the private rooms. "Welcome," Thea said. "How are you this evening?" Then she almost did a double take; the man looked so much like Father Gruneman in the soft light.

No—it *was* Father Gruneman, she realized, as he gave her the briefest shake of his head, a gesture that said, *Here you don't know me.*

"Hello," the woman said. "Nan isn't here tonight, dear girl?" She was looking down, searching inside her purse and then snapping open a cigarette case.

"Not tonight," Thea said.

"Well, can you get me a gin cocktail?" She was wearing clusters of carved ivory bangles at her wrists, diamonds at her ears, and a fur stole around her graceful neck. Such an elegant woman didn't look like she belonged at a table with humble Father Gruneman.

But then, the Father Gruneman she knew would not be at the Telephone Club, wearing a plain dark suit instead of church robes. "What about you, sir?" Thea asked him.

"Just a glass of port." He handed the menus to her before she could even gather them, his expression almost apologetic. It was a clear signal that she should leave them alone, so she did.

She felt as if the world had turned on its head, and she was the only one who noticed. Mother gone, Nan absent from work, and now Father Gruneman at the Telephone Club with some rich woman?

She brought the group in the next room the fresh fruits and cheeses they'd ordered, and then got the drinks. Onstage, the moon was singing her big star-crossed number about how she could never be with the sun, spreading her arms so that her spangled cape glinted in every direction. The Moonling chorus in white sang softly behind her on the stairs. Thea paused outside the curtain. Mr. Kortig would have her head if she were caught trying to eavesdrop on customers, but she had to know what Father Gruneman and the woman were talking about.

"She knew he was alive," the priest was saying. "That's why they took her away."

Was he speaking of Thea's mother?

"I think it's gotten too big for them," the woman said. "They're stretched thin, trying to keep up with all the loose threads. It's time to kill the witch. Cut them all in one blow."

"But we can't be hasty. We've already lost too many people by being hasty. If we act without enough intel and none of the workers can escape, they might cover up the entire operation."

"It's better than just sitting around talking while they take more people every day!"

"Don't you want to see your daughter again?" Father Gruneman said, more gently.

"You know I do," she snapped. "Don't say such a thing. But I need you on my side. Like you used to be."

The response was too soft to hear over the music. Thea's ears were already straining to piece the words together, and she didn't dare stay there any longer. She lifted the heavy curtain aside. Father Gruneman sat back.

"You know it's gone too far for mercy," the woman said.

Father Gruneman looked uncomfortable. Thea suspected she was part of the reason for that. "Nothing is ever too far gone for mercy," he said.

She put the drinks down and smiled at them, trying to act casual and happy, as if she hadn't heard a word and didn't find Father Gruneman's presence at the Telephone Club unusual in the least. "Did you need anything else? A bite to eat?"

"No, dear," the woman said.

"I'll come back in a bit to see how you're doing, then."

"Actually, would you bring us the check now?" Father Gruneman said.

"Why do we meet at all if you're going to be so eager to get rid of me?" the woman said.

He didn't answer her, just nodded to Thea. As the curtain closed behind her, she heard him say something about his congregation and guessed it might be about not wanting to speak freely around her.

"Fine, we'll speak at the Rouge," the woman said, sounding cross.

The Rouge. Thea had heard some of the revolutionaries talk about meeting at the Café Rouge.

Was Father Gruneman a revolutionary? She'd gotten the impression, from her childhood memories, that his life outside of church was nothing but cups of tea, books, and a dog sleeping at his feet.

Then again, his sermons did touch on rebellion and freedom so often, especially before the censorship rules. And he'd been visibly angry the Sunday after the church raids, when the government officials took all the hymnbooks away and replaced them with the "approved" ones. Anyone would be upset about that, of course—all those familiar, lovely old songs, and yet . . .

If he did know something about her father and didn't want to tell her, that could explain it. Her father could have been involved with the revolution.

Of all the nights for Nan not to be here! If anyone would know what to make of it all, Nan would.

How could Thea not know where her best friend lived?

At least she could visit Nan now, once she came back to work. Now that Mother—

Mother was gone. The thought of going home to an empty apartment crashed back into her mind.

Nan will be back tomorrow, she told herself, and plunged into work, trying not to let herself think.

SIX

Tuesday came and went, and Nan still hadn't turned up. Mr. Kortig didn't know where she lived, either.

"She probably got another job," Mr. Kortig said.

"But we were friends. She would have told me."

"Girls come and go all the time. She probably doesn't want to come around because she feels bad for cutting out without giving notice. I bet she has no idea you're fretting over her."

His lack of concern was probably meant to ease her worries, but it only made them worse. Mr. Kortig didn't understand. Nan wasn't the type of girl to abandon friends and leave her fellow waitresses scrambling.

Something must have happened. Nan always seemed so strong. But no one was invincible.

Thea thought she could try going to Father Gruneman. She ought to tell him what had happened to her mother anyway. But after the other night . . .

She was emerging from the kitchen with a tray of eels in wine sauce for table 72 when she almost collided with Freddy.

"Freddy!" she exclaimed. "You shouldn't hang around the kitchens. Someone might spill their tray of eels down the front of your suit, and I'd hate for that someone to be me. Can I bring something to your table?"

"Gerik's over by the stairs, talking to some old friends," he said, glancing at the balcony. "I was just looking around when I saw you duck into the kitchen. I hope I'll be seeing you again tonight."

"If you asked for me."

"I asked for Trouble." He crossed his arms. "Oddly enough, the hostess didn't recognize the name."

"It's Thea." She felt her cheeks warm.

"Thea," he said. "Sounds very modern. I imagined you as more of a Rosamunde or an Adelaide."

"Oh, no, no. I'm a very modern girl."

"Thea is a nice name, too."

"I detect a hint of disappointment. You're more of a three-syllable kind of gent?"

He laughed. "Maybe I just have provincial tastes. My parents were rustics from Irminau."

"Mine too." So he really hadn't meant it as an insult last time, when he'd called her a rustic. But it still didn't make sense. "Then Mr. Valkenrath is—"

"The city uncle," he said. "Really a third cousin or something."

"Very kind of him to show around a nephew from Irminau," Thea said. "I'd think he wouldn't want anyone to know he had rustic relatives."

"I suppose he feels bad that I don't have a father figure around," Freddy said. "But it's true; he doesn't like me to mention my background, so I wanted to say so when he wasn't here. You don't see the Irminau blood in me?"

"A—a little." She felt flustered. Wooing her with talk of low-born lineage was certainly a new one, but she had to keep her wits. She couldn't let him leave here twice without finding out if he had any connection to her father, and that meant she had to keep control of the conversation. "Well, that's a surprise, but I guess it explains why you don't seem like most of the other boys who come in here."

He smiled. His teeth were just a hair crooked, but she rather liked that; after all, she had that stupid tiny gap between hers. "In a good way, I hope."

She smiled back. *If I could just touch him and see if it happens again . . .*

"Well, look," he said, "I'd better get back. Gerik will think I'm showing poor manners coming down here, but . . . if I asked you to have coffee with me after work, what would you say?"

"I'd consider it."

"I hope so."

She let her smile fade, so as not to seem too eager, and started walking with her eels. It was a good thing the regulars who'd ordered them wouldn't care that they were getting cold.

She had never before agreed to meet a boy after work. She had her reasons this time, but he didn't know that. He might think this was a real date. And she had to be careful, certainly.

"Mr. Kortig said for you to go to the balcony," one of the other waitresses said, hurrying by her.

"I know, thanks."

Thea took Gerik's and Freddy's orders: once again, a drink for each and several rich dishes of food. She made casual banter with them, and when she brought their orders, she tried to find a way to brush one of Freddy's hands again, but he was still keeping them off the table. It was probably silly to think a boy's touch could give her visions of her father anyway, but it *was* strange that he wouldn't allow her the opportunity to find out.

"Have you had enough time to consider it?" he asked her when she brought their check.

"Consider what?" Gerik asked.

"Coffee, after," Freddy said.

"Oh, well, then," Gerik said. "You never asked me."

"I wasn't aware you were hoping I'd ask you out for coffee, Gerik." Freddy grinned. "Besides, you're the one who told me I should get out more."

"I guess I didn't realize how well you'd take to it," Gerik said, chuckling.

"Don't mind him," Freddy said.

"Fine," Thea said. "Coffee. It's pretty generous for me to give you more than the time of day when you've only been here twice."

"Then I'm glad I caught you in a generous mood."

SEVEN

After these past couple of nights of leaving work to go home to an empty apartment, it was nice to see Freddy waiting for her outside, with a gray fedora now covering his hair. He looked cross with Gerik, who stood a short distance behind him, smoking a cigarette.

"It looks like we're stuck with some company," Freddy said. "I can't seem to get rid of him, short of murder in the back alley, perhaps."

"Every lad has to learn his own ways to avoid his chaperone," Gerik said. "I can't make it too easy for you on your first date."

"You just enjoy the challenge, don't you? I know it isn't your strict moral code. I should probably be chaperoning you," Freddy replied. Then he told Thea, more softly, "Don't mind him. He's harmless. I've been on *dozens* of other dates, of course."

She had to smile at this rather backhanded admission that it actually was his first date. Not that it was a real date. Because that would have made it her first date, too.

No, they had important business to discuss, even if Freddy didn't know it.

"Do you have a place you like to go for coffee or something?" Freddy asked.

"Oh, I usually go to Café Tops because it's just around the corner. But it's—I don't know. Sort of a sad-old-man place, really. The prices are good; that's why I go."

"Gerik has a car, so we could go farther if you'd like."

She didn't trust them enough for that, but she didn't want to say so. "We could walk somewhere. I like a walk in the moonlight."

He looked up at the sky. The moon was nearly full. They couldn't see any of the stars with all the neon signs. "Sounds nice."

They started to stroll. Gerik stayed well back, so she could almost forget he existed.

"Have you worked at the club long?" Freddy asked, making small talk.

"About a year."

"Do you like it?"

"I do. Never a dull moment."

"In a good way, I hope. I heard someone mention that one of the waitresses went missing the other night."

The reference to Nan jolted her. Who had been talking about Nan? Everyone else seemed to brush off her disappearance. "Oh—well, yes, she hasn't come in for a few days. It happens. She probably got a new job." Thea didn't really want to talk about Nan. He didn't need to know how worried she was.

"You didn't know her, then."

"Does it matter?" *Why all these questions?*

"Not if it doesn't matter to you. I just wondered if you were worried, since it sounded like she vanished unexpectedly."

"I don't talk to the other girls very much," she said, but her voice was strained.

"A loner, are you? I am, too. It's difficult to talk to society girls. They've never worked a day in their lives, and they don't intend to, either. What do I talk to them about when they don't *do* anything?"

"What are you planning to do?"

"That's a sticking point," he said. "My father was a clock-maker. I'd like to follow in his footsteps, to honor him. But Gerik shudders at the suggestion that I'd go into a trade."

"But making clocks takes skill," she said, and then realized how silly that was to say. Of course a man from the upper tiers of society wouldn't care whether Freddy had the skills of a craftsman. "I think it's very respectable, anyway."

"I knew *you* would," he said. "That's why I'm buying you coffee."

They were turning away from the entertainment district, toward Frederstrasse, which lacked the wild abandon and abundance of neon lights but nevertheless had a reputation as a hangout for bohemians, with bookshops and small presses for poets by day, coffeehouses and bars by night. The street was lined with trees, men in artistically scruffy clothes spilled out of the bars, and somewhere in the distance she heard an accordion.

"Wonder where that's coming from," Freddy said, perking to the sound.

"It's an old song from Irminau," Thea said. "Did your mother ever sing it to you? Mine did. 'Little Cuckoo.'"

"Both my parents died when I was little," Freddy said, lightly enough, but she could tell it made him sad. She wished she hadn't asked him.

The accordion grew louder as Freddy led her right to it, through the door of a coffeehouse called the Hornbeam. She thought Gerik might protest the choice of a rustic coffeehouse, but he went right along. The musician's eyes were closed, as if he didn't care whether anyone was watching him. He was missing most of his teeth and needed a shave, but he played beautifully. Freddy led her to a table, dragging out a wooden chair for her. Nearly everything in the room was made of wood, and people drank their coffee by candlelight. Such a contrast from the sleek glitter of her usual environment, it reminded her of the country cottages of childhood summers.

Gerik took another table nearby and unfolded an evening paper from his coat.

They ordered cups of coffee, and Thea stirred cream and sugar into hers.

Gerik still wasn't paying any attention to them.

She gave Freddy's hand a light touch. "Thanks for taking me out. This is nice." She had planned the words, so they came out smoothly, but she barely heard herself say them. The vision returned. Weaker this time, but still more potent than anything in her imagination. Her father, eyes opening, drying blood on his uniform.

Freddy's reaction was restrained but obvious. He jerked his

hand back. His brows furrowed, and he looked at the spoon and napkin set on the table.

She stared at him for a moment until he had to acknowledge her eyes, and then she finally looked away. "You see it, too," she said softly.

"I don't understand," he said.

"It was my father. Why do I see my father when I touch you?"

"I don't know," he said, his voice quiet. "Are you sure it was your father?"

"I should think I recognize my own father. Do you—did you know him?"

"What was your father's name?" He was leaning closer. She got the sense he didn't want Gerik to hear them.

"Henry Holder."

"I don't know the name." He looked genuinely confused, but she felt he was holding something back. "Has he been missing?"

"He went missing in action eight years ago, during the war. They told us he was certainly dead, that a lot of men had to be buried unidentified in a mass grave. But my mother has always insisted he's alive."

"Maybe he is, then," Freddy said.

If she let herself, even for a moment, imagine her father walking in the door, imagine his laugh and the way his evening mug of beer used to smell and the piles of books he'd leave near his favorite chair and the way Mother kissed him when he came home from work . . . imagine all of that being *real* again . . .

"It's been so long," she said. "He would have come home by now. He'd *have* to."

"He could've been badly injured. Lost his memory," Freddy said, seeming to think along the same lines she once had. "It happens in books so often that it must happen in real life once in a while."

"Even if he lost his memory . . ." She drew back, letting her eyes drift to the accordion player again. "My parents were bound."

"Bound?" He cocked his head. "I thought that was outlawed."

"It is nowadays, but they were bound before that."

"Was it an arranged marriage?"

"No. They wished to be bound when they married, so they would always be connected."

Freddy looked interested. "I don't think that was done in my parents' village. I've only read about it."

"After my father supposedly died, my mother started losing her mind. When I touch her, the magic that binds them touches me, too. I have a bit of a connection to them both because of the spell, but it's not strong like Mother's. I just feel how disturbed she is, and I'm helpless to do anything about it."

Freddy's expression was dark in the dim light. Maybe she'd said too much. She didn't want him to pity her. She was supposed to be finding out why she saw her father when she touched Freddy, not confessing her own family history. Only, he wasn't giving her much to work with. She recalled Nan's comment that the revolutionary papers said Gerik was involved in terrible things. Was it possible he had anything to do with her father's death?

"Gerik's in the government," she said, switching angles. "What does he do, anyway?"

Freddy didn't seem to expect that question. "He's a domestic adviser or something. I'm not sure what he does, not exactly."

"I wondered if he had anything to do with the military. If maybe you'd seen the soldiers and just not remembered it. My father looks young in the vision, like he did when he went off to war, so you would have been young, too."

"No." Freddy stiffened.

She certainly couldn't let him stay stiff. She needed him to trust her, so he might tell her more . . . because there was more. There *had* to be more. "Well," she said, allowing some of her sadness and fear to show now. "That's too bad."

"I'm sorry," he said. "I know losing your father is a terrible feeling. I'll try to see if I can find out anything for you."

She nodded, but she wondered if he meant it. Although he seemed interested in her, he still held the cards. He could decide when to return to the club. It could be days or weeks. He could get distracted by society parties, or preparing for university, or whatever boys like Freddy did.

Maybe she shouldn't have lied to him about Nan. If he was asking, it was because he was either curious about the mystery of her disappearance or sympathetic that Thea might have lost a friend, and neither sympathy nor curiosity would hurt her tonight.

"That girl you were asking about earlier, the one who worked at the club?" she said. "She actually *was* my friend. My best friend. Nan."

He glanced quickly at Gerik. "Your best friend?"

"Yes."

"And you haven't heard from her?"

"No. And I never visited her at home, so I can't check on her, but I'm worried sick. I just didn't want to put a pall on the night."

"I see. Well, do you know her last name? Maybe I could look in the city records."

"Davies. And she's an orphan. Her guardian is named Horst, and I don't know his last name."

"I'll research it for you and find her address."

Thea didn't have to feign gratitude. She was genuinely glad she'd told him now—it hadn't even occurred to her to check the city records, and she wouldn't know how to go about it. "Thank you."

Gerik folded his paper and then walked up behind Freddy's chair. "Having fun, lad?"

"Yes. Good coffee here."

"You look pale. Maybe we ought to think of heading back."

Freddy emptied his cup. "Well, I'd better walk the lady home first, don't you think?"

"But of course." Gerik winked at Thea. She was in no mood to be winked at, but she forced a smile.

"It's a long walk from here," she said. "Maybe I should just get a cab." She didn't want Freddy to see that the wooden siding was crumbling off the apartment building and exposing old bricks beneath, or that Miss Mueller hung her underwear out the window to dry.

"We can take you home," Gerik said.

She shook her head. "I don't want to trouble you."

Freddy seemed to understand her reluctance. "She's a loner, Ger. She doesn't want to listen to your stories all the way home. I can't blame her."

Gerik laughed. "Just for that, I'm going to repeat the one about the ambassador's horse in excruciating detail."

Freddy was already lifting a hand to hail a cab for her. When one arrived, he opened the door. "I had fun tonight," he said.

"Me too," she said, and it was true, even with all the heavy things they had discussed.

"Maybe I can see you again sometime soon?"

"I'd like that very much."

"Until next time, then."

She slid into the backseat. Freddy waved and then turned away, his silver hair bright in the darkness.

EIGHT

"I'm impressed." Gerik lit a cigarette. "Where in the world did you learn to flirt?"

"Well." Freddy shrugged. If it took everything he had, he wouldn't let Gerik know his interest in Thea was anything beyond flirting. "I've had a good instructor over the years."

"I haven't instructed you. You never let me."

"I meant novels, not you."

Gerik snorted. "This girl—Thea? I like her spunk, but I wonder if there is something too earnest about her."

"What's wrong with that?"

"You're already too serious. What were you talking about over there with her?"

"Nothing much. Her family, work . . ."

"We're not trying to find you a wife here. Just someone who will bear you a child. Did you see that little blond waitress? She seemed more up for anything, if you ask me."

"I'm just not sure why you and Uncle are in such a hurry. When has my magic not been enough?"

"Insurance policy, Freddy," Gerik said. "If, god forbid, we

lost you, who would help the dead? And wouldn't you like a vacation yourself?"

"Not really."

Gerik sighed. "You ought to be begging me for a vacation. And I'm even *telling* you to rush into things with a pretty girl. Most boys have to do that on the sly."

From the moment Gerik first presented this plan, he had made it sound like a privilege and not something Freddy was being forced into. It was so simple, he had said. They could surely find a girl at the clubs. The girls were all pretty and respectable enough to hold a job, but they wouldn't be working there if they didn't need money.

"Nothing about this plan is respectable," Freddy had pointed out, but Gerik had waved him off and said he worried too much.

"It's very uncomfortable talking to a girl, thinking all the while that you have to ask her if she'd like children, especially when *I* really don't want children," Freddy said.

"She doesn't have to like children," Gerik said. "And neither do you. She just has to like money. I told you, we've already got a foster family lined up. I'm sure Thea needs money."

"But—not like that."

Gerik sighed. "Maybe falling in love would be good for you. And she seemed a little sad. A girl like that would give you something to protect."

"Please," Freddy said sharply. "Don't talk about her that way. For that matter, don't talk about me that way. You're making this sound like a game of courtly love."

"All life might as well be a game of courtly love." Gerik gave his hand a pat. "I only speak from experience. That was how I felt about the Countess of Ordzy. May she rest in peace. I truly loved that woman. Sometimes you take me so seriously that you remind me of Rory."

"I'm nothing like him." Freddy knew comparing him to Uncle was only a distraction from the real topic. "But I don't think Thea will like this plan any more than I do, no matter how much she needs money."

"We'll offer her enough for a brand-new row house with electric lights. She'd never have to work again. I bet she'll see the wisdom of this plan for that. Just as your parents like the money we give them, eh?"

"Money is nice," Freddy said. "But it isn't everything." *It isn't family.* He felt bad lying to Thea and saying he was an orphan, but it hardly felt like a lie to him. He rarely saw them, and he didn't know them.

Gerik had been bringing up his parents more lately, reminding Freddy of the favors they received in exchange for his service to the government. It made Freddy wonder if he could really trust Gerik, the man who had raised him, the man who had once insisted to Uncle that Freddy must keep his beloved cat and who had gotten on the floor with him to play with trains. Gerik always used to seem like he had Freddy's best interests at heart, but lately Freddy wondered if there wasn't something else going on.

"Gerik, you know that girl the other day, the one who attacked me?"

"How could I forget! Sometimes these suicide cases, you wonder if there's much hope for them."

"She was wearing a uniform just like Thea's. She worked at the club. But she never went back to work."

"Yes?" Gerik spoke as if he had no idea what Freddy was getting at.

"Well . . . why wouldn't she go back to work after I revived her?"

"Oh, lad, you know she killed herself. When we give someone a second chance, we encourage them to start a new life, so that whatever happened to bring them to that point doesn't happen again. That often means placement in a new job."

"But her old coworkers don't even know what happened?"

"Mr. Benson handles work placement. You've met him, haven't you, at one of those terrible gatherings Rory calls parties? Maybe not. I'll ask him, in any case, if he knows what became of her."

"Thank you, I'd appreciate that," Freddy said. Maybe he was overreacting, but whenever he thought of that girl, he felt her tie around his neck. He couldn't imagine why she would try to strangle him.

If only he could have asked Thea what kind of girl Nan was. Prone to violence? Involved in questionable activities?

Of course, then Thea would wonder why he was asking those questions.

And he wanted to see Thea again. He'd been dreading going to the clubs, imagining how fake and stupid all the girls would be, but she was easy to talk to.

"Anyway, about Thea," Freddy said. "She is a rustic. And aren't rustics more likely to have magic? Couldn't hurt to have magic running on both sides. But how am I supposed to get anywhere when you insist on chaperoning?"

"She likes the chaperone," Gerik said. "It makes her feel safer. And it also makes her think about how she'd like to get you alone."

"But still, I certainly can't ask her to—do what you want me to do—with you sitting a table away."

Gerik grunted thoughtfully. "Well, Freddy, I trust you, but Rory doesn't think I ought to let you out alone."

"You're the one who always says you never tell him anything if you can help it. Why start now?"

Gerik's eyes crinkled as a mischievous smile spread on his face. "Fair enough, lad. Fair enough. But you'd better work your charms quickly. People at those clubs like to gossip. I don't want them to start wondering just who you are and what you're doing there. Try to get her somewhere private and tell her the story we discussed, and we'll take care of things from there."

NINE

Nan woke in an unfamiliar place, with an unknown panic racing through her. Her head hurt, and her right shoulder, too, as though she'd wrenched something, but she couldn't move. She was strapped down, under bright, sterile lights. It looked like a hospital.

A sign was posted on the ceiling, obviously intended for the occupant of this bed. It said, INDUSTRY IS THE BACKBONE OF CIVILIZATION; WORK, THE JOY OF MANKIND.

What had happened? Where had she been?

The more she struggled to think, the more confused she felt. She remembered commonplace things: words and numbers and streetcar schedules and how to bake a loaf of bread. But she couldn't remember where she lived or whom she lived with. She remembered the world but not her place within it, which made it all seem hollow.

When she looked at herself, she saw only a white sheet, but underneath it, straps restrained her to the bed. She didn't seem to be wearing much, maybe a hospital gown. Something papery. A glance around revealed bare walls with lights shaped like triangles pointing downward to linoleum floors. Rows of cabinets and a sink. No clues.

She started tugging her arms from her bonds by inches. The straps scraped her skin, but she hardly noticed any pain. She was bony enough to work her way free, and strong enough to keep trying as long as it took, which felt like a long time. Once her arms were free, she flung the sheet onto the floor—just as the door opened.

"Don't do that, please." The woman marched across the room, picked up the sheet, and spread it over Nan once more. "Please relax."

"Where am I?"

The woman smiled in an automatic way. "You're in a safe place now. Can I ask you a few questions?" She started asking them without waiting for permission. "What is your name?"

"Nan Davies."

"And where are you from?"

"I don't remember."

"Where do you live?"

"I don't remember that, either."

"Do you remember anything?" Her tone was so blank Nan couldn't tell if the woman expected her to remember anything or not.

"My name, clearly."

"Anything else?"

"No," Nan said. At least, she didn't remember anything that seemed to matter.

"Count to ten for me, please."

Nan did.

"Very good." The woman turned back the sheet—Nan wondered why she'd bothered to replace it just for a brief line of questioning—and unfastened the straps from Nan's waist and legs.

"I'm going to give you some medicine." The nurse poured a little liquid into a cup and handed it to her.

"Where am I?" Nan asked before drinking.

"You're in recovery at the hospital here. You tried to kill yourself, Miss Davies."

"I did?" Was that something she would do? No. Surely it wasn't.

"You've been here for twenty-four hours, but don't worry. You're fine. Drink your medicine, please."

Nan looked at the medicine a moment. It smelled like something sweet beginning to ferment. She didn't want to take it. "What does it do?"

"It will calm you down and ease your aches and pains."

"I don't think I need it. I feel all right."

"Doctor's orders. You won't leave my care until you've taken your medicine."

Nan gave it another suspicious sniff. The woman looked impatient and quite ready to force the liquid down her throat. If it was that important, she could have done it while Nan was still strapped down. Nan drank it in one swig under the woman's waiting eyes.

"Good. Now you can get dressed." The woman opened a drawer and took out a pile of clothes and some work boots. "In a moment, someone will come to show you to the dormitories."

"Dormitories?"

"Where you will live."

"Where did I live before?"

"I don't know. It doesn't matter. It's safer, in light of your suicide attempt, if you remain here. You will be well taken care of." The woman stared at her for a moment, as if daring her to ask another question, but just as Nan opened her mouth to ask one, the nurse quickly went out the door.

Something was very wrong. But without her memories, Nan couldn't grasp exactly what it was.

Nan saw the world in what people called black and white, like a film, and yet the sprightly contrast of dark gray flowers on the light gray background of a pretty dress was a world away from the lifeless gray of the clothes the nurse had left for her. She slipped her arms and legs into the one-piece work suit. She had never worn anything like this before. She was sure of that.

The door opened again without any warning—good thing she had changed quickly—and now a man entered. His hair was no longer than the stubble on his chin, and he had a small scar on his cheek. He didn't look like he worked in a hospital. His outfit looked more like a police uniform, except it had no badges or insignias. "Follow me," he said.

They walked down a hall blank of anything except the triangular lights. No windows. They passed through a door and turned a corner. Nan kept looking for landmarks, but there was nothing to go on except numbered doors: she had come from thirteen, now down this hall were the twenties. . . . She tried to keep track of the twists and turns, aware of a slight downward slope.

The man didn't say a word. They took another turn and

went down a long hall. A steady hum grew louder, and periodically Nan heard clanging and hissing, and then some shouting.

"Where are we?" she asked.

"We are passing by one of our factories."

"Our?"

"The city's." He was not a man of many words.

Nan heard an approaching rumble on the other side of the wall. It sounded like a subway car. But the subways had been shut down after the war, when she was young . . . hadn't they? She knew this as a fact, like the streetcar schedules, but the knowledge was disorienting when she couldn't remember what the war had meant to her or where she used to ride the streetcar.

The man noticed her change of expression and gave her a severe look. "Are you feeling all right, lad?"

Nan laughed. "I'm a girl."

"I can't tell the difference anymore," he muttered.

"It might help if I wasn't wearing this shapeless rag."

His eyes turned on her again. "I'd keep comments like that to yourself from now on. They'll decide what you are now."

"Who are 'they'?"

"Right now, *I'm* 'they.' You ask too many questions."

After another few minutes of silent marching, he finally stopped at one door in a hall full of doors. "I'll put you here, then, since you're a girl; there's been a vacancy in this room. Your roommate will show you where to go and what to do. My advice is not to cause trouble, or they'll find a *better* place for you."

He opened the door to a room no larger than a closet, with

one electric light hanging from the ceiling. Then he gave Nan's back a small shove and shut the door behind her.

Nan's roommate stayed huddled in the corner of the bottom bunk. She murmured a brief introduction—her name was Helma—and directions to the bathroom, and that seemed to be the extent of her interest.

"So what do you do around here?" Nan asked, trying to get something out of her.

"Work. Eat. Sleep. That's about it." Helma picked at her nails. "You should probably get ready for bed."

"Bed? I just woke up."

"Well, it's almost bedtime, so you should try to sleep. You'll be glad you did tomorrow when you're working."

Nan knew she wouldn't be able to sleep, but she wasn't sure what else to do. She changed into the pajamas that were folded on her bunk, made from cheap cotton that held sharp creases even after she put them on. Helma turned out the lights, and within moments her breathing turned deep and slow.

My name is Nan Davies.

That felt like all she had. Just a name.

But the memories weren't gone completely. They were close enough to taste. They were hidden around a corner. If she could only find a path to them, she would understand what had happened and why she was here. Commit suicide? That couldn't be right. Nan had never wanted to die. There must be some mistake. An accident, maybe.

Horst will worry about me. He shouldn't, but he will.

The thought burbled to the surface as though it had slipped

through a crack. Just a name. She felt as if he was the person who had raised her. He wasn't her father; she was quite sure she didn't have a father or a mother.

But what had Horst looked like? What did he do for a living? What sort of things did he say? She couldn't remember.

She was breathing fast in the still of night because she needed this memory back, needed all her memories back. She felt almost as if there was something she had meant to do.

But after what seemed like a long time of struggle, all she could recall was the smell of his cigarettes.

She had to escape from this strange place. The memories would come back if she could only see the real world teasing at the edges of her mind. There must be a way. If she'd gotten in, she could get out.

TEN

In the morning, a crackling voice on a speaker in the hall announced that it was time for the day to begin. Twelve girls shared a bathroom. They had to stand in line just for the privilege of using a toilet and sink, and even looking in the mirror.

The hall was lined with bedrooms, their doors hanging open to show identical bunk beds. A stairwell led down.

"Where do the stairs go?" Nan asked the girl standing in front of her.

"Tracks for the old rail lines, but they don't go anywhere anymore. They've been walled off," the girl said. "And the tunnel's full of rats."

"And worse!" said Helma, behind Nan. "Monsters and ghosts."

"Oh, I'm sure," another girl said.

Nan got to the front of the line and met her own face in the mirror. She remembered it, but not so pale and exhausted. Her cheeks and jaw were angular, lips thin, hair cropped very close to her head. In the real world, she had worn dark lipstick and lined her eyes; she remembered doing it—just yesterday. Yes. She was sure that yesterday she had been free. Now she could see why that man had taken her for a boy.

Nan followed the crowd to a huge cafeteria roaring with voices. This room had once been a juncture of the subway system, Nan thought. Probably a hub, judging by its size. All the signs were gone, and all the stairs save one had been blocked off, but Nan recognized the shape of the room—the arched ceiling, the places where there would have been benches and a shop or two and a map posted on the wall. The stairs would have led down to the tracks. In fact, just as she thought it, she heard the rumble of an approaching train below. "Are the trains still running?" she asked Helma.

"Only the workers' rail," Helma said. "It takes some of us off somewhere. A slaughterhouse, I heard. If you do anything wrong, they'll threaten to send you there." She was peering around the crowd, spotted a boy across the room, and wandered away from Nan without another word.

Nan rolled her eyes and followed the crowd by herself, taking a bowl and a cup and holding them out to be filled with drink and soup, as everyone else did. The servers, bored-looking women in white dresses, talked very little. The soup was lumpy and clotted. The drink had a slight syrupy thickness to it.

At the center of the space were long tables in rows, where several hundred men and women in identical work suits hovered over their bowls. Their voices echoed in a din among all the tiles and concrete.

She hated having to choose someone to sit with, but there

weren't any spots completely apart from other people. As she scanned the rows of people, her gaze paused on a girl with a head of unruly dark curls. That tumble of hair, she felt, almost seemed familiar. The girl was sitting near a column, so there was no one to her left, and she wasn't talking to the woman on her right. The seat across from her was empty, so Nan took it.

"Hello," Nan said.

The girl looked up. "Hello." She didn't look entirely pleased to have her solitude among the masses disrupted. Her accent was unexpectedly aristocratic. But after a moment of studying Nan, she said, "I'm Sigi," and offered a hand to shake.

"Nan." Nan shook the offered hand, even if the gesture seemed formal in this coarse place. Sigi had a strong grip that matched her stocky build but not her socialite voice. Her eyes, under long lashes, turned slightly upward at the corners. She looked like the kind of girl who could throw a punch or care for an abandoned kitten with equal skill.

"You're new here, I take it?" Sigi asked.

"Yes. I came last night."

"Who's your roommate?"

"Helma."

"Oh. Helma. With the boyfriend? Watch out for that one."

Nan shrugged one shoulder. "I don't think we'll be friends." She mucked her spoon around in the soup, trying to summon some kind of appetite. "How long have you been here?"

"About three months, I think. Brigitte marked the days— she was my roommate—but I haven't kept up."

"What happened to Brigitte?"

"She threw herself into a fire."

"Into a fire?" What sort of place was this?

"At her work. They didn't tell me details." Sigi shuddered. "I can't imagine, but Brigitte wasn't quite right in the head."

"But why would she do that?"

"It's the only way to kill yourself. They do something to us, so we can't easily die. Hanging doesn't work, I heard. Some people have tried it."

"Is this . . . some sort of mental asylum?" Nan asked.

"Good question. I'd love to know, myself."

"Do you remember anything from before?"

"Nothing important. Sometimes I'll have snatches of memory—a dress I used to have, or someone's face, or bits of a song. But it's not anything I can really go on. They don't want us to remember anything. One girl started to remember her husband. She was going on and on, crying to the rest of us. A guard overheard her. They took her aside for a day, and when she came back, she'd forgotten him again."

"What's the point of all this?"

"Oh, come on, they don't tell us that, either. They just tell us what to do. They *say* that they saved our lives, and now we must work and work. That's about all you'll get out of anybody in charge."

"Do you believe it?" Nan asked, although Sigi's tone was already cynical.

"They said I tried to kill myself and my family doesn't want to see me anymore. Maybe it's true." Sigi shrugged. "But I certainly don't believe they saved my life. All this? It's not a life."

"They told me I tried to kill myself, too, but I wouldn't do that," Nan said. "I don't do things without a good reason."

"Do you remember anything?" Sigi asked.

"No . . . not really."

"You seem to be very calm for having just arrived. Most of the time, the new girls cry buckets of tears."

"I don't cry."

Sigi smirked. "Ooh, how very rugged of you."

Nan felt chastened. "I just . . . don't, that's all; it's not that I'm proud of it."

"I bet you are proud of it," Sigi said, still smirking. "But it's an admirable quality. I wish I didn't cry."

"I could swear you seem familiar," Nan murmured.

"Oh?" Sigi said. "That's funny. Do you think we knew each other before?"

"I don't know," Nan said. "You sound rich, and I sound like a ruffian."

Sigi's nose flushed. "Maybe I liked to spend time with ruffians, then."

Nan grinned, but all the while she was desperately trying to recall whether she had known Sigi.

Sigi filled her spoon with soup. "We'd better eat before we run out of time, and you'd better drink that."

Nan sniffed her cup and immediately recognized the sickly sweetness of the medicine she'd been given before. "What is it?"

"The serum."

"Serum?"

"You'll get sick without it. Besides that, you'll get a reprimand."

"From who?"

"Trust me, just drink it."

"Is this what causes us to forget things?"

"It couldn't be, could it?" Sigi said. "We'd forget each other every morning at breakfast. What a mess." Sigi suddenly hunched into her bowl, and a heavy hand fell on Nan's shoulder. She turned to see a man staring down at her, the only man wearing a suit and tie. In fact, everything about him was distinguished, with his slenderness and height, watch chain, and slicked-back hair.

His voice, when he spoke, was gentle but not kind. "Is there a problem here?"

"It's my first day." Nan lifted her chin. "So tell me what I'm in for. What does the serum do?"

He squinted back. "What's your name?"

"Nan Davies."

"Nan Davies, you're an impudent little thing, aren't you?"

"You tell me what I am—I can't remember. Isn't that the idea around here?"

Sigi kicked her under the table, and it *hurt*. Nan shot her a look before she could think better of it.

"You, miss, seem like a sensible girl." He gestured to Sigi, who quickly looked at her soup. "Why don't you take Nan Davies under your wing and explain matters."

Sigi grunted.

He raised his brows. "Have we regressed to the primeval era down here? Well, Miss Davies, I will tell you, if you'd like to see what happens if you don't drink your serum, you are welcome to do so." He walked away, and she could almost hear a collective exhale around her.

"You are in so much trouble," Sigi said when he left, but there was a streak of admiration in her tone.

"Who is he, and why are you so afraid of him?"

"Don't say it like *that*. I don't want to be afraid of him, but it can hardly be helped. That's Valkenrath. He's the overseer of all this," Sigi whispered. "And he's heartless."

"What happens if I don't take the serum?"

Sigi hesitated. Now she really did look afraid. "You'll get sick. Really sick."

"Like a fever? What does that mean?"

"Just weak and . . . sort of crazy. You don't want it to happen to you, believe me." All the animation seemed drained from her face, like even having a personality was dangerous with Valkenrath prowling the room.

Nan frowned into her cup for a minute and reluctantly took one sip

Sigi abruptly stood. "I need to use the powder room before we go to work."

Nan almost smiled at the idea of anyone needing a "powder room" in this place, but she wished Sigi wouldn't run off. So many secrets around here.

She finished her soup, but she didn't touch the rest of the serum. When the speakers announced that it was time for the start of the work day, and everyone rose, she switched her cup with an empty one from another table during the commotion. Whatever that stuff was, she'd take her chances without it.

ELEVEN

"This is your station!" The man had to scream at Nan to be heard over the rhythmic cacophony of machines, steam hissing from valves around the beginnings of rust. There were no windows, just a sickly glow. "All you need to do is watch the lights on this panel, and if one of them comes on, you pull the lever next to it. Do you understand?"

"What does that do?"

"Doesn't matter. You just need to pull the lever. If you have trouble with this, we can send you down to work in the slaughterhouse."

Nan sat down hard. He walked away, leaving her with the panel. There were six lights in a row, each one numbered, and each with a corresponding lever. She stared at them for a moment, and then number five lit up. She pulled the lever. It stayed down for a few seconds, and then it popped up again, but now the light was out.

Now number two lit up. She pulled that lever. And number four.

Three seconds passed by. Four. Five. Six.

Number two lit up again. She pulled the lever.

One. Two. Three.

Lever five.

One. Two. Three. Four. Five.

Lever two. Stubborn thing.

One. Two. Three.

Lever five.

Lever one.

Nan fell into a rhythm, just like the machines that churned and hissed and thumped and clacked all around her, almost the way she imagined dance music sounded to other people. Nan had never been able to hear music properly. It sounded like off-kilter noise. The only time music ever sounded right was in her dreams, but it wasn't like any other sound in the world. It was slow and haunting and heartbreakingly beautiful. She could never remember it exactly when she awoke, but it was never entirely forgotten, either. Nan had often felt so alone in the world, but whenever she woke to the fading sound of that music, she knew she was not alone in the universe.

As the moments went by, the music of the machines seemed to blend into the song of her dreams, a pattern of slow, resonant tones underneath the clamor. The more she focused on it, the calmer she felt, but it was a purposeful calm.

I have a reason for coming here. I'm sure I do.

I know what this place is.

At least, I did know. If only I could remember. . . .

A memory floated, like cream, to the top of her mind. This was a stronger memory than the one of Horst. She'd been walking with a friend of hers—her only friend, she thought, a girl who always seemed a little sad but quick to laugh.

Thea.

I always had a hard time relating to people, but not to her.

Nan remembered Thea telling her that her mother was sick. Bound-sick. *The spell,* Thea had said, sounding almost ashamed. *It went wrong somehow.* The term *bound-sick* had been unfamiliar to Nan then.

At first, Thea said, it had not been so bad. Her mother insisted her father was alive, and seemed out of sorts, but life still went on as it always had. The bound-sickness grew worse each passing year. Thea didn't even know how long she'd be able to work. Thea, who always seemed so strong, had let Nan see her cry. Nan never cried, but she also had never comforted, until that day. It was a powerful feeling, to comfort someone.

Nan remembered feeling an almost overwhelming urge to do something. She'd wanted to rush home with Thea and grab her mother and . . . and . . . fix things. Somehow. But Nan hadn't known what she could do. She had never even heard of this magic before that moment.

It was a familiar feeling, that stirring of fire inside her. She felt it now, too.

A buzzer squawked behind the panel, making her jump, and the light blinked. Quickly, she pulled the lever, and it stopped. Nan's mind had wandered too far away, but at least she had one memory now, and if she ran her mind over it again and again, maybe it would lead to more.

Her arms burned. The levers had enough resistance that pulling them once or even ten times was hardly an effort, but after a hundred times, she dreamed of being anywhere else.

A dozen other girls were in the same row, performing the same rote task, all under the inanimate glare of the hulking machines, with their buzzers and lights.

One of the girls kept setting off the buzzer, and after a number of mistakes, the supervisor stalked over. Nan couldn't hear the conversation until the end, when the man barked, "Get up!"

Meekly, the girl rose and followed him out. A few moments later, another girl took her place.

Nan's arms shook with exhaustion as she pulled the levers. She wanted to do something about this. She wanted someone to fight.

⊙–⊙–⊙–⊙

Two days passed just like the first. In the morning, Nan was given serum and thick, tasteless soup. She pretended to sip the serum, but she quickly realized that at the end of the meal, all the workers gathered their trays and tossed them into a bin to be washed, and in the chaos no one would notice a full cup of the stuff. She always ate with Sigi, chatting about other workers. Then she pulled levers for hours. For dinner they were given bread, milk, and more of the same soup, but no serum. Nan was beginning to dream of roasted pork and apples, but she didn't feel sick, weak, or crazy without taking the serum at breakfast.

On the third day, when the workers shuffled back into the cafeteria for dinner, Nan heard a concerned murmuring that swept back through the room to where she stood.

"Oh, no, who is it this time?" a girl asked, glancing around.

"Are they punishing someone?" Another girl turned pale and covered her eyes with her hand. She grabbed the arm of the girl beside her. "I won't look!" she cried, a frantic note in her voice.

"You can look," the other girl retorted. "It's only been a day. It won't be bad until tomorrow, at least."

A cage like a prison cell had been placed just past the cafeteria line, so everyone would see it. A guard stood beside it, his eyes resting briefly on each worker who passed by with dinner. A girl sat on the cage floor, sobbing, arms clinging to the bars above her. A boy was hunched behind her. When Nan got closer, she realized it was Helma.

Most of the people moving through the line tried to pretend they hadn't seen, but a few stopped to look at the pair with sympathy. Helma wailed at anyone who would look her way, "Help! You know I didn't do anything. I didn't do *anything*." One of her arms reached out between the bars, her fingers waving desperately.

A passing man took a step closer and shook his head. "You'll get through it," he said, rather insistently.

"Move along," the guard said.

"Is this really necessary?" Waving his hand, the man looked at the guard. "I mean, she is young! They are both young, and they're very new here. Look at—"

"*Move along.*" The guard poked the man with the end of his nightstick.

The man huffed, abruptly turning away.

Helma looked at Nan. "She's my roommate," she said,

gesturing to her. "Tell them! Tell them I wasn't sneaking around seeing any boys!"

Nan wasn't sure what to say. She'd known Helma only a few days— and *known* was a generous word to use. Nan had been sleeping too heavily to notice what Helma did.

Sigi's hand hooked Nan's elbow and dragged her away from the scene. "Oh, for heaven's sake," she said. "Don't get involved. I'm surprised it took this long for her to be caught. When she didn't have a roommate for a couple of weeks, she was even inviting her boyfriend into her room. Talk about asking for trouble!"

Nan drew back from the grip. "But why are they in a cage?"

"There aren't enough guards, so . . . this is how they keep us in line."

Nan could still hear Helma screaming as though the world were ending. "Why is she carrying on like that? What will they do to her and the boy?"

Sigi grabbed an empty seat. She tore her bread into several pieces. "They'll—go without their serum for a few days, that's all."

"And get sick," Nan said. "That's what you said earlier. But it doesn't make sense."

Sigi's voice was low. "They are going to . . . decay."

"Decay?"

She nodded. "As if they're dead. And then . . . they'll get some serum, and they'll come back."

Nan rubbed her arms. All her hair stood on end. "Has it ever happened to you?"

Sigi shook her head vehemently. "No. No. Hopefully never. I don't even let myself think about that happening. You can't go around in fear of it. Sometimes they punish people for what seems like no reason at all."

"So *are* we dead, then?"

Sigi averted her eyes. "I don't know for sure, but . . . I feel like I am."

"And there's no way out?"

"Well, Brigitte said . . ." She trailed off.

"What?"

"She said she tried to run away. She said the rails beneath the men's dorms are still in use, and if you follow them left from the platform, they eventually split. You can go from there. At least, you can try, if you aren't afraid of rats and bones and well . . . getting lost without any serum."

"For someone who doesn't want to escape, you certainly remembered those directions." Nan thought she recognized a bit of the rebel in Sigi.

Sigi half-smiled, half-winced. "Well, sure, I've thought about escaping, but even Brigitte decided burning to death was a better way out. What am I to think of that?"

"Better think you'd be more successful at escaping than Brigitte was."

"Maybe."

Nan didn't press Sigi. She didn't want to say that she had yet to drink another full dose of serum since her first day.

TWELVE

Nan could hear the moaning and screaming before she even reached the cafeteria.

This morning Helma and the boy were both at the bars, reaching out with awkward, flailing arms. Their eyes were beginning to sink. Their skin was discolored, darker and sort of shriveled, so their bones stood out. The change had been alarmingly rapid.

It wouldn't have been as awful if they weren't moving, if they simply decayed quietly like the dead. But the pair didn't really look dead; they were something else entirely. Their desiccating flesh moved; their pathetic, shriveling eyes darted; their mouths opened. "Help . . . help . . ." Helma sounded hoarse, as though she'd been screaming all night.

The boy clutched the bars now, lunging his body against them when he saw Nan's eyes on him. "Just a taste . . . so hungry . . ."

The guard never looked at them, never stopped them from reaching out or screaming, and he didn't stop the workers from staring, either, although few did. He just kept the workers from getting close enough to touch the prisoners.

Nan watched for a long moment. She wasn't even sure why. It didn't do any good, but she stood there as if she could do something about it, if only she had a moment to think.

Sigi tugged on her sleeve. "Nan, come on. Let's eat," Sigi said. "I'd hate being looked at if—"

Helma's eyes rolled to Nan. "Please . . ." she breathed. "Please. I'm so hungry. . . ."

Nan's fingers clenched her cup of serum. She fought an urge to throw the cup or yell at the guard. Her insides felt all twisted.

She noticed Sigi's eyes move to a point behind her. Valkenrath was at her shoulder. "Miss Davies, would you come with me, please?" A guard stood with him.

"Why?" Nan asked, as she felt Sigi squeeze her fingers.

He gave her a tight smile and no answer. The guard put a hand on the pistol at his hip. Nan got the message. Sigi reluctantly let go of her, then almost dropped the tray she'd been balancing on one hand.

"I'll be fine," Nan said softly. Sigi seemed so worried.

Would they put her in the cage with the couple? Their withering fingers reaching for her . . . She forced this thought back as she followed Valkenrath down a maze of halls and finally through a door. The guard had followed them and now waited at the entrance. Valkenrath handed her a pile of clothes—nice ones: a dress, stockings, and heeled shoes.

"I need you to do something for me, Miss Davies," he said.

"I'm going to take you to see the boy who brought you back from the dead."

"So, I am dead?"

"Well, not anymore," he said impatiently. "And very lucky you are, after what you did to yourself. But this boy wants to know that you're well. He'd be upset if he realized the extent of our program."

"What program?" Nan struggled to grasp exactly what Valkenrath meant. "And what did I do to myself, anyway? Just tell me what the hell's going on!"

"Calm yourself," he said, sounding excruciatingly calm himself. "It's very simple. You committed suicide. Freddy brought you back from the dead. You are in our work program, and your memories have been taken from you, because if you went right back to the mental and physical place that caused you to kill yourself, you might do it again."

"So all the workers back there killed themselves? Do they ever get to remember anything, or do anything else? I've heard some of them have been there for years!"

"Some of them have no place to go."

He was lying, and it was plain to see, because none of this made any sense. But he was a very good liar—she'd give him that. He spoke as if he believed all he said, and he never lost his cool. "Maybe you should let them die, then," she said. "What kind of life is this? Who are you to decide they should live?"

"Would you like to die, Miss Davies?" For a moment, his eyes came alive with threat. "I could arrange it, if it's what you truly wish."

"No," she snapped.

"Get dressed, if you would, and I'll tell you what to say when you see Freddy."

I made my own dresses, and they were better than this one.

She remembered the satisfaction of putting on a new creation. Of following a pattern. She liked patterns. Everything laid out so clearly, and yet it felt like art at the end. Nan had such trouble with art most of the time—her world was colorless, and music jarred her ears—but the symmetry of sleeves and seams made sense.

Even though she hadn't made this dress, wearing silk again was nice. Not that she had much time to enjoy it.

The guard tied a cloth around her eyes so that she couldn't see and led her down more corridors and up some stairs. When he removed it, she was in a house with sunshine streaming through glass windows. The outside world, just steps away from where she'd been.

But it wasn't really the world she had known. The house felt quiet and insular; she didn't hear the voices of passersby or the rumbling of motorcars. She imagined this gilt-and-brocade interior must belong to one of the wealthy houses in the city's finest districts, set back from the street and surrounded by a gate. No one had to tell her that if she cried for help, she wouldn't get any.

She heard murmuring male voices in a different room, and after Valkenrath delivered his instructions, the guard led her there.

"There she is!" A thin old man with a mustache sat at a table with a cup of coffee and a slice of pastry. The smell of the coffee was sharp and familiar and made Nan feel suddenly very homesick for a place she couldn't quite remember. "Looking very well indeed."

The younger man must be Freddy. He looked at her rather gravely. She didn't want to say any of the things Valkenrath had told her to say.

"Nan?" Freddy said.

"Yes," she said, glancing around. Dark oil portraits gazed upon her from the walls. The wealth and well-kept age of everything felt unfamiliar and uncomfortable.

"Are you feeling better?"

"It will take time for her to recover from the suicide, but she's happy at her new job, aren't you, Miss Davies?" Valkenrath said.

She held herself stiffly. "It's all right."

"Where are you working?" Freddy asked, leaning forward in his chair, clutching his cup of coffee.

"I pull levers all day," she said. Valkenrath had told her to smile, but she was not smiling. She could feel his cold gaze on her.

Freddy looked like a question was blazing on his lips. One he couldn't ask.

"Not much of a party girl, are you?" the mustached man said with a chuckle. She didn't quite understand the situation, but it almost felt as if the mustached man was making fun of her. As though she would think the job fun if she were a different kind of girl. But no one would find that job fun, or anything about that sunless world.

"There isn't much opportunity to party when you have

nothing of your own," Nan snapped back. "Not even good food. What would we party with?"

"Thea's worried about you," Freddy said. The mustached man frowned at him.

Thea! Before she could ask him how he knew Thea—or for that matter, how *she* knew Thea—Valkenrath turned her shoulder to the door. "She's ill-tempered, Freddy, but otherwise well," he called as he forced her out. The guard was waiting just outside and grabbed her arms behind her back, holding them secure with one hand while roughly pulling the blindfold back around her face with the other. She stayed half limp, not trying to fight. There didn't seem to be any point right now, when the guard could easily overwhelm her.

"You didn't say a single thing I told you to say," Valkenrath whispered as they led her back into the depths.

"Why would I?"

"I could make your life much worse."

"So Freddy brings us back from the dead, but he doesn't know anything about it afterward," she said softly.

"I'll tell him the truth someday," Valkenrath said. "When he's old enough to understand why we do it."

"Why do you do it?"

"For the good of the city, Miss Davies. But I don't expect a troubled, suicidal girl to understand." They had stopped walking, and he pulled off the blindfold. They were back in the room where she'd changed out of her work suit. A nurse was waiting, with as much animation in her face as a coatrack, and he nodded at her.

"I wasn't suicidal."

"I wonder why you poisoned yourself, then." He turned away from her, opening a cabinet. "Why you chose to die alone in some squalid alley."

The fire inside her was white-hot. He could lie all day, but she knew her own essence. She knew she had never been troubled and suicidal. She didn't have to remember to know. "I would never do such a thing. If you take all my memories, you can tell me anything, but you can't make me believe it."

"You're sharper than most." He watched the nurse prepare a syringe. "There's something special about you. I do sense it. You were probably quite a charming girl in your life before. Used to getting your way. But trust me. You just haven't been here long enough."

"This is ready, sir," the nurse said.

Valkenrath's eyes indicated the guard should restrain Nan again, holding one pale arm out for the syringe. Her throat tightened, and she had to force herself not to struggle and fight, knowing it would only make things worse.

"Over time," Valkenrath said, "you will believe anything."

The needle entered her skin.

THIRTEEN

On Thursday morning, Thea changed into a day dress to try to catch Father Gruneman at his breakfast table. After the other night, she was nervous to see him again, but if he knew anything more about what had happened to her father, she owed it to her mother to find out.

When her father was alive, the whole family used to have dinner with Father Gruneman on occasion, but it had been so many years ago. In her childhood memories, his house was practically a mansion, but in reality it was a cottage, with a steeply pitched roof and two dormer windows. The walls were weathered, the roof patched. Like the church, it was a remnant of an earlier age when the city had not yet spread this far.

She rapped on the door.

Father Gruneman opened it promptly. "Thea," he said. He was still . . . friendly, but not as easy with her as before. "I wondered when I'd see you. I just heard about your mother being taken away."

"I need to talk to you."

He glanced at the street behind her before motioning her in.

His windows were all curtained, even though the sun was up. The house was furnished with sturdy wooden furniture, the kind that would be passed down through generations, and there were piles of dusty books. It should have seemed comfortable and lived in, but the pent-up darkness was uninviting.

"Would you like some eggs?" he offered. "A glass of milk?"

"I'm not hungry, really," she said. "But don't let me stop you from eating breakfast."

He briefly shook his head and motioned for her to take a chair. "I had no idea you were working at the Telephone Club."

"It's a good job," she said, trying not to sound too defensive.

"For a young woman, I suppose. But where do you go from there? I hate that you left school for your mother's sake."

"Well, I had to do something. The veteran's widow checks aren't even enough for the rent, and the savings are long gone." She looked at him carefully, almost expecting to see a stranger, but it was still her Father Gruneman, with gentle eyes. "Never mind me. I—I had to talk to you. The other night—"

He interrupted. "I didn't mean for you to see any of that meeting."

"But I can't unsee it now." She laced and twisted her fingers, wishing she could blurt out all her questions, tell him what she'd overheard him say. "Who was that woman?"

"That was . . ." He hesitated as though he was deciding how much to tell her. "Arabella von Kaspar."

"How do you know her?"

He stared at the ashes in his unlit hearth. "My dear Thea, I only want you to be safe. You must be patient. Your father was a good friend, and I want to help your mother, but if you ask too many questions and walk down a dangerous path, I would never forgive myself."

"But you do know something! How can I not ask? You're the one who told me they took Mother away to erase her memories! Every day that goes by—" She swallowed. This was an idea she tried not to face.

He sat back with a sigh, stroking his weathered cheeks. "Let me put it this way. You know me at church. When I'm there, my role is to speak the word of God, as much as I am capable, not to lead you into danger. But away from that—my own personal quest, if you can call it that—is to *live* the word of God as much as I am capable. To fight for peace and freedom and love. That is what led me to the revolutionary movement in this city. But it is not an easy business. I've put myself in danger, and I've sometimes succumbed to my own darker motives—revenge, or anger—because I've lost people in this. Your parents, of course, are among that number."

"But you won't tell me anything about it?"

"How could I tell your mother, if something happened to you? She'll need you when she comes back."

"Shouldn't I fight for peace and freedom and love, too? You don't want me to actually learn anything from your sermons?"

"I did walk into that one, didn't I?" He met her eyes, and she was taken aback by the steeliness in his gaze. "Look, Thea, I understand and admire your impulse to help. But I will not put Henry's daughter in danger. I know what I'm doing, but I also know—" He shook his head. "Just lie low. Wait. I will help your mother. I promise you that."

"Will you just answer one more question?" she asked. "Then I'll leave you alone."

"If I can."

"Was my father . . . part of what you're doing?" Her whole body was rigid. She had to know if he was alive. If he was in prison.

Father Gruneman caught her hand. "No. It was the war that led me to this work. And he was already gone."

She bit her lip. "But he could still be alive, couldn't he?"

"I don't know for certain."

Of course he would say that. There was no body.

But she had heard him say, at the club, *She knew he was alive.*

He'd been talking about her mother. It must be. But if Thea confronted Father Gruneman, he would know she had spied on him. And it was obvious he had no intention of letting her in on the other half of his life.

Still, she couldn't just sit back and do nothing. All the things that had happened so quickly seemed to be leading her on this path, whether or not she wished it.

"Are you sure I can't offer you a bite to eat?" he asked, obviously trying to move off the subject.

This time she accepted, just to be polite, but she was already thinking ahead. Maybe it was better to pursue the answers alone. He wouldn't be putting her in danger, then. She would be choosing to get involved on her own. She knew the revolutionaries met at the Café Rouge, and if she happened to take an interest, could he really stop her?

FOURTEEN

"I'd like a Starlight, and she'll take a Milky Way Twist. Will you still have the Starlight when this show ends? It's my favorite cocktail in the world now."

"They might give it a different name," Thea said. "But I'll mention it to the bartender."

"Thanks," the girl said as the telephone on her table rang. Thea started to inch away, but the girl waved her back. "It's for you. You have an admirer at table seven."

The waitresses, despite uniforms suggesting the career-girl clothes of a telephone operator, were not actually supposed to use the telephones. Thea's eyes strained through the haze of smoke to table seven, finding a flash of silver hair.

She walked over to Freddy. "Down here with the rabble tonight, are you?" she said with a smile, but she was burning to know if he'd found out anything about Nan. She still hadn't shown up, and with every passing day Thea was surer that something awful had happened to her.

"I insisted. Gerik likes the balcony better than I do."

"Noisy down here," Gerik said with a glance at a nearby woman with a constant whooping laugh.

"In all your stories of your crazy youth, no one was ever loud?" Freddy asked.

"No one was loud in the imperial days," Gerik said. "All the whispering was much more exciting. But don't mind me." He turned to watch the chorus line of dancing girls dressed— barely dressed—like stars.

Freddy caught her eye and mouthed, *Later*. He mimicked picking up another cup of coffee.

She nodded, but tonight was Monday, the meeting of the revolutionaries at the Café Rouge. She'd already asked Mr. Kortig about leaving work early. She couldn't miss this one and have to wait another week to attend. She took Freddy's and Gerik's orders and rushed off. Supposing she could get Freddy alone, she wondered if she should bring him with her to the meeting.

She didn't know the least thing about revolutionaries, really. She'd always assumed a lot of artist types would talk about intellectual concepts she didn't understand and say *the bourgeoisie* this and *labor strikes* that, and not actually do much. But she couldn't imagine Father Gruneman talking that way.

Freddy might tell Gerik and bring the whole thing down. Perhaps the best thing to do would be to see if she could get him to walk with her on some other pretense, and decide as they talked.

She brought the drinks out, a slight smile playing on her lips, shooting an occasional glance at Gerik. "You're becoming a regular, you know. I hope it isn't just for the science lesson."

"Certainly not that," Freddy said, grinning wryly.

She leaned in closer and said, just loud enough for Gerik to hear, "Too bad you can't seem to ditch the chaperone. I asked to get off early today to go to a party some girls I know are throwing. Ought to be a heck of a time. They have a phonograph and lots of music."

"I've never been much for parties," Freddy said.

Did he not understand what she was getting at?

"Freddy!" Gerik barked, with some exasperation. "When a girl asks you to a party, you don't need to act like such a stick."

Ah. Now she understood. He knew how to play Gerik, too. She tried to toss out more encouragement for Gerik to let him go. "It'll be a nice time. Fifteen, twenty other kids, and some dancing. A bit tame for my taste, really, but she's an old school friend who just moved into her own place with a couple other girls."

Gerik waved his hand. "I suppose you can't get in *too* much trouble without me."

"Hmph," Freddy said. "You wish I would."

"Can you meet me out front of Café Tops at ten thirty?" Thea said.

"The sad-old-man place?"

She laughed. "Exactly."

"Sure."

The night was brisk, a northern wind whipping down the street and keeping the crowds light, which was part of the reason Mr. Kortig had agreed to let her go early. Thea shivered as she hurried across the street. Freddy was waiting inside, alone among the sad old men. He had coffee and a pastry, in spite of having already polished off a plate of smoked-meat dumplings at the club. Even for a boy, he certainly ate a lot for someone so thin!

"Well, Gerik's gone, or at least spying from a comfortable distance," he said.

"Goodness, he'd better not be."

He smiled, but it did make her wonder. "I need to change," she said.

"How far away is this party?" he asked. "Because I need to talk to you."

"Well, me too. Just wait."

She hoped there would be a crowd at the revolutionary meeting and Father Gruneman wouldn't notice her, but just in case, she didn't want to look too Thea-ish. In the bathroom of Café Tops, she slathered her eyelids in kohl and wiped off her usual red lipstick. She had bought a new hat just for the occasion, bonnet-style with a curved brim that shaded her face, and pink flowers all over. She thought it was awful and would never wear it again, but that was just the idea. Then she wrapped her mother's long black scarf around her neck. Father Gruneman might still recognize her coat, but among a lot of people no one would notice coats.

"That is quite a hat," Freddy commented.

"It was the ugliest one I could find."

"You didn't tell me it was an ugly-hat party."

"It's a masquerade. But only for me. I'd rather not be recognized."

"Hmm. I hope the lighting is bad wherever we're going,

because I don't think anyone would consider an ugly hat a disguise."

"It's the best I can do on short notice!" She moved toward the door. "Let's go."

The weather, unfortunately, was not welcoming to conversation. They walked fast, Freddy keeping a hand clamped over his own hat against the wind, and their teeth chattered. "Maybe we should h-hail a cab?" he said.

"N-no. Just t-tell me what you wanted to tell me. All the cabs look occupied, anyway."

He squinted ahead. They were approaching the Lampenlight District's traffic light, one of the few in the city's busy intersections. Automobiles halted, turned, and proceeded in their usual dance.

"I . . . I saw Nan," he said.

"What?" The vigor rushed out of Thea's step. "How? Where?"

He looked upset. Not at her. But at something. "Gerik . . . he has some involvement with the hospital. They have a sort of rehabilitation program for people who attempt suicide. And Nan . . . was there."

"But Nan wouldn't—she couldn't—I mean . . . !" She thought she'd known Nan well. "She had ambitions. She spoke of becoming a dressmaker, and she was so clever and brave. And she never seemed depressed or unsure. It wouldn't be like her at all."

"Maybe she had trouble talking about it. Are you sure?"

"*Yes,*" Thea snapped. He didn't know Nan, but *she* did, and she was certain. "Nan was solid as a mountain."

"I'll admit that something doesn't add up. . . ."

"And you said you saw her at the hospital?"

"Well, yes, but—"

"Which hospital?"

"I don't know. I wasn't paying attention on the way—didn't realize where we were going."

"But you don't know the name of it?"

"No."

She was walking fast again, and she didn't seem to feel the cold much anymore. "Speaking of something that doesn't add up," she said, "how could you not find out the name of the hospital once you knew Nan was there? Even after you'd seen her there, you didn't think to look for a sign?"

He didn't say anything, just kept walking along with his head down against the wind. His expression was pained.

"What are you not telling me?"

"I need to think. It doesn't make sense. . . ."

"If you tell me, maybe we can make sense of it together."

He hesitated, glancing around again. "I cannot underestimate the gravity of it," he said. "The danger we would be in if you told anyone I'd told you. You have to swear to me you won't act on this information."

"If—" *If it's about Nan, or my father, I can't swear that.* But she had to know, even if it meant breaking Freddy's trust. "I swear. B-but we have to walk faster. I'm shivering again."

"All right," he said. "It's just this: ever since the war, when people die from suicide, and sometimes murders and executions, the government has been reviving them. The city has been in need of manpower since the war, and suicide is no good way to die, so it benefits everyone."

"Reviving them? After death?"

"Yes. So they can have a second chance. And do some good work for the city. That's where I saw Nan. At the rehabilitation center. Gerik has a hand in it, but I can't breathe a word to anyone."

"Nan *died*?"

"It's all right, though! She was revived. She's fine. But they won't send her back home as long as they think there's a risk she might hurt herself again."

"How could they ever send her back if it's a secret?"

He paused. "I'm sure they must do something to their memories."

"Who's doing all this? Who has that power?"

"I don't know, some of the government sorcerers, I suppose." He looked uncomfortable. "I know it's a shock. And I knew you'd want to save her. But if Gerik or anyone knew I'd told you, they'd probably have to lock you up and tamper with your memories, too."

She walked in silence for a bit. They were getting close to the Café Rouge. It was at the cheap end of Lampenlight, behind Kuka-Kasino, known for having a caged parrot above every table that squawked for the bill. She could see the neon bird on its sign in the distance.

"What about my father?" she asked, although she was almost afraid. The vision of him she kept seeing—could it be his revival? "Tell me truthfully: have you ever seen him?"

Freddy hesitated again, and that was answer enough.

"You *have*." She caught his sleeve. "Tell me you have."

"Yes . . . I did. Years ago. I—I witnessed his resurrection."

"He was in his army uniform," she prompted. "But I know he wouldn't have committed suicide."

"They said when a soldier was brought back, it was only following execution for an act of treason. But . . . maybe they made a mistake." He said this, clearly knowing he could not suggest to her face that her father was a traitor. She wondered if he really believed it. He showed more emotion than Nan, really, and yet he was harder to read.

She pulled her scarf closer around her face, trying to understand what she had heard. He was saying her father was alive. He was saying that, wasn't he? Her father had been brought back from death. And they thought he was a traitor and wouldn't let him go home. Her mother had been right all along.

She wanted to cry, to run, to strike Freddy—no, nothing seemed right. It was such an unbelievable, amazing, horrible thing that she found herself looking up at the moon above them, as if she might see something written in the stars. Her jaw trembled.

Freddy was looking at her warily. "I want to help you," he said. "I'll try to find out more." And then, "Are you all right? Well, that's a stupid question, but—"

The wind was preventing her eyes from tearing up, but she quickly wiped them with her scarf anyway. "I'll manage. We have to keep going."

"Not really to a party, I hope."

He must trust her, to tell her all of this. So she ought to trust him, too. "To a meeting. Of revolutionaries."

FIFTEEN

The address for the Café Rouge matched a narrow four-story brick building painted green and sandwiched between similar buildings. It had no sign, so the only indicator that she had the right place was the cluster of young bohemian types milling around out front.

A man was guarding the door. Thea stopped at a distance, watching him greet and nod at some people and stop others. He talked for several minutes with one girl, even after she produced a piece of paper from her purse.

"Do we need some kind of pass?" Freddy asked her.

"Well, I know the revolutionaries are always looking for more members. If I talk to them . . ." But she worried Father Gruneman might see her at the door and turn her away.

"I'll admit, with that hat, you don't look likely to be part of a police raid."

"If you tease me about this hat one more time . . ."

"I'm more concerned I might be recognized, if anyone's seen me at the club with Gerik."

She turned around to face the street again. "You're right.

A lot of revolutionaries go to the club. It's too risky to try to talk our way in."

"Are you suggesting espionage?"

"Well, 'espionage' is a strong word."

"I like it. Maybe Trouble is an apt name for you after all."

She smacked his arm gently and then took his elbow. "Well, let's not stand here any longer, in case we're noticed. Maybe there's a back entrance."

They made their way around the row of buildings to the back alley. The café sounded packed by now—she could hear the rumble of conversation even through the door, but the words weren't intelligible. The back door was locked. A fire escape ladder dangled temptingly above them, the bottom rung low enough to grab.

Thea looked higher up, chewing her lip. The first fire escape was cluttered with potted plants and junk. "It looks like apartments above. I don't want to break into someone's house."

"I see doors," Freddy said. "They might open into a hallway for more than one apartment. We just need to have a reason for poking around. Like we live down the street, and we lost our cat, and we just saw him on the roof."

"I guess that might work."

Freddy hung from the rung. "So, are your arms strong enough to haul your entire body up to that ladder?"

"No." She cast around the alley. "We need something to stand on. A milk crate won't be enough, will it? We have to hurry! If we miss the meeting, it'll all be for nothing."

"If you grab on, I can support your feet," Freddy said. "You can go ahead."

Thea didn't much like the idea of sneaking around the building alone, but they had already come this far.

The ladder rattled alarmingly as Freddy boosted her up, but she managed to hook her heels over the thin rungs and clamber onto the platform. As she glanced around at rusted tins that housed herbs and a few scattered tools, her eyes alighted on a crumpled sheet. Perhaps it was meant to cover the plants on cold nights.

"Freddy, there's a sheet here. Do you think if we knotted it, you could use it to climb up?"

"Maybe. Toss it down."

She tied the sheet around the top of the ladder and looked left and right. "This is looking really suspicious now."

"Hurry, hurry."

He quickly made a slipknot in the sheet, to use as a foothold. She crouched to try to help him up. Her body shivered from the cold, but she was too nervous to truly feel her discomfort.

Moments later, she was grabbing his arms, helping to support him as he climbed his way up, grimacing. Once his foot was over the railing, she was so glad to have managed it that she almost forgot the whole point of the endeavor.

"Let's never do this again," she said, laughing with relief.

"You don't have to tell me. Whose idea was it?" He tugged her hat brim over her eyes.

They untied the sheet and put it back in its place. Freddy looked in the small window at the top of the door leading from the landing. "It *is* a hallway." He opened the door.

As soon as the door opened, the voices from the meeting became audible again. Thea was breathless with triumph as she stepped into the warmth of the indoors. The smell of cigarettes, coffee, and perfume trailed upward from the interior staircase.

She turned to Freddy. "What now?"

"We're not going to be able to sneak in, so I think we should just act like we belong here."

Thea tried to look confident and breezy as she took the steps. The door to the bottom floor hung wide open, and people were crowded into the lower stairwell. Indeed, the girls on the stairs, who looked to be about her age, didn't seem to think it was strange for Thea and Freddy to come in behind them, even though Thea's heart pounded as fast as a jackhammer.

Father Gruneman and Arabella von Kaspar were standing on a small dais in the corner of the stuffy room, which was packed wall to wall with revolutionaries, some of them at tables, but most standing. "We are at the point now where we know what must be done," Father Gruneman was saying. "We *must* free our brothers and sisters. It is simply a matter of working out the how. According to our intelligence, when the workers are freed, they may not have their memories."

"Workers?" she whispered to Freddy. "Are those the revived people you were talking about?"

"Maybe." He tapped his chin, thoughtful, almost nervous.

"Should this prove true," Father Gruneman continued, "it will take considerable organization to reunite them with their families. We must all do our best to protect them, and each other, when the time comes. This will be our opportunity to—" He stopped as Arabella sidled up next to him and put a hand on his arm.

"Do you hear what Viktor asks of you?" she said to the

crowd, her voice fierce and furious, where Father Gruneman's had been firm and calm. "We have spoken of revolution for years, but the hour is almost upon us. I am prepared to fight and to die, if I must, for the thousands who have fought and died before me. For my daughter. For your son. For your father, your grandfather, your friend." She met eyes as she named relations. "We must not tremble when the hour is upon us. We must not hesitate when the enemy is before us and the gun is in our hand. Because if we do, they will squash us as they have squashed so many others, this 'republic' of ours." Her voice rang throughout the room, and the crowd around Thea stirred like the leaves of a tree touched by the wind. "Do you hear the call?" she asked the crowd, pounding her fist to her palm, the bracelets on her arm clacking. "Will you fight?"

The crowd responded with hooting, shouting, murmuring. Drinks were lifted to the ceiling.

Father Gruneman shook his head. "I don't want our focus to be bloodshed. We risk killing innocents. Our loved ones need our help."

"Our loved ones do need our help, yes," Arabella said. "But it isn't going to be pretty. This is war, and the person responsible for this needs to pay."

"Is she talking about the person who has been bringing back the dead?" Thea asked Freddy.

"Perhaps." His already pale face was a shade paler.

"What's wrong?" His reaction reminded her that he might know more than he had told her. "Do you know who it is?"

Some of the crowd were beginning to murmur now.

"I agree that this won't be bloodless." A bearded man

standing near them lifted a hand. "But we need to stay on topic, and that's assigning task forces. We know from Karl's reports that we're going to see widespread power outages. I'd like to form a response team to deal specifically with that side of things."

Even though Thea's apartment didn't have electricity, just gas, she felt ill at the very suggestion of power outages. But if it meant saving her father—well, she would sit in the dark or stand in breadlines again. Whatever it took to have him back.

"Yes," a young woman said. "And we need to talk about safe houses for the workers. I've been talking to Mr. M. about different locations where we could shelter them as we help locate their families."

"We won't have time to shelter them and locate their families!" Arabella said. "I don't care what Viktor says—it's impossible! They won't have their memories, and there are too many of them."

Father Gruneman was locking eyes with Arabella, and Thea had only seen him look so angry when the old hymnbooks had been taken away. He was standing as straight as his slightly hunched old back would allow. "It's been our mission from the beginning to find out what happened to the missing people and then to save them. Well, now we know what's happened. If we give up, if we indulge in some violent impulse, our chance is gone. Sigi is gone with them."

"I told you not to speak of her." Arabella turned from him.

"And I tell you, you should. I know it pains you—" Father Gruneman put a hand on her shoulder, but she pushed it off.

"It doesn't pain me. Don't you turn 'Father Gruneman' on

me, Viktor. I've seen far too many sides of you for that."

Thea was startled by Freddy putting an arm around her shoulder and whispering, "Let's go." When she didn't move at first, he said, "I don't think we'll learn much more."

"But we've been here only a few minutes, after all that trouble to get up the fire escape!"

"At least it'll be easier to get down again. And I need to talk to you. Alone."

SIXTEEN

The cabdriver was whistling a jaunty tune, seemingly oblivious to the heavy mood of Thea and Freddy in the backseat. Out of the corner of her eye, Thea could see the city lights racing across the strong, straight lines of Freddy's face.

In this quiet moment, she began to move the pieces in her mind, to see how they fit together. Freddy, with his silver hair, bringing a strange vision of her father and an odd story about Nan . . . and this talk of a sorcerer who could revive the dead . . .

It couldn't be him.

Surely it couldn't be him.

He wouldn't be here with me if he had that kind of power. They wouldn't even let him go out.

But —

The cab pulled up in front of her apartment building and they both got out, but Freddy walked around to the driver's window and exchanged a few words before giving him money.

"Sending a message to Gerik," he explained as the taxicab drove away.

"He won't worry that you're out so late?"

"Not if I tell him the right thing."

Thea approached the stairs apprehensively. These were dank, poorly lit stairs trod by well-worn shoes, and she hated to bring him here. But when he had asked if there was a private place where they could discuss things, the only truly private place she could think of was her apartment. Although it sounded strange to call it that. It wasn't really *her* place. It was still paid for, in part, by checks from her father's military service. It was waiting for her mother to come home.

"Step quietly," she whispered. "If Mrs. Weis or Miss Mueller hears me bringing a boy up, heaven knows what." She fished out her keys.

After she hung up her coat and lit the gas lamps, he looked around curiously, as if her apartment were an exhibit. She cringed inwardly. The apartment was dusty, the floor grimy, dishes piled up and needing attention. . . . Mother had been cleaning less reliably in recent months, and Thea really hadn't felt like picking up a broom or a rag since she was taken.

His eyes wandered to the photographs on the ledge—her parents' wedding photo, and another of Father in his army uniform. Freddy picked that one up. "This is your father?"

"Yes."

Freddy studied the picture for a long moment. "I remember," he said. "I always remember."

Thea stood near the table, not knowing where to put her hands. "Remember what?"

"It's a wondrous, humbling thing, bringing someone to life," he said, his voice trembling. "Why would I be granted such a gift? But I was. I brought back your father, and Nan."

It's true.

She wanted to sit down. But she couldn't bear to make all the noise of dragging out a chair. Instead, she took the picture from him. Father's smile looked out at her. *Mother* was *right. All along. I never should have doubted her.*

"It *is* you, then," she said. "You're the sorcerer the revolutionaries are looking for?"

"It was probably stupid of me to walk into their den. But then again, it was probably the last thing they'd expect." He looked at her kitchen. "Would you mind if I had a bit of that bread? I'll give you money for a new loaf."

"Is this really a time to be eating?"

"It just—it makes me hungry all the time, the magic. Gerik says it eats away at people, and so sorcerers are always eating away at something else. Magic does things to a person. It turns hair silver, too."

"I didn't realize."

"Not many people do. Strong magic has never been common. I still try to keep my hat on unless I'm someplace where it would be too conspicuous to wear a hat, like the dining room of a nice club."

She took a deep breath. "So . . . these people you bring back . . . where do they come from?"

"Gerik and Uncle—Gerik's brother—bring them to me."

"And they're the ones who told you all the people committed suicide?"

"They must have," he said. "I mean—it must be true. Why would they bring so many people back otherwise? I'm giving them a second chance."

"But are you?" Thea grabbed the bread for him and started slicing it; at least it was something for her hands to do. "My father hasn't come back."

"Well, Gerik isn't a *monster*. He wouldn't want to bring back soldiers who fought for this country and never let them see their families again."

"Wouldn't he?" Freddy was wrong. He had to be wrong. "My mother isn't the only woman in the parish who was bound-sick, you know. Surely not all these men were cowards and traitors or suicidal? And even if they were, why wouldn't they at least tell us the men were being held somewhere, instead of letting their wives get sick? If my mother could just see my father here and there, she wouldn't be sick." Her stomach was churning the more she thought of it. "What does happen to them, then? The revolutionaries mentioned . . ." Well, they hadn't mentioned many specifics. "They spoke of getting them out. You said Nan was at a hospital?"

"No, actually," he admitted. "Uncle brought her into his parlor."

"So it isn't too far away, I imagine."

"When I saw Nan, she said she was working in a factory and the food was bad. After I revive them, they're led off through the basement."

"Underground?" She thought of her mother trying to enter the subway. The subways that were all shut down after the war.

This image of her father and Nan trapped beneath the streets was too much for Thea to bear. Her father had been gone for eight years. Her mother had been losing her mind for eight years. And it could have been prevented. It wasn't death that had torn them apart; it was the government. The same government that had called her father up for military service in the first place. Moving like a mannequin, she handed a plate of buttered bread to Freddy.

"I'm sorry," Freddy said. "I didn't know."

"Maybe you should have thought about it sooner." She jerked back when he tried to touch her. "Don't. Please don't." She couldn't bear to even think of his hands on her, knowing what they could do—and what they had done.

"Are you afraid of me?"

"I just don't want to be touched right now. Not by you."

He stepped back again. "But . . . maybe there's just been a mistake. Maybe—"

"How could it be a *mistake* to take everyone I love away from me?"

He didn't answer.

She felt small and wretched, like it was the first time something truly awful had ever happened in her life, all over again. But she wasn't a child anymore, and she couldn't give in to it. "We have to set them free," she said. "You have to tell your fake uncles that you won't bring anyone else back unless they let the people go free."

"I can't . . . just . . . do that."

She drew a breath deep enough to lift the buttons on her

dress, and then said, "Well, we have to do something. And you can't bring people back from the dead anymore. Surely you can't, knowing this now?"

He didn't respond.

She was still shuffling through all the ramifications. "So . . . you can really defy death, for good?"

"Well . . . almost," he said. "The only thing is that they need to take a magical serum. It keeps the magic going. Like a medicine."

"Do you make the serum, too?"

"No," he said. "Gerik and Uncle make it. Or else they know someone who makes it—I'm not actually sure. It just appears, as far as I'm concerned. I give it to my cat."

"Your cat?"

"Yes. He died some years ago, so now he gets the serum."

"Your cat is *dead*?"

"Not anymore."

"And what happens if your cat doesn't take the serum?"

"I've never actually bothered to find out."

"So . . . the people you've brought back need Gerik and his brother, or whoever makes the serum, or the magic might fail and they'd die again."

"I think that's true."

This was a sinister new development.

"And you never thought to ask about these things?"

"I was a child when all of this started, and it's been going on for so long. Why would I have thought anything was wrong?" His expression turned stern. "Don't get angry at me. I was taken from my family when I was three years old because of this. My parents *are* alive, but I see them only once a year, with Gerik accompanying me. And I'm hardly permitted to leave the house, because they're so afraid the wrong person is going to find out what I can do. But it's a sacrifice I make to keep this city going."

"Why did Gerik take you to the Telephone Club, then, if you have to stay so secret?"

His expression twisted, and she had a sinking feeling he was going to drop a new surprise in her lap.

"They want me to father a child," he said, avoiding her eyes.

"A *child*? And is that what he thinks you're up to with me tonight?"

Freddy nodded. He looked a little flushed. "I'm afraid they won't let me see you much more if . . . Well, Gerik took me to the Telephone Club to find a girl. Just any girl, he said, somebody pretty I could pay off. But I didn't want it to be like that."

She sucked in her breath. "Why? Why a *child*?"

"To duplicate my magic. It's hereditary." She had put the bread in front of him, but he didn't touch it.

"You aren't good enough for them?"

"That's what I said. But they figure two revivers are better than one. Not that there's any guarantee the magic would pass on. I believe they intend to keep trying if it doesn't work the first time."

"This is ridiculous." She pressed her hands against her head, crumpling her waves. "Gerik thinks I'm the kind of girl who would have a baby with someone I didn't even know? For *money*?"

"He actually warned me that you seemed like the kind of girl who might not be amenable to this plan."

"But he still thinks—he let you go tonight because he thinks that's what we're doing?"

"Look, none of this was even remotely my idea."

It made her sick to remember the way she had flirted with Freddy in front of Gerik, knowing now that all the while he was considering whether she would be "amenable" to this despicable task. She wanted to smack Freddy. Maybe he hadn't meant to dupe her, but she felt duped all the same. Hot tears flooded her eyes.

"Thea! I've just told you all the things I'm never supposed to tell anyone!"

"I believe you, but you don't seem to understand how all this sounds to me. You let Gerik think awful things about me, you asked me about Nan without telling me you'd actually seen her, and worst of all, you—my father—"

"What do you want me to do?" he said, his voice flatter now.

"You have to stop reviving people. You have to tell Gerik you refuse. It's *your* magic. What can they do without you?"

"They could threaten my family."

"But have they? Have you tried to think of a way to stop this, or are you just going to give up?" she said. "I don't think you truly realize how much your magic has hurt me. I thought my father was dead. This is much worse."

"Thea . . ." He seemed at a loss for words.

She shook her head. "Why don't you just go?"

"Go? But we should—"

"I want to be alone right now. I need to think. You've lied to me. Maybe you had reasons, but it was still an awful lot of lies, Freddy."

"Fine." The word was like a dull blade cutting into her heart. He opened the door and left her to face these dark revelations alone.

But, of course, that was exactly what she had asked for.

SEVENTEEN

When Freddy arrived at home, he went straight to his room. He brushed off Gerik, pleading exhaustion and a headache.

"Do you need some medicine, lad? You don't sound very good."

"No. Just some rest." Freddy shut the door behind him.

Amsel, sleeping on the bed, got to his feet with an eager meow and pressed his head against Freddy's hand, getting up a good purr. Freddy glanced at his desk. He spent many hours, which otherwise would have been idle, repairing clocks. It was the only way he could connect to his father, and to the life he might have had without his magic. Gerik indulged him by sending them his way. Amsel was the enemy of half-repaired clocks, and sure enough, he had swatted gears and parts all over the rug.

"You're terrible," Freddy said.

Amsel chirped through his purr and climbed into Freddy's lap. The cat was the only thing Freddy had been allowed to take with him when he left home. Freddy would never forget clutching Amsel, wrapped in a blanket, in the back of Gerik's car when they drove away from his home forever.

When Freddy woke one morning shortly after his tenth birthday to find Amsel a stiff corpse curled up at his feet, he didn't cry. He simply put his magic to use. Thinking back on it now, he remembered Gerik's anger when he saw that Freddy had revived the cat. "He'll need serum every day!" Gerik had said.

"What serum?" Freddy had asked.

Gerik had quickly calmed himself, explaining the serum and saying it was fine, *just fine, good lad, of course you want your old cat to stick around, you can just mix it into his breakfast. . . .*

That was a slip on Gerik's part, wasn't it? He didn't even mean for me to know about the serum. But I didn't think about it at the time.

Usually Freddy slept as well as he ate. Magic was a strain on the body, but a satisfying one.

Now he felt his conscience battling his body, telling him, *You must not do this.* He spent the night staring at the crown molding of his bedroom ceiling. In the morning, the whole daily cycle began again: a heaping tray of breakfast, a freshly pressed suit, Gerik knocking on the door and asking if he was ready to head for Uncle's.

"How was the party last night?" Gerik tapped impatiently on the steering wheel, waiting for a nursemaid to walk a baby carriage across their driveway. Unlike most wealthy men, Gerik hated being chauffeured around. He owned several sporty cars and drove them himself, so they had complete privacy behind the doors of a swank coupe.

"Just fine."

"Good music?"

"I guess it was all right." Freddy looked out the window, avoiding Gerik's eyes. Thea was on his mind, telling him he must take responsibility for his own magic.

"Records, eh?" Gerik said. "I tell you, when I was young, we always had someone singing, playing the piano. If Alex Korsky was there, we even had a mean violin. Not the same anymore. But after that, she invited you back to her apartment? I hope that went somewhere."

This just kept getting more painful. "I kissed her," he lied. "But she's not the kind of girl who rushes into things, I think. She doesn't want to be thought of as . . . you know." He tried not to think of her shame last night. "I think next time I should drop by her apartment with something nice to eat, when she isn't at work." Whenever he saw her again, he didn't want to be at the club and he didn't want Gerik around.

"Yes, that's a fine plan," Gerik said. "But if it takes much longer, we'd better find another girl. Rory's not very happy I'm letting you pick the girl yourself, and he has no idea you've been gallivanting around town. You wouldn't have any fun at all if I weren't around."

That was certainly true.

⊙–⊙–⊙–⊙

"How is the quest to provide Freddy an heir coming?" Uncle asked, without even a "good morning" first, when they walked into his impeccably kept parlor.

Even though Freddy saw Roderick Valkenrath at least once a week, the man always remained a distant figure, even down to the fact that he wanted to be called "Uncle" rather than his given name. He was Gerik's brother, younger by just a year, but he looked much younger—broad-shouldered beneath his trim suit, handsome in a severe way, and clean-shaven.

"Quite well," Gerik said. "We have a likely prospect."

"A 'likely prospect'? I don't understand why this is taking so long. How hard is it to find a woman willing to accept a sum to bear a child?"

"Well, this will be Freddy's first experience with a woman, Rory. I don't want to take that from him."

"*You* would think that." Uncle sniffed. "But Freddy is not you. And he isn't going to be young forever. We've scoured the country for someone else with reviving magic. I know there were once half a dozen at any given time, but they've disappeared. All the common country witches have wised up and hidden themselves away. But we have Freddy. And he is a boy, thank god," Uncle said.

"'Taking so long'?" Freddy said. "I've only seen Thea twice." The more they pushed this on him, the more he wanted to push back, and yet he couldn't forget about his family.

"Thea?" Uncle said, as if he disapproved of the girl's having a name.

"I think she's a fine choice," Gerik said. "She looks like good stock."

Freddy supposed it was nice of Gerik to stick up for Thea instead of describing her as rustic and too earnest, but he couldn't stand hearing her described as "good stock," and it brought yesterday's terrible conversation with her rushing back.

Uncle glanced at Gerik, his face remaining utterly impassive, and Gerik glanced back at him. They seemed to be communicating something they weren't letting on.

"Freddy, I know sometimes it seems like a burden," Uncle said. "But part of having power is giving up freedom. In the old days, that was the job of the prince. Princes grow to become kings and emperors. Their lives are never their own, but they understand what they have to do. You must find a way to accept that, too."

"But I didn't ask to be a prince."

"No one *asks* to be a prince. They are born into it, as you were. Think of your family if not yourself. Because of you, they will never be hungry, never be cold, never know the fear of having an illness or accident and not being able to take care of their own. We take care of them because of you."

Gerik and Uncle never used to use his family as a bargaining chip. *But,* he reminded himself, *you never asked questions before, and you never refused to do anything they asked.*

"We don't ask that much in return," Uncle continued. "But if this girl isn't interested in the deal, I can find you one who is."

Gerik snorted. "Do you even know any women of child-bearing age, Rory?"

Uncle glanced upward briefly, as if he didn't want to indulge Gerik with a reply. "All I know, Freddy, is that the next time you have a date with this girl, I want you to bring her back with you, fully informed about and willing to do what's expected. Now, we'd better not dally any longer. Lots to be done. There are fifteen bodies today."

This was the moment where he ought to refuse, Freddy thought. The moment where he ought to start demanding honest answers to his questions. He could imagine himself doing it.

He could also imagine the look on Uncle's face. Evasive answers and more veiled threats. Freddy's magic might belong to him, but what else did? Not just the roof over his head but the roof over his parents' heads had been granted because of his magic. And the only people who even knew he was alive, besides Thea, of course, were the chancellor and other government officials. They could lock him in his room without food until he gave in. It was that simple.

"Maybe we ought to hold back five or so for tomorrow, for the boy's health," Gerik said. "Fifteen is a fair number for one day."

Uncle waved a hand. "I suppose."

However I look at it, it would be stupid to defy them outright. I have to think of some other way.

Freddy held his tongue and shoved open the workroom door.

A middle-aged man awaited his magic touch. The man's eyes were still open, his face slack and slightly pudgy. Freddy's fingers itched, eager to work. The way his magic flowed from him was almost seductive—warm, potent, living.

Now he placed his hands on the man's callused, cold ones. They weren't cold for long. The magic felt so right, even as it left Freddy feeling slightly light-headed.

Life entered the blue eyes of the formerly dead man. He gasped. "Where am I?"

Freddy had always tried to calm the people he revived. He would say things like "You're fine" and "You're in a safe place."

He had believed those things. Now he wasn't sure how to answer. He didn't want to tell a lie.

He showed the man to the side door and turned him over to the guards. "They'll show you where to go," he said. The guards stayed very close now, since Nan, but Freddy had told Gerik he couldn't work with them in the room, which was almost true. His magic flowed easily, but it felt very personal, and he hated doing it with anyone watching. He shut the door again as he heard the footsteps disappear.

The parade of fresh bodies continued. Some of them showed plainly the method of their death—gunshot wound, or a wrong twist to the body, as though the person had fallen from a roof. But the rest could have died from any number of causes that left no mark.

Freddy wondered about that, in a serious way, for the first time in his life. If Gerik and Uncle were lying about where the people went, did they also lie about where the bodies had come from? Maybe all the people didn't really die by suicide.

The fifth person he revived that day was a young woman— a pretty one, healthy-looking despite the threadbare elbows of her coat, with the blush of cosmetics giving her cheeks color. When life came into her eyes, and she asked the usual where-am-I question, he hissed into her ear: "What's the last thing you remember?"

"I was . . . what? I was at a demonstration. . . ." She seemed addled. People he revived often did.

"What kind of demonstration?"

"Near the university . . . The police broke it up, and—let me think—gosh. I thought someone shot me!" She looked down at her clothes and found blood, and then looked up at him with wide eyes. "What happened?"

"Shh, don't talk too loud. You're fine, you're fine."

A guard opened the door. Maybe he'd heard the girl, or maybe he just had good intuition. He shot a stern look Freddy's way. It might mean nothing—the guards never smiled—but Freddy still felt deeply disconcerted. He took her arm. "I'm sorry. Follow them, they'll . . . they'll help you." He faltered on the last words, the way she was looking at him, her made-up face and waved hair reminding him of Thea's.

He revived the remaining five without trying to question them.

EIGHTEEN

A man in a plain uniform showed Nan to a room that he said was hers. Everything felt both familiar and wrong at once. A girl was springing off her bunk just as the door opened, and she threw her arms around Nan.

"Oh, Nan, are you all right?"

"I know you, don't I?" Nan clutched her head, which didn't ache, exactly, but was definitely out of sorts. She was sure she'd been here before, but she couldn't fit anything to an actual memory.

"Yes! It's Sigi! I decided to take your room while Helma's being punished. She'll be happy enough to have my room when she gets out. It's known as 'the party block' because there's a deck of cards." She shut up abruptly as Nan looked blank. "They erased your memories again? So soon?"

"Who's 'they'?"

Sigi groaned. "The people who run this place!"

"What is this place, anyway?"

She groaned louder still. "Those beasts! Come on, sit down. I can't believe they've done this to you. I don't know what you could have done to deserve it in just a few days' time. You're in the old subway tunnels—"

"Oh, yes." Nan remembered this, once Sigi said so.

"—and you work in a factory every day."

"That's right."

"It's extremely dull and there are no days off. Well, actually, there are two holidays a year. I don't think I told you about that yet. They're holidays mainly because we get cake."

"I do something with levers," Nan said.

Sigi's brows lowered. "Have you lost your memory or not? It seems like everything I say, you're nodding and remembering."

"I start remembering it as soon as you say it," Nan said. "But until then, I have no idea."

"Hmm," Sigi said. "Makes you wonder how good their memory spells really are, doesn't it?"

"But everything you're telling me happens here," Nan said. "Even if we can remember things as soon as we have them explained to us, it's no use if no one here remembers anything that happened before."

"I guess." Sigi sighed.

"Tell me more. Why are we here?"

"We don't know that," Sigi said. "But the food is awful. And every morning we have to take a serum."

"Except me."

"No, everyone does."

It suddenly occurred to Nan that she must have been keeping this secret from Sigi. Only Sigi couldn't tell her that, of course.

Sigi had a distressed look on her face, fingers pressed to

her lower lip in a gesture that seemed oddly ladylike with her unkempt curls and drab work suit. "Or . . . maybe you're right. I never have actually seen you drink it. But everyone needs it." She blinked up at Nan. "There is something different about you, isn't there? Like you're alive and the rest of us are . . . dead, or at least sick."

"I don't know," Nan said. "I think it would be bad for me if anyone found out. I don't think I meant to tell you. This is so—disorienting."

"Oh, Nan, I won't tell anyone, of course I won't," Sigi said, grabbing her threadbare pillow and hugging it against her. "In some ways, I really hope it's true, because you keep talking like you're going to do something about this place. And if you don't need the serum, maybe you really will. Maybe you could get us back to the real world."

"The real world," Nan murmured, trying to capture what that looked like. She tipped her head back against the wall and stared at the framework of her top bunk. All her memories seemed to dance before her, just out of reach.

It was not until the next day at work, among the clamor of machines, that one fluttered close, and she caught it.

Nan had served Arabella von Kaspar before. Her name was well known in radical circles. Nan had never spoken to her, beyond taking her order. Until tonight. Tonight Nan heard the term bound-sickness *cross the woman's lips, and she stopped.*

"What is it, dear girl?" Arabella asked, her voice soft and yet cold. No matter what she said, her voice rested on a bed of steel.

Nan supposed a notorious revolutionary like Arabella could never let down her guard.

"'Bound-sickness,' you said. I know someone with it."

Arabella waved her closer. She was sitting with a younger, scruffy-looking man. "Tell me. Perhaps I can help." She reached for Nan's hand, but Nan drew back. She didn't like to be touched, particularly by strangers. And this woman was an intimidating figure; even Nan recognized that, although she was rarely intimidated. Dripping wealth from every diamond at her neck, secure in her beauty even though she was certainly past forty, Arabella looked more like an heiress than a revolutionary leader.

"The mother of one of my friends," Nan said. "And she keeps getting worse. I get this sense that something is wrong, beyond a spell gone awry. I want to help her, but I don't know how."

"You sound like a good candidate for joining us."

"I'm not usually a group person. . . ."

"Maybe you've just never found the right group."

"Maybe." Nan wondered at that moment why she was not with the revolutionaries. She liked to work alone, but what good was working alone when you didn't know where to begin?

"I'd love to speak with you further." Arabella opened her small purse and fished out a card. "Maybe we could talk more easily about it elsewhere."

Nan pocketed the card, noncommittal.

Later, as she walked home from work, she heard a pair of heels behind her and turned. Arabella was following her. Nan's hackles rose.

"I hoped to catch you," Arabella said. "I ask to have you as my waitress every time, you know. You're usually quiet, but there's something about you."

She was far from the first person to say this. Nan got a lot of "There's something about you." As if others saw something special, not the awkward, antisocial creature she often felt like on the inside.

"You don't have magic you're hiding, do you?" Arabella said.

"No."

"But there is something, isn't there?"

"It isn't special at all. I can't see colors. Or hear music correctly. My guardian took me to an oculist, but we were told there wasn't anything wrong."

"That is curious," Arabella said. "I might be able to help you, and perhaps your friend's bound-sick mother as well."

"How? Tell me. I'll help if I can."

"You're like me." Arabella smiled. "A fighter. And I'll tell you exactly what we're fighting. But not here on the street. Come visit me at home."

The vision was disturbed by a guard marching a new worker in. It was a man with one arm amputated above the elbow, still bandaged. The guard sat him down and told him what to do, and he started pulling the levers.

In Nan's old life, she never would have stared at a man with a missing arm, but he was sitting beside her, doing just the same task; it was almost like looking in a mirror.

He glanced at her. "They had me working with machinery, and it got the better of me," he said shortly. "I'm glad to be here."

"Don't talk like that," Nan said. "Don't say you're *glad*. This isn't fair work. We're slaves."

Her panel buzzed. She yanked the lever hard.

"Don't end up like me, kid," he said. "Pay attention. Could be a lot worse."

"But it could be a lot better," she retorted. She did have a purpose in coming here; she felt sure now, remembering Arabella. Arabella and the revolution . . . there was something there. If only she could remember everything, maybe she would know what she had to do.

NINETEEN

Nan waited a few nights before attempting an escape, to be sure she didn't need the serum. Each day without the serum, more little memories of her daily life before trickled back into her mind, and she felt sure that Valkenrath must have some of the memory potion slipped into the serum, too.

She also felt sure now that she didn't need it, that she was different not just in her mind but in her body. They couldn't scare her with the threat of decay.

When she heard Sigi breathing softly, she lifted the covers away and put her feet on the floor. She grabbed her boots and tugged them on in the dark. Slowly, she crept to the door and turned the knob, slipping out into the quiet hall.

The lights were still on, but the only sound was a distant thrum; now the hall almost reminded her of a school after hours. No guards to be seen. Still, she knew there might be a few making rounds.

She had seen some of the workers who were on cleaning duty using a broom closet in the hall. She slowly coaxed the door open wide enough so she could grab the mop inside.

Behind her, a door creaked. She glanced back, heart thumping.

"It's just me," Sigi whispered. "Are you going down to the tunnels?"

"I want to do a little poking around. Don't worry about me," Nan said, praying Sigi would just let her go without protest. She didn't want to feel responsible for anyone else's fate.

"Can I come with you? You might want company. It would be safer with two of us."

"Sigi . . ." Nan hesitated, looking toward the stairs. She didn't want to spend much more time talking, in case a guard did come prowling. "I can handle it on my own. I don't want to get you in trouble."

"But the underground is dangerous. If you run into some trouble, I bet we could take care of it between the both of us."

"True." It would be good to have a companion in the dark, rat-infested tunnels. "But I—I feel like I should do this on my own."

"Because you don't need the serum," Sigi said, her face falling. She understood. "I thought you might say that. I just—I want to see the sunshine again. So badly, I . . ." She shook her head. "And I don't want you to go."

Sigi would be nice to have around in a cold tunnel. "All right," Nan said. "I might not try to escape tonight, anyway. This might just be a scouting mission."

They moved to the stairs. It was a constant balance between moving swiftly and silently in their heavy boots. At least the floors and stairs were solid here—all metal and concrete, no creaking wood, but still plenty of echoes. The hall led to the cafeteria one way, to the men's dorms another. They headed down the stairs toward the subway track, keeping their ears pricked for guards.

The lights were still on in the subway station. The signs still hung on the walls: B-2 NORTHBOUND TO WALNUT HILL.

They passed the gutted remains of a newsstand, with broken glass windows and empty racks that had once held magazines. Some papers were scattered across the floor of the place, but the roof leaked, and they were yellowed, sodden, rotting away.

No guards to be found. Nan knew she ought to be relieved, but instead the lack of guards was disconcerting. They really weren't afraid anyone would try to escape here.

Nan knelt and brought her legs over the edge of the platform, noting the live third rail. It was far enough away that she didn't think they needed to worry about it, but she reminded Sigi just in case.

"Oh, I know," Sigi said. "I'm more afraid of it *not* killing me than killing me. One guy tried to kill himself that way and he couldn't, but I heard it was awful."

Nan kept the mop close, the nearest thing she had to a weapon. The electric lights continued until the track split. Signs posted on the wall marked the dark offshoot as the B track, while the lights of the B-2 continued to shine.

"This is where the adventure begins, isn't it?" Sigi said. She seemed to be trying valiantly to remain cheerful. It almost made Nan grin.

"I'll lead the way with the mop." Luckily, the tracks provided a relatively predictable walking space, and although the handle of the mop wasn't an ideal tool for probing their way through the shadows, if she held it out in front of her, it served as an additional warning against anything dangerous. Nan doubted this track was live, but she still kept close to the wall, just in case.

They walked for a time in increasing darkness. The only sounds were moist and inanimate—a chorus of occasional drips that echoed with different tones, some near and some far. Sigi gasped when one fell on her cheek.

When all light was gone, they heard a shrill rat noise. Not too close.

"How big do you think the rats are?" Sigi whispered.

"Oh, tiny. No bigger than your thumb."

"Thanks for lying."

The track curved. How long had they been down here now? Time seemed meaningless. Nan guessed it was an hour since she'd left the bedroom.

"I was so tired I had to force myself out of bed to go after you," Sigi said. "Funny, now I'm wide awake. I feel like I've had three cups of coffee. And a cocktail besides. Do you remember cocktails? The little olive? I almost wish the memory loss was more thorough. Sometimes I feel like I'd give anything to have a cocktail."

"Yes, I remember those very well."

"I'd love to have an olive almost as much as the cocktail itself. So salty. They never give us anything salty here." She sighed and then said, "I'm sorry to prattle on. I do it when I'm nervous."

"I like your prattling. I certainly prefer listening to you over the rats."

Sigi laughed nervously. "It is always a goal of mine to be more interesting than rats."

A rat suddenly raced right past them; Nan felt it jar the mop. She froze, and Sigi bumped into her from behind. Sigi didn't scream, but Nan could almost feel them share the sensation of strangling their own voices. Both of them went completely still, pressed together in the dark, breathing hard.

Sigi was trembling. Nan found her hand. "It's all right. It's gone."

"Oh . . . I'm—I'm fine." She was still breathing terror, leaning against Nan. "I'm glad you're here."

"You wouldn't be here if you hadn't followed me."

"I know, but I've always wanted to explore down here, and I was too scared to do it on my own. I think about escaping every day. It's so much better to be free. Even here. I don't want to die *there*."

Nan spoke as soothingly as she could. She felt the waves of panic rippling through Sigi's body. "You won't."

"I have to see the sunrise one more time."

"I promise you won't die here, either," Nan said softly, feeling a sudden protectiveness toward Sigi.

"Okay," Sigi said, hushed. Her fingers slowly uncurled from Nan's.

There was a faint source of light ahead.

Nan hoped against hope it might be a window. She dreamed of finding a window to some remembered sunshine world. But no, it was only a single, dim electric light. It illuminated a ladder that led to a door above the tracks. Nan climbed up to investigate, with Sigi just behind her.

"It's probably just an old power station," Sigi said. "Maybe they have to service it or store things here or something."

She was right. The door opened onto some massive, dusty machinery, barely made visible by the electric light shining outside. Nan scuffed her feet along the floor, and something crunched under the soles of her shoes. Bones? She knelt to touch them. No, just the hulls of some hazelnuts.

"What's that?" Sigi hissed.

When Nan went still, she heard faint footsteps. Shuffling. Unnatural. And headed right toward them.

TWENTY

Nan tugged on Sigi's pajamas, urging her to get down in the corner of the power station with her. They were beyond the dim glow of the electric light, hiding behind some squat construct made of cold metal.

The footsteps took a long time to reach them. Or maybe it just felt that way. Sigi's breathing was very loud beside her. The anticipation heated Nan's skin.

A figure moved past the doorway. Nan smelled death.

And she could see it, the sunken eyes and the emaciated limbs, moving awkwardly, wearing workers' pajamas with a rip in the knee and dried blood staining the shirt brown.

Keep moving, she inwardly begged the thing. *Just keep moving.*

But it had stopped in the doorway, and now it sniffed.

It could smell them, just as they could smell it.

It spoke. "What is that? Who is there?" The voice was scratchy and strained.

Nan and Sigi remained utterly still, not even breathing.

The thing reached into a pocket and brought out an object. Sudden light blazed in their faces. A flashlight! There was no hiding anymore.

Sigi was on the outside of Nan, closer to the awful thing, and she let out a wild scream, as if she could repel it with her voice, while she sprang to her feet and struck it like a barroom brawler. The flashlight clattered to the floor, its light whipping around wildly, and Nan dove for it. She switched it off and stuffed it in her own pocket. She didn't want to look at this half-alive thing wandering free in the dark tunnels.

It reeled from Sigi's punch, stumbling back out the door. Sigi lunged after it, Nan just behind her.

The creature made its own sound, a strained shriek, and pushed back at Sigi, who howled in pain. She clutched her hand. Blood trickled down her palm. "It's got a knife!"

Nan could see the blade now, a small one, flashing in its hand. The being couldn't move very fast or well. She swiped at it with the mop, and it reeled, trying to dodge her. She could see now that it was a man—or had been a man. It was hard to think of him ever having been a person. Somehow he'd gotten free to wander, without serum.

"Stop," he rasped. "Don't hurt me. You're one of us. . . . I'm one of you."

"You cut my hand!" Sigi said.

"You attacked me. . . . I didn't know. I thought I smelled fresh blood, but you're—"

Nan had the flashlight out, thinking maybe she could deflect the knife with it, but the man was cowering now.

"Fresh blood?" she said, seeing now just how bloody he was. His clothes were crusty with it, his hands and face smeared with it, all dried and flaking.

"It's—it's not as tidy as serum . . . but it works. I've been down here for years. They won't get me."

"You're killing people?"

"I have to."

"What people?"

"People in the tunnels. Poor people. They don't have homes anyway. They'd have to be crazy . . . to come down here."

"What about the rats?" Sigi said, her voice small. "You could eat them."

"Oh, no, no, no. No rats. Not good enough. When I must. But they're not good enough. No, no." He leaned closer to Nan, nose-first, whispering, "I do. I smell it. Fresh . . . and sweet."

Nan edged back.

"Have you found a way out?" Sigi asked.

"Oh, there's a way out. There's a way in, so there's a way out. But I don't want to go out there in the world. I'm trying not to eat children." His breathing was growing louder, more ragged, while his voice grew softer, a mere mutter. "I need help. I don't want to eat them. But I have to."

Nan wasn't exactly comforted by his words. He was still looking at her hungrily. And he was killing people in the tunnels.

He wasn't supposed to be alive like this. His desperation, like his decay, almost had an aroma, like slimy mushrooms.

"Where is the exit?" Nan asked.

"Down . . . way down." He pointed farther into the depths

of the tunnel. "All the way in the old Vogelsburg station. . . ."

"Thank you," Nan said, taking a step back.

She wished she knew how to send him to a peaceful end. She felt she glimpsed his captive soul behind the wild eyes straining in their sockets.

His rotting arm lashed out at her, his voice snarling with sudden anger. "Give me back my flashlight."

Nan threw the flashlight to Sigi, who caught it with a bit of flailing.

"Give me your *blood*." He lunged at Nan, teeth bared.

Nan whacked him with the handle of the mop so hard the handle cracked. Sigi rushed to grab a handful of his clothes before he could get a grip on Nan.

"Stop!" Sigi said. "Stop! We're dead! We don't have any blood for you."

"*She's* not dead." His eyes bugged out at Nan. "I can smell her life. Please." He clasped his hands. "I just need"—he struggled and twisted in Sigi's arms—"a taste. A taste!"

"We don't want to fight you," Nan said. "And I don't think you really want to fight us. Just . . . let us go." She spread her hands.

He went still, but his eyes remained on her—wide and gleaming, a wounded animal in the dark. Sigi let go of his clothes and began creeping back toward Nan's side. Nan suddenly grabbed Sigi's arm and broke past him. Enough of this! They could run faster than he could. She could run all the way to Vogelsburg and see the sun or the moon or whatever was shining now!

Sigi shrieked, losing her footing. Nan turned and saw that

the man had grabbed her arm, scratched her with his finger-nails. Sigi shoved him hard, and he fell backward, almost onto the tracks. Nan kicked him down with her boot, and he crumpled, unmoving.

Nan's hands were shaking.

"Oh my god," Sigi said.

"I didn't know what else to do! I—" Nan crouched. "I'm sorry!"

"No." Sigi touched Nan's cheek, drawing her into her gaze. She shook her head. "No, Nan, this is not your fault. It's awful what they did to him, but—he would've hurt you."

Nan stared at his fallen form and exhaled sharply, then dropped back down on the tracks. He still wasn't moving. She got the knife from his limp fingers. Quickly, she searched his pockets. Nothing but a few coins and a book of prayers. She could envision him reading prayers by the weak light, trying to hold on to his humanity even while he hungered for blood. Her hands were covered in the flecked blood that had come from his skin and clothes. She brushed her hands together again and again, but she just kept feeling it.

"Let's get out of here," Sigi said.

Nan's eyes were still lured by the way ahead. She wanted, more than anything just now, to feel sunlight on her face. "He said there's a way out."

Sigi's jaw clenched. "Nan, I think I should go back."

Nan looked at Sigi a moment, and she felt a sinking in her stomach that never seemed to stop. Eventually Sigi would turn into a hungry thing, smelling Nan's blood.

But she had promised Sigi that she would see the sunshine again, and she hesitated to break the promise and go on without her. Sigi couldn't die down here alone.

"We can . . . we can try again later," Nan finally said.

"Thank you," Sigi whispered, and Nan thought she knew the truth, deep down. Next time, Nan would have to go alone.

TWENTY-ONE

The Telephone Club had premiered a new stage show on Friday night, packing in larger-than-usual crowds. The theme was now mythology, the costumes designed by a twenty-seven-year-old fashion designer who went by a single name. Girls fluttered around the stage in white tunics and bare legs, and the thin plot involved archery and snakes. Thea kept half an eye on it, happy for the distraction of different costumes and music and dances; she was trying so hard to forget the argument with Freddy.

But nothing cheered her—not serving a famous actress, nor being showered with compliments by charming young men. Everything she said felt forced, every smile pained.

She came home that night to an apartment so quiet that dropping her keys into her coat pocket seemed a disturbance. The gas lamp in her bedroom hissed, and she stared at the shadows, feeling her mother's absence more keenly than ever.

She needed someone. She had to act on what Freddy had told her, but Arabella von Kaspar had spoken only of violence. And Father Gruneman wanted her to stay away from the revolutionaries altogether. She needed a friend—like Nan. But no use thinking of that.

A knock roused her from bed late in the morning. When she opened the door, Freddy stood on the other side with a serious expression.

She wasn't ready to see him.

But he is the key to everything. He is the key to my father.

His magic had torn his family from him, too. Difficult as it was to confront the truth, they should be working together. She slowly opened the door wider, stepping back, a wordless acknowledgment that he could enter.

"I thought about what you said the other night," he said, taking his hat off but holding it to his chest instead of hanging it on the rack, keeping his distance from her. "I don't know if you want to see me, but there's too much at stake, and I don't have anyone else to trust."

"No, I—I think I'm glad to see you."

A touch of relief lightened his features. "Good. I knew it was a shock, everything I told you last time. And you were right. I feel like . . . there must be something we can do together. I don't know if it's possible that I might escape and get a message to my parents to hide, too."

She let her shoulders loosen, realizing she had stood almost frozen since letting him in. "Surely it's possible. If we only had somewhere for you to hide. . . ." Yet another moment to wish Nan were still around. "We should talk to Father Gruneman," she decided. "He didn't want me to get involved in this, but obviously it's too late now. He wants to limit bloodshed, and surely he'll know many places you could hide."

Freddy looked grave—she understood how hard it was to commit to something like this. "That sounds like a good plan," he finally said. He clamped the hat back on his head.

Thea grabbed her coat. "His house isn't far."

The sky was gray and wintry, but in a way that almost made her look forward to snow and pots of stew, and not dread the frigid walks home at night and endlessly cold hands. It was hard to even imagine winter, though; the longest night of the year was still more than two months away, and anything could happen between now and then. So much had already changed so quickly, and she feared the worst was yet to come.

I mustn't think that way or I'll lose my nerve altogether.

They walked and talked, catching each other up on everything that had happened since they last spoke—more on his end than hers—and soon they had reached Father Gruneman's house.

She knocked, then returned her hands to her pockets, rocking back and forth on her toes. When he didn't answer, she knocked again.

"Hmm," she said. "What day is it? Saturday? Maybe he's at church. There's an evening service . . . but it's barely past noon."

Freddy was looking at the handle of the door, though, as if he were thinking of just barging in.

Thea tried it. It swung open easily.

Freddy gently but firmly moved ahead of her.

"Is something wrong?" she asked him.

"I hope not," he said, doing nothing to reassure her.

"Father Gruneman?" she called.

Freddy moved to the stairs. "Stay here a minute," he said. His words sounded almost like an order. As he hurried up the stairs, she heard his steps creak on the boards above her head, and she started to follow him.

This moment, she thought. *This moment when you're almost certain something awful has happened and you still have a shred of hope . . . I can't bear it.*

Who would hurt Father Gruneman?

But she knew now that he was not just a kindly old priest but also Viktor the resistance leader. She stopped on the landing at the top of the stairs and looked past the open door of the office to see Father Gruneman slumped at his desk and Freddy taking his hand.

"He's been shot," Freddy said. "Probably just this morning."

She rushed into the room. "Oh, no, no!"

His monolithic old chair kept his body propped up, but his head was slack. He wasn't dressed to go out, still wearing a robe, now covered in blood. His eyes and mouth were open; he looked as if he had been in the middle of saying something.

Death was ugly. She had never met it like this before. Maybe it was better, in the end, to see it, to know, and not to be left wondering, as she did about her father. But just the other day she had seen Father Gruneman full of life and fight, and now the twinkle in his eyes had been snuffed out.

Beside her, Freddy seemed unnaturally calm.

He had no reason to be afraid of death, she realized. He could undo this with a mere touch.

"Someone murdered him," Freddy said. "We have to find out what happened."

"Wait—but—he'll need serum! And you don't have any, do you? We'd have to turn him over to Gerik! We have to think about this first."

"But we can't just let him go, without knowing who killed him."

"I . . . suppose," she agreed, but it didn't feel like her choice to make.

Freddy glanced at her. "I don't usually revive people with anyone else in the room."

"Do—do you want me to go?"

He paused. "No. I think you should be here."

She hadn't thought of it as a personal thing—using magic. But clearly it was. What would it look like? No matter how Freddy explained it to her, she still couldn't believe this was something he could actually do. What was it like going through life knowing you had such power flowing through you?

Freddy took Father Gruneman's hand and stood over him for a moment.

Life returned suddenly to Father Gruneman's eyes, and he drew a sharp, surprised breath, as though he'd been saved from drowning, and despite all her concerns, Thea felt relief when she heard it.

Father Gruneman clapped a hand to his bloody chest, and then he noticed Freddy, who had let go of his hand. "What happened? Who—"

"Father Gruneman . . . it's me, it's Thea," Thea said, hurrying to his side.

"Thea?"

"Henry's daughter," she prompted, shooting a look at Freddy. Was this normal?

"People are usually confused when they come to," Freddy said.

"Thea—yes—Thea—what are you doing here? You shouldn't be here. Something just happened. . . . It might be dangerous."

"You . . . you *died*," she said. She meant to say more, but her throat closed up.

"Someone shot you," Freddy agreed. "I brought you back."

Father Gruneman looked down at his torn, bloody clothes, and then around the room, his features setting into resolve. He seemed to be remembering. He furrowed his brow at Freddy. "You're the one," he said. "The reviver. It's true. But are you the only one?"

"I am the only one."

"And, Thea, you know him?"

She nodded. "How do you feel?"

"I'm not in pain," he said. "But how did you know to come here?"

"We didn't," Thea said. "We were coming to talk to you, to tell you about Freddy and ask you what to do."

"Well. Why don't you tell me now, if . . . I suppose it's safe. She's long gone, I hope, now that she's gotten rid of me."

"We didn't see any sign of someone here," Thea said. "Who killed you?"

"Arabella von Kaspar. You remember her, Thea. We were eating together at the club that night. . . ."

"But why would she do something like this?"

"She felt I was in the way of what must be done." He seemed to be wrestling with how much he wanted to reveal to her. "The workers—you know about the workers? I want them to reunite with their families. I don't want our group to focus on instigating a civil war. It might happen as a result, yes, but I think we should let the people carry the revolution, and we should focus on protection. But Arabella feels that we should actively pursue violence." He looked at Freddy. "And I fear for your safety if she were to find out you are here. She would probably kill you in a heartbeat, were it not that all the workers would die with you."

"Are you sure they would die?" Freddy said. "I mean, I've already revived them."

"They need your magic to live. You know, when I was a boy, a reviver lived in the neighboring village."

Freddy's expression lit with interest. "My grandfather was a reviver, my mother said. But he died before I was born. My mother told me he didn't use his magic much . . . but she doesn't seem to like to talk about him, or any of my family, really. I always wondered how revivers could have normal lives back in the old days. Why weren't they overwhelmed with people wanting their loved ones brought back?"

"God help us," Father Gruneman said, rubbing his head. "I can't believe they would abuse you like this and let you believe such a lie! You can't defy death, my boy. You don't bring back the dead. No one can. What you can do is revive them for a brief time, no more than a day. It's a gift that allows people to say good-bye to a loved one, or ask one last question. I don't know how they're able to keep these people alive longer. Our intelligence has been unable to get to the heart of the operation."

"It's a serum," Freddy said. "It keeps the dead alive, but I don't know where it comes from."

"Serum." Father Gruneman looked over his desk restlessly, as though he wanted to start taking notes. "Some kind of healing magic? I see now how these Valkenraths have become so dear to the chancellor, if they have figured out a way to keep your magic going." He looked thoughtful. "But at the core, the power is still in your hands. You can choose to let all these people go."

"To kill them? But what about reuniting them with their families?"

"Oh, yes. I want them to be able to escape first. But it can only be temporary."

"But, Father Gruneman—my father and Nan!" Thea couldn't believe he was suggesting something so terrible, but then she also understood, and that was what made it so awful. It wasn't right for people to come back from the dead. She just couldn't bear the thought that—Nan! Nan, of all people, could not be dead. She was only sixteen, and she was the kind of person who ought to live to be ninety and have lots of adventures. Thea and Nan were supposed to have some of those adventures together, or at least keep talking about having them.

"I know, Thea, I know." He rubbed his chest where he'd been shot. "It's so important I make you both understand, and I don't have much time. But I think that even when things seem to be at their worst, someone is looking out for you. The people you love are never far away."

"But they *are* far away," Thea said, unable to accept such

145

lofty comfort. "I'll never see them again. And I—I miss them so much." She stopped, afraid she would start to cry if she went on.

"But I believe if your father was released from the magic tethering him to this world, your mother would be back to her old self again."

"Yes, but Father's life must have been so awful all these years, I just . . ." She didn't know what to say. "He deserves better than that."

"He deserves peace now," Father Gruneman said gently.

"So what do I do?" Freddy said. "How would I 'let them go'?"

"It should come naturally, if you let it," Father Gruneman said. "Now that you've brought me back, if you think about it, you should feel the magic that connects my life to you."

"I know that feeling," Freddy said. "I remember all the people I've revived."

"Exactly. You just have to break the connection and release them. Perhaps you can think of it like snipping a thread. And you'll have to practice with me."

Thea bit her lip hard. She knew she couldn't fight this. Freddy was quiet.

"Thea, may I speak to you alone for a moment?" Father Gruneman said.

"Of course."

"I can wait outside," Freddy said, moving to the door.

She touched Freddy's arm as he moved past her. His eyes were distant.

When the door shut, before Father Gruneman said anything, he put his arms around her and pulled her close as her father would have. No one had embraced her like this in a long time. Mother had been too addled to notice when Thea needed comfort. She choked on her tears. Regret pierced her. She should have been more open with Father Gruneman. She should have visited more often. He could have been like a grandfather to her after her father died, but she had been too shy and proud. It was too late now. And he loved her anyway. . . . She felt that he did.

"I'm looking forward to seeing your father again," he said.

She took a handkerchief from her purse and dried her eyes.

"It will be all right," he said. "But I wanted to have a moment alone with you. I never wanted you to be involved in this. It's too late for that, I see. You must know, Arabella and I agreed on some things. Most important, that in the end all the people Freddy has revived must die properly. When the time is right, Freddy *must* let them go. You might be the key to it all. That boy . . . he seems to like you and trust you. You must make him do what needs to be done."

She swallowed. "I understand," she said. She didn't want to lose her father. But if it was the only way . . .

"But first the people must see, with their own eyes, the ones they loved and thought lost. They must know the extent of it."

"What is the extent of it?"

"I'm not sure of the numbers, but they must be substantial. The government likely began reviving the dead during the war, picking bodies off the field, and then they passed the Funeral Relief Act."

The Funeral Relief Act, Thea knew, meant that if a person of low income died, the family could opt for a cremation fully paid for by the government. "They use it to collect bodies?" Her voice matched Father Gruneman's hush.

"Yes, and recently people have started disappearing. They have targets, I think. Even some of the people from our group who went to search the underground never returned."

He suddenly moved to the desk and took a gun out of the drawer. Her eyes widened. She certainly had not expected him to have such a thing.

"You should take this," he said. "In case you have any trouble. I bought it in the event I needed, shall we say, a negotiation tool. But that didn't work out very well."

"I don't know how to use it."

"Hopefully, you won't have to. But I want to leave you prepared, as much as I can. It's loaded. Be careful with it."

"I certainly will," Thea said, putting it in her purse gingerly, as though it were a grenade.

She followed him out of the office, her movements automatic, her face feeling like a plaster mask. Freddy waited in the hallway, approaching her when they emerged.

"I'm ready," Father Gruneman said.

"I don't know if I can do this," Freddy said.

"Of course you can," Father Gruneman said. "In fact, you're the only one who can do this. But . . . let's go to the parlor. I'd rather have my favorite chair."

They went to the parlor. Thea barely realized she had gone down the stairs. Her heart thumped, strong and scared, in her chest. She wasn't sure she could bear to watch Father Gruneman die again, but Freddy would need her support. He thought himself a giver of life, and she couldn't imagine how awful it would be to bear the burden of knowing he had to do the opposite.

Father Gruneman reached for Freddy's hand. "Don't be afraid."

Freddy's eyes remained open, but they seemed to look inward. His shoulders hunched slightly. She could see him searching for that thing—that thread of magic—that connected him with Father Gruneman. Thea's hands trembled, and she put them in her pockets.

Father Gruneman looked at the ceiling, and the life seemed to flow out of him, softly and gently. He closed his eyes just before it was over, and he was left with an expression that was not quite a smile but a look of deep peace.

But still she cried, choked and angry tears that threatened to break out of control. She forced them back, because of Freddy. Another person gone from her life. Nan and her father still to come. The world going all to hell, and she didn't know if she even really believed in heaven. She went to church every week because of Mother and because she wanted something more meaningful than work, but some days the world seemed too unfair, too random, and too ugly for faith of any kind. Other days it was too beautiful not to believe in something. And in a moment like this, she wasn't sure which it was.

Freddy's arms suddenly went around her, and she leaned into his warm, tall embrace. His clothes smelled of somewhere rich. She managed to pull herself together, looking up into his pale face.

"Are you all right?" he asked.

"I'm—I'll manage. I'll have to. But what about you?"

"I—" He lowered his gaze. "I can't do this. Letting all those people die. There must be a better way."

She drew back. Father Gruneman had told her she had to persuade Freddy to let them go. But what if there *was* a better way? "I don't know if there is."

"So you expect me to just let your father and Nan die? I've already unwittingly hurt so many people, and this is such a huge decision. I have to find out more about the serum. Maybe there's a way to save them."

TWENTY-TWO

Nan's days had become almost like the levers. One day. Two. Three. How long had she been here now? Two weeks?

But it couldn't go on forever. *I have to try to escape again, and I can't take Sigi.*

If everyone underground was dead except for her . . . then to leave here was to return to the land of the living. To leave Sigi in a sunless tomb. Nan might never see her again. And she still had the feeling that she had been meant to do something here. In another day or two, she might remember it.

That night, in the space between consciousness and dreams, Sigi appeared in her memories.

Arabella's home was the most lavish place Nan had ever seen. The Telephone Club may have glittered, but under that glitter was the smudge of desperation. These rooms were open, full of sun and sculpture. From the art on the walls to the carvings on the staircase, the colors were warm and bright, the lines soft. Elephant tusks hung over the fireplace; a window of stained-glass trees framed the real garden plot behind the house.

"Have a seat." Arabella gestured to the sofa. "Let me start by telling you something about magic. If you see enough of it, you will begin to recognize it, even when it's hidden. I see it in you, my dear."

"But I've never—"

Arabella held up a hand. "Before you say anything else, listen. Some of our members are descended from witches of the court. They have saved thousands of books and documents from destruction by the new regime. I asked a colleague if he knew anything about people who could not see colors or hear music. We spent a day poring over his library, and we found an account from the court of Queen Sofie."

Nan vaguely remembered the name from her school days, but as nothing more than a parade of royal names in history class.

Arabella continued. "Queen Sofie kept witches locked in her castle and forced them to use their magic for her own aims. A lot of what she dabbled in was quite dark—curses and death. She had many enemies. There are accounts of a charming young woman who came to the court claiming to be from a faraway land. Queen Sofie seemed intrigued by her and allowed her to stay the summer. According to the other ladies of the court, she asked for help selecting clothes, as she could not see colors. She also would not dance and was curiously uninterested in the men of the court."

"That sounds like me," Nan murmured.

"Additionally, Queen Sofie's guard caught the woman sneaking into the private chambers where she kept her witches. The woman said she was a guardian of fate, half-human and half-spirit, and she had come to stop Queen Sofie from abusing the gifts of the spirit world—magic. It sounds like she could be an ancestor of yours, doesn't it?"

"But how would she know she was a guardian of fate?"

"Of that I'm not sure," Arabella said. "But many types of magic mature only in adulthood. I think it's worthy of further investigation."

"I do . . . get these feelings," Nan said. "I can't explain them to anyone. Just an intuition that something is wrong in the world and I'm supposed to do something, only I don't understand what to do."

"Perhaps you do have a calling," Arabella said. "If you are a guardian of fate."

Nan wanted to believe in an answer. "But how could I be sure? Is that all you found? Just a few old stories from hundreds of years ago?"

Arabella smiled faintly. "It was only one hundred and thirty-five, to be precise. Look, my dear girl, it's only a beginning. I will try to find more answers for you."

"What can I do now? You said you'd tell me what we're fighting."

"You can come to one of our meetings. We know quite a bit about what's going on, and we can certainly find you a task while we look for more information for you."

Elsewhere in the house, a door swung open and footsteps thumped down stairs. Arabella twisted around and called, "Sigi?"

"Yes?" A girl appeared on the landing.

"What are you doing?"

"Going somewhere."

Arabella sniffed. "Yes, but where? Just come down so we aren't shouting." She smiled apologetically at Nan.

The girl's gray suit was slightly rumpled, her hat floppy and *unfashionable, with untamed dark curls beneath. She was thickset and a little tanned, but not in an on-purpose, seaside vacation way. The Telephone Club would never hire her. But Nan preferred girls who weren't polished beauty queens. "I'm just going for a walk," Sigi said. "Do I need to sign a log now?" She looked startled when she noticed Nan. "Sorry—I didn't know you had, um, a visitor."*

"Not at all. Nan, this is my daughter, Sigismunda. Sigi, this is Nan."

"Yes, call me Sigi, please. Sigismunda? Really now." She hesitated. "So what brings you here?"

"Nan is curious about our group," Arabella said. "I told her she could come over and I'd answer some questions. I see you have your camera."

Sigi put her hand on the boxy leather bag slung over her shoulder. "I always have my camera."

"Well, just be careful," Arabella said, but her attention had already absented itself from Sigi and she was looking at Nan again.

"Yes," she said. "You were worried about your friend's mother. You're just the sort of girl the revolution needs. You have your eyes open to the city's dark secrets, even if you haven't been able to puzzle them out alone. Can I trust you not to speak of these secrets?"

"Of course," Nan said. "I swear it. I just want to do something."

"Sigi." Nan spoke into the darkness.

"Wha—?" Sigi replied sleepily.

"I just remembered where I know you from. I knew your mother. I knew you."

"My mother . . ." Sigi sounded distressed.

"Do you remember your mother?"

"No, but as soon as you said you knew her, I had an unpleasant feeling. I don't think we got along." The bed creaked as Sigi sat up. Nan came down from the top bunk and climbed onto the edge of her mattress.

"I think you're right," Nan said.

"What else do you remember about me?" Sigi asked. "Maybe I'll remember, too."

"You had a camera."

Sigi sucked in a breath. "Oh—my camera," she said. "Yes. Now that you say that—I can't believe I don't have it. I'll never use it again. They don't give us anything down here. No art. No art at all."

Sigi reached for Nan's hand.

"My camera," she repeated, and she sounded heartbroken. "But I can't remember my pictures. I can't remember them."

Then she didn't talk anymore, and Nan didn't try to make her. Although Nan usually didn't like being touched, she didn't really mind when it was Sigi.

It was too dim to see much of Sigi's expression. Finally, she heard her sniff. But when Sigi spoke, her voice was level. "Maybe it's better if I don't try to remember. I should get back to sleep."

Nan felt a pang that she couldn't do more for her. She drew her hand back and stepped onto the ladder to her bunk. "Remember, I promised you that you won't die down here. I meant it. It'll be all right."

TWENTY-THREE

The next day, Nan had breakfast with Sigi and worked as usual. But when she went to dinner that evening, a frenzied murmur passed among the workers in line, and she knew someone must be in the cage.

Sigi.

When she saw Sigi in the cage, she felt as if she'd run head-first into a wall. She took a step back. *No . . .*

Sigi caught her eyes and shook her head quickly. *Don't worry about me,* she mouthed.

Nan looked at the guard. "Why is she here?"

He regarded her silently, eyes cold.

"Just go eat your dinner," Sigi said. She was standing straight, arms crossed, trying to look brave, but she couldn't entirely hide the fear in her voice.

"She hasn't done anything wrong," Nan told the guard. "She's my roommate! I'd know."

The guard's eyes lifted to some point beyond Nan's head. She turned and saw Valkenrath crossing the room toward them. People scurried off when he passed them, but Nan held her ground.

"Is there a problem here?" He seemed to be asking the guard, but his eyes moved to Nan as he spoke. "This is your roommate."

"Yes," Nan said. "And I'm a light sleeper. I would have noticed if she ever left her room."

"What makes you think we're accusing her of leaving her room?"

"Well—what else could it be?"

"Maybe she was defiant on the job. Maybe she fell asleep. Maybe she was caught having a rendezvous."

"Nan, just don't worry about it!" Sigi snapped.

"Or maybe we found her carrying a flashlight," Valkenrath continued. "I wonder if you have any surprises in your pockets. Come with me." He started walking with the apparent assumption she would follow. He slipped out a side door into a hall that was much quieter than the cafeteria.

She had the pocketknife tucked in her boot. Sometimes their rooms were searched while they worked. But it was reckless for Sigi to carry the flashlight around. Nan should have kept it. She felt like the reckless one for ever letting Sigi follow her to the tunnels.

"Turn out your pockets," Valkenrath said, almost like a teacher scolding a naughty child.

Nan did. He grabbed the crumpled bits of fabric jutting from her hips and gave them each a quick shake to see if anything was hidden in the folds. Then he nodded curtly. "Please tell me what you know about your friend. Where did she find a flashlight?"

"I don't know."

"If she tries to escape, she won't have serum, and I'm sure you understand the consequences of that."

As he spoke, Nan could imagine him rotting and dying like the man in the tunnels. He thought he was above her. He thought he was safe from such fates. Maybe he was for now, but death would get him, too, in the end.

"Are you going to say anything?" he asked.

"You've made up your mind that Sigi did something wrong," she said. "I don't think there is much I can say to change that."

"I might be persuaded to help your friend if you're honest with me."

"What makes you think I'm being dishonest?"

"I am very, very good at sniffing out lies, Miss Davies."

She could feel her aggression, simmering deep down, but she kept it back. For a moment he didn't say anything, either. Her face remained placid. A twitch of anger played across his features, but when it passed, curiosity was left behind.

"Are you not afraid?" he asked.

"No." She hurled the word at him. What did it matter anymore?

"Why not?"

"You're just a mortal man. One day you'll rot, too."

His hand flashed out and struck her cheek, so hard that tears of pain welled in her eyes.

"Your honesty could have saved your friend," he said. "But since you won't speak, how would you like to suffer with her?"

Nan stared at him as if she could will him to leave her alone. "Come with me." He grabbed her arm. She twisted, but she couldn't get away. She kicked him, catching him in the kneecap, but that was all she managed before a pair of guards appeared behind her. They dragged her back into the cafeteria. Her fellow workers gaped at her a moment, then turned away. The door to Sigi's cage rattled open, and they tossed Nan in.

TWENTY-FOUR

When the workers finished their dinner, the room cleared out except for a cleaning crew that came through with mops and rags and pails of soapy water and scrubbed down the tables and the floor. When they finished, the guard left with them, shutting off the lights, leaving the room pitch-black.

The darkness was hard to bear. It was so deep it almost felt like something physical pressing on Nan's eyes. She slid her hands down the bars, which were just a few inches apart. She groped until she found the lock, and pushed her arms between the bars to get at it. But the lock felt far too solid for the blade of a pocketknife to do any good.

"Sigi, I don't suppose you know how to pick a lock?"

"No . . ."

Nan tried anyway, and she could feel something wanting to give and click; but the knife was neither strong enough nor long enough.

"Any luck?" Sigi asked.

"No." She pulled her arms back in and sighed, finally sitting down. "He's got me," she said, angry enough to break something, only there was nothing to break. "And there's not a damn thing I can do about it."

"He's got all of us," Sigi said. "But you have an element of surprise, at least. If you really don't need serum, he isn't going to know what to do with you. You're so . . . strong." Sigi breathed faster. "This will be my first time. I wish you weren't here. I don't want you to see me."

"Sigi, I know it won't really be you," Nan said, but her stomach churned at the thought of what Sigi would become. Sigi's eyes sinking. Sigi lurching stiffly. Sigi moaning hungrily.

"But I'm afraid. I can bear anything except you seeing me turn into a—a monster."

Nan reached out in the dark until she found Sigi's shoulder. She was crying silently. Her skin was already turning cold, but it was still perfectly supple. "Whatever happens, Valkenrath can't touch your soul."

Sigi swallowed. "You think there is such a thing as a soul?"

"I do."

"I wish I could feel sure about something like that. What good is a soul if life has no meaning? And I don't trust that anything has any meaning at all."

Nan put her arm around Sigi, remembering the first time she had seen the girl's mischievous eyes. She had always known there was something great beyond her earthly existence; she heard it in the music in her head. But she couldn't give that gift to Sigi. "I wish I could show you what I mean," she said softly.

A shiver passed through Sigi. "I don't mean to sound so tragic, anyway. When we were in the tunnels, we protected each other." She laughed drily. "I actually enjoyed that night. It was terrifying, of course, and we didn't really get anywhere, but it felt so liberating to walk away from this place, just the two of us."

"Yes, but I shouldn't have let you go with me. I knew from the start that I was different. Like I was meant to fix things."

"Oh, Nan, could you really fix things anyway? Even if you don't need serum, there is only one of you."

"What's the point of being different if I don't have a purpose?"

"Maybe nothing has a purpose," Sigi said. "You see . . . that's what I'm afraid of."

Nan swallowed. "No. Everything has a purpose. I firmly believe that."

"I wish I could believe in something like that. That's my problem. I doubt everything."

Now Sigi was so close that her curls tickled Nan's cheek. Her voice was soft in the dark. She sighed. "Oh, Nan . . . promise me again that I won't die here."

"You won't."

And gently Sigi's fingers touched Nan's face, questing in the dark, and she kissed her.

Nan froze with shock.

Nan had been drawn to Sigi from the day they met—both times. Sigi was earthy and soft, the opposite of Nan's cool angles. She felt things, and she expressed them, even wordlessly, with the twinkle of her eyes and the intimate nudge of her elbow. But Nan hadn't thought of her like this. And she hadn't realized Sigi might see her as more than a friend. Nan didn't even know how to read the signs when someone cared for her.

She liked it when Sigi took her hand. She liked protecting Sigi, imagining she might free her from this place and show her the sunshine.

She wanted to surrender herself to this kiss. But she couldn't. Inside, she felt strong and purposeful—and alone.

Sigi touched her cheek. "Nan?" Her voice was full of hope and fear. "Maybe I shouldn't have done that. Considering the circumstances. But I've wanted to for so long. You're the most striking girl I've ever seen. And if something did happen to me here . . . I'd want my last act to mean something."

"I—"

"I was presumptuous, wasn't I?" Sigi spoke faster now. "I thought you might like me, too. I feel so comfortable around you, like I've known you forever—maybe because we had met before. And I thought we were two of a kind, but if you'd rather just be friends—"

"Sigi, I—I can't. It isn't you. I told you there's something different about me, and part of it is that I just don't . . . feel for people, the way others do."

"Oh," Sigi said, her voice flat.

"Your mother thought I wasn't quite human." She needed Sigi to understand. "She said I might be a guardian of fate. Because it isn't just that I can't seem to—to feel." Nan groped for words. She *did* feel. She felt loss and loneliness, but she didn't feel love. "I also can't see colors. Just gray. I don't want to be this way, but I am. And I think . . . if I were wholly human, I think I could . . . we could . . ."

Sigi was silent for a moment, and then she said, "You don't have to say that just to make me feel better."

"You don't believe me." Nan was afraid of this. And could she blame Sigi? It sounded so far-fetched. A guardian of fate? Even Nan didn't know what it meant. "But it's true. I—I liked you from the first moment I saw you."

"I thought so, too, but what good is it if—" Sigi didn't sound bitter, just broken. "God, I'm stupid. I guess I believe you. I thought you were just . . . I don't know. I thought we got on so well."

"Sigi, we do." Nan reached for her hand.

"No!" Sigi shook her off. "Just leave me alone. Let's forget it happened at all. I just had a foolish moment, and I'm sorry about it now."

"Don't be sorry. I'm the one who's sorry."

Sigi made a sound somewhere between humiliation and despair, then drew even farther away.

Nan could feel the emptiness inside her grow and grow, until it seemed to swallow her whole. Everything, everything was so cold. She could hear, faintly, the solitary thrum of music that seemed to belong to her alone, and memories of Sigi drifted into the space between thoughts and dreams.

Nan had arrived only half an hour ago, and the cigarette smoke, the loud voices echoing in the grand room, and the press of people already threatened to smother her. These were the luminaries of the revolution, the people Arabella so wanted her to meet—scruffy young men with university slang and poetry books, their older equivalents with thick glasses and world-weary expressions, society women with a rebellious streak and too much money for their own good.

These were not Nan's people.

Not that she had people, anyway.

A lot of them approached her and introduced themselves. They had heard about her from Arabella. They seemed interested in her, welcoming, complimenting her dress.

She felt like a hand thrust into the wrong size of glove, discomfited by the attention, wondering why these people cared. She was just a sixteen-year-old girl. It made her wonder if Arabella had found more in those books than she'd said.

Nan slipped up the stairs, above the smoke and the noise. Down the hall she heard rummaging, which stopped at the sound of her footsteps.

Sigi's head poked out from a door. "Oh—it's only you. I'm sorry. I thought it was Mother."

"Just me," Nan agreed.

"Aren't you enjoying the party?"

"I needed some air."

"Your hands are empty, I see. Here's a tip: go get a cocktail. It'll help." She smiled and ruffled her hair. "But don't mind me if you need a quiet moment."

"I don't mind," Nan said. She had walked closer and could see that Sigi had a suitcase open on her bed and clothes strewn about. "Are you going somewhere?"

"I'm moving in with my friend Margie. She just got her own apartment."

"To get away from your mother?"

"Well, that's blunt," Sigi said. "I don't want to complain about her to a member of her crowd."

"I'm not in her crowd. She just seems to know more than most."

"That's true, I'm sure. Mother likes to know everything." Sigi folded a jacket artlessly and put it in the suitcase, pressing the pile down with her palms.

"I just get the feeling she might not be telling me everything."

Sigi glanced up. "What do you want to know?"

"Well—" Although Sigi felt easier to trust than her mother, she also seemed too practical to speak to of vague feelings and guardians of fate. "I have a strange condition. I can't see colors. Your mother found something about it in an old book, but . . . she didn't really tell me much. I wondered if she's holding something back."

"We could check her office. . . ."

"Please. Where is it?"

Sigi stepped out the door, checking the hall. The party downstairs was noisy, but this upper floor seemed empty. "It's just ahead," she said.

Inside, the desk was piled with books and papers. The walls were lined with mounted birds, their staring glass eyes giving Nan the sense of being watched. She quickly rummaged through the papers and books, Sigi beside her.

"Do you know what the old book was called?" she asked.

"No," Nan said. "But—" She uncovered a dusty tome, The Mystic in Our World. A bookmark poked out from the pages. Nan opened the book, finding a passage that was underlined—

*

In times of trouble, the guardians of fate, sometimes referred to in old texts as the Nornir, will appear as humans and step in to influence destiny. They always appear in female form, and in appearance they are indistinguishable from other women, but their senses are troubled by the human world—our music is abhorrent to them, they dislike being touched, and they cannot see colors. Having a connection to the realms of gods, their powers are considerable and should not be trifled with. If the fates have marked you for death, woe betide you, for even death will not stop these women. Their human bodies are only shells, and they will return in some other guise.

*

In the margin was a scribbled note: NAN? Could she be immortal? May be. answer to our prayers.

"Did you find something?" Sigi asked, peering at the page. Nan snapped the book shut so fast the dust made her cough.

"Just—the same thing your mother already told me," she said. Her heart raced. She couldn't speak of this to Sigi—or Thea—or anyone who might be a friend. If it was true, if she really was some kind of mystical creature in a human shell, it explained why she had such trouble identifying with people. But she wasn't indifferent to them—she wanted to be a part of this world. This book didn't help her with that, so why even speak of it?

"What did Mother say, anyway? You look awfully pale."

Nan put the book back in the same spot where she'd found it, covering it with the other papers. "She thinks I might have magical powers of some kind. It was just nonsense. I want real answers."

"I don't blame you. Do you want to keep looking?"

"No. I don't want her to find out we were in here."

Sigi shrugged, moving for the door. "I'd take responsibility. I don't care. I'm leaving anyway." Then she spoke more shyly. "But I wish I could help you out. I'd love to photograph you someday. Just because—you know—that's what I do. I like taking pictures of people who look like they have a story."

"Do I look like I have a story?"

"Yes," Sigi said. She looked at Nan for a moment, her eyes seeming almost as if they were the camera, focused, shuttering with a blink, and then looking down again.

"Of course you can photograph me," Nan said.

"Not here, though," Sigi said. "Maybe you could come to the apartment sometime. It's at Eighty-Five Richter Street, number six. If you give me a ring the day before, I'll even make a torte."

They were walking back into Sigi's room now, and Arabella suddenly appeared at the top of the stairs. "There you are, Nan! Is everything all right?"

"Yes."

"Don't mind Sigi; she's leaving anyway. Sigi, are you taking only one suitcase?"

"I can always come back. But I don't need much. I should've been born into a family of tramps."

Arabella shook her head and motioned a hand to Nan. "I must introduce you to someone."

TWENTY-FIVE

Sigi didn't talk to Nan anymore. She curled up in the corner, occasionally staring out in a way Nan didn't want to admit was unnerving. Nan sat and watched breakfast and dinner go by.

Minutes. Each so very, very slow. She would have been happy to work, just to escape Sigi's slow decay.

No! Not happy. That was how they got you to accept, or even appreciate, the fate they forced upon you.

In the middle of the second night, she heard Sigi groan gently, rousing from sleep. Nan wasn't sleeping. Her bones ached from the cold floor.

"Help . . ." Sigi's voice scratched the darkness, and in another moment, it was her fingernails on Nan's arm.

Nan jerked away and got to her feet. "What is it?"

"I remembered something, Nan. Nan, *help*!" Her voice was a pained rasp. "Hold me, hold me, it's so cold. . . ."

Nan froze. This didn't sound like Sigi anymore.

Sigi slumped to the floor, hugging herself. Nan could hear her more than see her, hear her fingers scratching at her clothes. "I'm starting to remember. . . . I did it, I killed myself." Her

voice was high-pitched and choked at once. "I was so alone. . . .
I didn't think it would really work. . . ." She cried, "Now I'm
dead!"

Nan shook Sigi's shoulder. Her skin didn't feel right; it was
cold. "Sigi, please—it's all right, I'm here. You're here."

"I need help. . . ."

"What kind of help?"

"I don't want to be dead, Nan, I don't want to be dead!"

Nan rubbed Sigi's back, trying to keep her from descending
into complete hysteria. "You're here. It's okay."

"You know that man . . . in the tunnels?" Sigi grabbed
Nan's shirt.

Nan's heart was hammering. "Yes?"

"I won't be like him. I won't."

"I know you won't."

Sigi let go. She got quiet again. But Nan could hear her
breathing—it was labored and loud. Nan didn't hear her inner
music, and she didn't sleep. She just waited.

It was some hours later that Sigi bit her.

TWENTY-SIX

Nan shoved away the face, her finger brushing Sigi's eyeball—still soft and moist in contrast to her withering skin. "Sigi!"

"I'm sorry. . . ."

"Don't make me have to fight you. Please. You're strong, Sigi, remember."

"I forgot who you were."

"What?" Nan grabbed the bars and got to her feet again. She felt dizzy and desperate for light. The whole world felt as if it were tilting, slowly. "Please. Remember."

"I'm just so . . ." The voice trailed off and then flickered back in like a radio. "You smell like *life*, Nan. Like . . . honey and cinnamon . . ."

Nan heard Sigi moving—only it just wasn't Sigi anymore. It could be Sigi again, but right now it was a terrifying thing, half-dead and hissing and hungry. Sigi was scrambling to her feet, not moving all that fast, but still Nan was trapped with her and she didn't know what she could do. If she fought back, she could wound the thing that wasn't Sigi but would be Sigi again.

"Please let me just . . . just . . ." Sigi said, and Nan imagined a hand coming at her in the dark.

Nan felt sick. She took out the knife and unfolded the blade with an audible click. "Don't come near me. I have a knife. Do you remember when we got the knife?"

"Yes." The voice was expressionless.

"I could hurt you," Nan said, trying to keep her voice steady.

"You won't. . . ." The voice turned slightly cajoling. It didn't even sound like Sigi anymore, but it still had her accent with her aristocratic vowels.

And then the Sigi-thing lunged at Nan. It moved stiffly and yet it was ferocious, tearing at her collar until the button at her throat broke. Fingernails dug into her tender skin. The pain sharpened everything. She slashed the knife at the assaulting arms, and the raspy voice howled like a sick child's.

"Don't touch me again," Nan said, her words harsh with fear. She had known Sigi would become this, and she thought she was ready, but this was worse than she had imagined.

"So hungry," it wailed, and it tried to grab her shirt again, but Nan dodged. She didn't know what to do but dodge. She didn't want to hurt Sigi.

"Please remember, Sigi! I'm Nan. Remember how—how we—the tunnels." Nan wondered if some primal part of Sigi's brain was angry at Nan for not returning the kiss. "Sigi, *please*."

Nan tried to push Sigi back with one hand and get in a punch with the other—maybe just enough to knock her out—but it was so hard in the dark, and she didn't really want to touch that dead flesh.

But it wanted to touch her, and when Nan tried to simply back away, they were on her again—those little scratching, questing fingernails. They were gentler now, but that was almost worse. She batted the hand away.

And screamed. Finally. Finally, she had to scream. She didn't even know such a dreadful noise could come out of her own mouth.

Were there any guards around? She just wanted someone to let her out. She could deal with Valkenrath if she could just get *out*.

When the door to a lit hallway was flung open, the wash of relief made her feel as though she had been trapped in some confusing childhood night terror. A candle, warm milk, a blanket tucked to her chin on a cold night . . . the opening door was better than all that. She put her knife away and grabbed the bars.

"Please," she cried to the two silhouettes framed against the light beyond. "She's—I'm—I'm not like her. I'm alive!"

"See, sir, it's just as I said. She was screaming bloody murder; they don't scream like that. Couldn't if they wanted to."

"Hmm," the second man said—Valkenrath. He took a step into the room and looked to both sides. "Where is the light switch in this place?"

"Here, sir." The guard hurried to switch on more lights. Nan squinted. Sigi was making some awful, unending moan. Nan didn't look at her.

Valkenrath approached the cage, frowning slightly. He needed a shave and looked quite tired. Sigi's hand suddenly caught the leg of Nan's pants, tugging sharply. "Help," she said, her voice barely a groan.

"All right, Nan Davies," Valkenrath said, and he quickly unlocked the cage and yanked Nan out by the elbow. He slammed the cage door before the Sigi-thing could stir itself to escape.

"Thank you," Nan said, before recalling that Valkenrath was to blame for the whole thing in the first place.

"I remember when they brought you in, cold and dead," he said. "How did you trick me?" He waved the guard away. "You may leave us. We're fine."

"Are you sure, sir? This is the one who tried to strangle Frederick."

"We're fine."

"Who is Frederick?" Nan asked. She had tried to strangle someone? Some of her memories still eluded her, and she felt they must be the most important ones.

"Never mind that. Is there some substance that can safely mimic death? Did someone help you? Tell me anything you remember."

"I don't remember anything," Nan lied. "All I know is that I haven't taken the serum since I arrived."

"I made a mistake having your memory wiped rather than questioning you," he said. "It's fairly common for the revived dead to be a bit hostile, so I merely assumed you were a particularly violent case. But it's certainly not common for anyone to truly come back from the dead without . . . consequence."

"I don't know what to tell you."

"I suppose the first question is, were you ever dead to begin with?"

When Nan saw his hand move toward his jacket, she rushed him, tackling him just as he brought out the gun.

He let out an "oof" as she knocked him to the ground, obviously caught off guard. The gun was still in his hand. Nan grabbed his wrist, and for a moment they twisted and struggled. He was much stronger than she was. Could she get out the knife? If she took her hands off him, he'd shoot her.

It didn't really matter, anyway. He growled, breaking from her hold, and clocked her in the temple with the butt of the gun. Stars swarmed her vision, but she was conscious enough to hear the shot and feel the force of it tearing through her heart, but there was no pain.

There was nothing except the familiar thrum of music, drawing her away, away, her soul like a tiny ship on an ocean of sound. . . .

TWENTY-SEVEN

Gerik was sitting in the back parlor, reading a newspaper, when Freddy came home. On his way upstairs, Freddy had to pass him.

The paper was folded and cast aside. "Come talk to me, lad."

"Surely it can wait until morning," Freddy said, but he knew Gerik wouldn't accept that.

"No, I don't think it should wait. But it won't take long." He motioned to the seat next to him.

Freddy sat down. He kept reliving, again and again, that moment when he let Father Gruneman slip away forever. Father Gruneman said he had to let all those people die, but he didn't even know if he could sever a thread of magic without touching the person. He wondered what it would feel like. When he let Father Gruneman go, it was like the snap of a strained cord—both painful and a relief.

"Tell me what happened with Thea tonight," Gerik said. "You don't look terribly happy, so I assume it didn't go well."

"Of course it didn't. I'm not ready to do this."

"You wouldn't feel that way with the right girl, Freddy. The right girl can make all the difference."

"But Thea was the right girl. The circumstance is what's wrong."

"She might be the right girl for later. But not now."

Freddy growled. "I can't reason with you."

Gerik cleared his throat and patiently drew his cigarettes from his pocket. Once he had one lit and had taken the first drag, he said, "I'm the only one you can reason with, at this point. If Rory knew how permissive I'd been with you, there would be hell to pay for both of us."

"Permissive? Oh, because you let me have a life for—let me count—four nights? So that both of you can get something you want?"

"*Permissive,*" Gerik said, lifting his voice into a more forceful timbre, "because I don't want to tell him where you've been going with this girl. But I also realize I cannot let it continue."

Freddy wasn't about to admit to anything until he determined how much Gerik really knew. "So you were following me, I suppose."

"Of course I'm not going to let you go without keeping an eye on you! You're far too important. Thea is one of those anti-establishment rebels, am I right? You sneaked into one of their meetings, where your head was no doubt filled with outlandish theories and plans."

"Well, if you know where I've been, you'll know I didn't stay long. Thea is not a revolutionary at all. She's just trying to figure out why people keep disappearing and why her mother is bound-sick."

"And that's also why she took you to the home of a rebel leader today, I suppose?"

"He's also the priest of her church. Thea was worried because he was supposed to stop by and check on her since her mother is gone, and he hadn't."

Sometimes Freddy surprised himself with how easily the lies came. He had never thought about all the lies he told Gerik. Most of them had felt not so much like lies as ways to keep a part of himself private. Gerik and Uncle could own his magic, but not all of him. Now he had become truly deceitful. And the reasons were still the same.

"Every lad needs a taste of freedom," Gerik said. "I'm sorry yours was short. You know I'd rather give you a different kind of life. I'd rather you had much more fun. But it just can't be. I hope you can at least see the advantages we've been able to give you." He sighed. "Maybe not now. But in time, perhaps."

"So that's it? I'll never see Thea again?"

"You can't see Thea again. She's obviously wrong for the task. I'll find you someone who's right."

Freddy stood up, feeling a blinding anger. "Why even loosen the leash if you're just going to jerk it back? Am I expected to spend my entire life in a handful of rooms?"

"Not once you have an *heir*," Gerik said.

"There is no guarantee of an heir. You know that as well as I do."

Gerik wasn't meeting Freddy's eyes anymore. "I don't know what else to say, lad. It is what it is."

"Fine. Don't answer my questions. Just dismiss me. I get it. I'm just a pawn and it doesn't matter what I want; I need to shut up and do whatever you want me to do. But this is *my* magic."

"Lad, I know you're upset. Why don't you go to your room, have a bite to eat, and calm down?" Gerik got up and moved to the door, avoiding the conflict and the tough questions, and Freddy didn't know what he could say to stop him. And behind the scenes lurked Uncle, unwilling to even engage with Freddy much of the time, yet in most ways he was really the one pulling the strings.

The power is still in your hands, Father Gruneman had said. Who really held the strings, in the end? If sending all those people to their deaths was the right thing to do—the only thing to do—then it was his choice.

But he still wasn't sure it was right. He had brought back thousands of people and been proud of each one.

He left the room in silence. The two rooms that were his—a bedroom and a sitting room—seemed so small after he had walked the streets freely. He sat at his desk, where the same clock was still dismantled, and stared for a long moment at all the gears and parts and tools. If only life could be so straightforward.

A housemaid stopped in at the door. "Would you like me to bring you something from the kitchens, sir?" she asked. Usually Freddy was hungry when he returned from any outing.

"Just bread and butter."

"If you're sure."

"Yes."

He moved to the window, gazing out at the motorcars driving around the square, just visible over the fence from his third-floor view. It reminded him of the balcony of the Telephone Club, where he could see all the people mingling below him—but Gerik kept him apart. Privileged but alone. Until Thea walked in. He would never see her again unless he escaped. But if he escaped, he needed a plan. He could try to get underground, but the only thing he could do from there was to release the spell and kill all the people he'd ever saved from death.

He needed the serum. It must be made in mass quantities. Vats and vats of serum. And someone would have to keep making more.

What happened to the dead without serum?

He looked at Amsel, sleeping soundly on his bed, his breathing slow and deep, his whiskers occasionally twitching with dreams. Freddy had a test subject. Right here in his room.

TWENTY-EIGHT

After his breakfast the next morning, Amsel followed his usual schedule of sitting in the window and staring at the birds that flocked in a nearby tree, and then curling up against Freddy's pillow and falling fast asleep. Amsel had not been a young cat when he died, and he was not very active in his second life.

Freddy, meanwhile, did not have his usual schedule at all. No one woke him in the morning to go to Uncle's. Gerik didn't come around until well after breakfast.

"No revivals today, lad," he said, lingering in the doorway uncomfortably. "I told Rory you ought to have some space today, since things didn't work out with Thea. He only had two anyway, so you can do them tomorrow. Just get some rest. Work on your clocks."

Freddy didn't respond, but Gerik didn't stay long enough to notice.

Freddy was certainly not interested in clocks at the moment. He wanted to see the people he had brought back. Maybe he could find a way to save them, if he could get down there. There must be an entrance beneath Uncle's house where the guards took the revived people away. But there were always so many eyes on him.

The sun was beginning to set when Amsel suddenly lifted his head from sleep and began to sniff the air.

"Amsel?" Freddy went to him, and Amsel started grooming Freddy's hand. Freddy stroked Amsel's back, noticing that his fur seemed dull and he no longer felt so nice to touch. He felt sort of dried out, somehow. His eyes, too, looked odd— his pupils were dilated with excitement, but his eyes looked sick. Freddy couldn't pinpoint it exactly. He didn't look dead. But—wrong.

Amsel's jaws suddenly clamped on Freddy's hand, and when Freddy jerked away, he was bleeding from several deep gashes. Amsel often nipped at Freddy in play, but he never bit or scratched. Amsel's jaws reached for another bite, and Freddy shoved the cat into the pillow reflexively.

"No!" Freddy shouted, pulling a handkerchief from his pocket to catch the blood. Amsel suddenly bolted under the bed with a low growl.

Freddy got on the floor, seeing Amsel's eyes gleaming in the shadows. He hissed when Freddy reached for him. Freddy drew back, reaching instead for the thread that connected him to Amsel.

Amsel was scared. Freddy felt it. He hadn't felt Father Gruneman's feelings like this, but maybe, he thought, because of his years spent so close to Amsel, or maybe because his animal mind was unguarded, Freddy understood that the cat was confused—he didn't want to hurt Freddy, but he was hungry.

And Freddy was food.

Freddy yanked open his desk drawer and took out the serum. He opened the bottle and held it out. "Come on, boy. Medicine."

But plain old serum offered no temptation to the cat.

Freddy put the bottle away and yanked the bellpull. The maid appeared in a moment. "Yes, Master Linden?"

"Can you just bring me some bread and pâté?"

She didn't even blink at the idea that Freddy might want food at this hour. Nothing he ate ever stuck with him for more than an hour or two. "Of course."

He sat on the bed. It looked empty without Amsel curled up on it. He kept remembering Amsel's fear and confusion.

He wondered if people felt that, too, without the serum.

Forgive me.

This was wrong. He felt the wrongness of it now. He understood how the people in earlier generations with reviving magic would have known not to hold a person to the earth—even if they were tempted, the sickness and the hunger would have forced them to cut the thread.

No one was supposed to live beyond death.

The maid brought the plate, and Freddy mixed the serum into the pâté. He slid it under the bed and Amsel gobbled it hungrily. When he was done, he licked his lips and his paws, and then he came out and pressed his head against Freddy's leg.

Freddy gathered him up. The cat's fur still felt a little strange, but he was purring and content now. He held Amsel against him, close enough to feel his heartbeat. "Thank you," he whispered. "Thank you—for being here. I was never alone with you here. Amsel . . ."

In his arms, Amsel sighed—tired, but content.

Freddy cut the thread.

TWENTY-NINE

Late that night, a rough hand shook Freddy from sleep. He rolled onto his back, opening his eyes to see Uncle looming over him in the moonlight.

His first thought was that Gerik had told him about Amsel. Gerik had been angry and suspicious about the cat. "We'll discuss it later," he had said, but now it was the middle of the night. Something else must have happened.

"Beg your pardon, Freddy, but this is important," Uncle said in a tone that did not seem to be begging any pardon at all. "I want you to revive someone right away. Get some shoes on and meet us in a moment. Don't dawdle, please."

"Who am I reviving?"

Gerik was standing behind Uncle, tugging thoughtfully at his sideburns. "We'll talk about it when we get there, lad."

A few minutes later they were in Gerik's car, whipping down the empty street behind Uncle's chauffeur. Once inside the house, Uncle led the way, not to the workroom but to what appeared to be a guest bedroom, blandly furnished with heavy drapes and antique furniture. A body awaited on the bed, partially unwrapped from a swath of blankets.

Why would they need to bring him to a different room? He didn't see any guards around, and Uncle seemed a little rattled. Whatever had happened, it seemed he didn't want anyone to know.

Nothing had been done to clean up the body—there was blood on its drab one-piece work suit, and even on the floor. Uncle was frowning at . . . her—Freddy was close enough now to see it was a girl, and not just any girl.

It's Nan, damn it—it's Nan. What did they do?

The last time, she had been unmarked, and her face had been like that of someone sleeping. Now there was blood everywhere, and her expression remained one of shock. When he got closer, he saw there was a wound in her chest, like she'd been shot in the heart.

He looked at Uncle. "What did you do to her?"

"Who said *I* did anything to her?" Uncle's eyes moved to the wound, a slight frown tugging at his mouth. "Remember how she tried to attack you? Well, she tried it with me. One of the guards shot her."

"Where did this happen?"

"Just revive her, Freddy, and we'll talk about it later," Gerik said impatiently.

"Why do you even want me to revive her again if she attacked me and then you? There's more to this, isn't there?"

"It isn't your concern." Uncle sounded angry. "I only ask this one simple thing. Revive the girl."

Freddy's magic felt as itchy and urgent as ever. He took her hand, trying to see if he could sense anything strange. A current of discomfort passed through him. He had never tried to revive the same person twice. Maybe he wasn't supposed to do such a thing.

"I need privacy to concentrate," he said. If this worked, he didn't want to talk to her with Gerik and Uncle in the room.

"Why don't you try doing it with us here," Uncle said, pushing Freddy toward the bed. "After all, she tried to kill you last time, so I'd rather not leave you alone."

Magic tingled in his hands. *No, not yet.* He forced his magic to stay back. He could feel it beginning to work, and jerked his hand away from Nan.

"The magic is making him sick," Gerik said. "Look how pale he's gotten. Come on, let's just step out for a minute. It's all right, Freddy. We'll be right outside if you need us."

"Why don't you let me handle this?" Uncle snapped. "Your soft approach has caused far, far too much trouble as it is. Freddy . . . you remember. The welfare of your family depends on your cooperation. You understand that, don't you?"

"Of course I do."

They slipped out the door. Freddy knew he had only moments, but if he could get Nan out of here, bring her somewhere safe . . .

He noticed the fireplace behind him. Quietly, he drew the poker out from its stand. His hand clenched around it. He would have only one chance to strike at Uncle and Gerik. One chance without a guard at the door.

He hurried over to Nan and grabbed her hand. A warm rush of magic flowed from his hands, and he exhaled with relief.

Her fingers stirred beneath his touch while a wave of nausea rippled through him. His ears filled with a resonant thrum like a bow drawn slowly over the strings of a giant cello. The sound was beautiful, like the very sound of magic itself, and he felt as if something were taken from him and given, both at once. As if some greater force than his own magic worked through him. "Nan—" His eyes filled with stars, and he kept clutching her hand, even when he couldn't see, reeling under the waves of power sweeping through him. It had never felt like this before.

She coughed, sounding weak.

He staggered backward, fumbling for the wall so he could lean against something solid. The room was swirling.

The door flew open.

"Freddy!" Gerik had a hand around him. "What's happened?"

"I don't quite know," Uncle answered, when Freddy couldn't find his voice. "It looks like magical backlash. As if he tried to tap into something too strong for him. It's like something is working through that girl."

Freddy couldn't focus, couldn't even stand anymore. The room seemed to have turned sideways, and all he could see were swirls of color. He felt Gerik grab him under the shoulder and nearly drag him toward the door, away from Nan.

THIRTY

"All right, lad, we're here. Have a rest."

Freddy felt the edge of a bed and collapsed onto it. He shut his eyes, letting the spinning room wind down like a top. He didn't have time to feel ill.

"What happened?" Gerik asked again. "Was she violent again? Why were you holding a poker?"

Freddy shook his head. He didn't want to talk, especially not to Gerik, who was happy enough to call him "lad" and tell him to rest and eat, but not to answer a single question worth asking, much less truly take his side.

"All right. Well, just get some rest." Gerik patted his shoulder and left the room. Freddy lay still, waiting for his head to clear. He had to get back to Nan before he lost his chance.

⊙–⊙–⊙–⊙

Suddenly he was coming to.

The day had warmed. The sun had moved dramatically.

Damn it to hell.

He'd missed his chance to fight back and run Nan out of there, but then, she hadn't exactly popped off the bed, either. Maybe neither of them was much good for a hasty escape. If she was still in the house, she might be feeling better now. Could he find a way to sneak her out?

He crept to the door, hearing footsteps somewhere distant, but when he peered out, the hall was empty. He didn't know the layout of Uncle's upstairs floor well, but she must be in a different bedroom nearby.

He heard voices and footsteps approaching, and scrambled back onto the bed, closing his eyes. If Uncle knew he was feeling better, he'd probably find a way to keep Freddy from further exploration. The door creaked open.

"Looks like he's still asleep," Gerik said softly. "Maybe we should just let him rest a bit longer."

"Not too much longer. I have a few more revivals for him."

"Really? Do you think he ought to do any more of that, after what happened earlier?"

"He skipped yesterday! It's unpleasant when we leave them for too long. Anyway, he's fine. He just had a reaction to the girl. What *is* she? Is she even human?" They were whispering now, and the voices became fainter as the door gently shut behind them.

Freddy would not be dragged off to revive yet more people. He was going to find a way out of here. Now. No matter what he had to do.

When he heard Gerik's and Uncle's footsteps go down the

stairs, he rushed into the hall, passing empty bedrooms. One door at the other end was closed. Even as he turned the handle, he heard Nan groan.

"Nan?" he whispered. "Are you all right?"

Her hands and feet were bound, and she had a gag in her mouth. Her eyes were barely open. He could smell the metallic tang of her blood.

He pulled the gag from her mouth. "We have to get out of here. I know about the underground, the scrum, everything."

She looked at him, eyes glazed. Did she understand?

"Freddy," she said slowly. "I'm sorry I tried to kill you . . . before."

"Don't worry about that. Let me get you out of here." He reached for the bonds at her wrists and worked the knot free.

"I don't think I'm strong enough to escape. . . . I can feel myself knitting back together, and it's—it's awful." She winced as she spoke. "But you—you need to go. There's an entrance to the underground in Vogelsburg. It won't be guarded."

"Vogelsburg?"

"You have to save them. Let them . . . see the sun before they die. Get Sigi . . . out of the cage. Please." Her eyes shut tight, and a spasm racked her body. He touched her arm, instinctively trying to soothe her, but she flinched. Was she going to die, even with his magic? "Just—be careful. There are . . . *things* down there."

"I will," he said. "But who is Sigi?"

She had already gone limp again, her eyes open but glazed, and then they shut, and she breathed heavily.

The sound of a maid's voice elsewhere in the house pulled his attention from Nan. "Mr. Valkenrath, sir?" she was calling. "There is a woman downstairs to see you. Mrs. Arabella von Kaspar."

THIRTY-ONE

He hadn't expected Arabella von Kaspar. But Uncle wouldn't be expecting her, either.

As Freddy left the room where Nan lay unconscious, he caught his name amid the conversation drifting from downstairs.

"I know who he is . . ." Arabella was saying. He couldn't catch every word. "But of course, we both . . ."

Murmur, murmur.

". . . boy." She was talking about him. Freddy edged farther out on the landing to hear. From where he stood, he couldn't see them and they wouldn't see him, but there was the risk of servants' noticing.

"I know what you're involved in these days," Uncle said. "I don't know what brings you here, and I don't care to. I must ask you to leave."

"Oh, I see," she said. "Well, if you'd rather I be direct, don't think I don't know what *you're* involved in, Rory."

"Please leave," Uncle repeated. "Or I shall have to ask my guard to assist with your departure."

"Just one guard?" she said, her tone now as hard as his under its false politeness. "I think I can manage him."

"Where is Wolff?" Uncle asked the guard.

"He'd been at the bottle last night, sir. Passed out in the kitchen," the guard said with some reluctance.

"Go get Wolff!" Uncle barked at someone. Maybe a maid; he surely wouldn't send his single guard out of the room. If Uncle had only one guard available, well, this was definitely Freddy's best chance for escape. Uncle's house would have at least one back set of stairs. He checked the bedrooms until he found an inner door. Although it was made to look like part of the wall, the door's outline was still visible.

Downstairs he heard some low, harsh words exchanged, and then Arabella called, "Freddy! Please come out. I know you came to see us last week! I won't hurt you."

He opened the door to a narrow stairway and hurried down into the servants' quarters. A boy of Freddy's age was walking by with a tray of household silver. "Master Linden!" he exclaimed. "What are you doing here?"

"Where's the back door?" Freddy growled.

"I can't tell you that!" The boy looked behind him. "Somebody, help! Master Linden's escaping!"

Freddy knocked the tray of silver so it scattered on the floor. The boy gasped and seemed briefly frozen between gathering up the valuables and stopping Freddy. Freddy found a door that led up stairs to a narrow back alley. He started running for the nearer exit just as Uncle's guard rushed into it, blocking the opening. Freddy quickly turned the other way. But the alley was much longer in that direction, running past several large houses. He pushed his legs—farther, farther—hearing the man coming closer behind him.

A hand caught his shoulder, and the other grabbed his arm.

"I'm actually a spy for the revolution," Uncle's guard hissed in Freddy's ear. "Come peacefully and Arabella won't hurt you."

Freddy lunged, trying to break free, but the guard caught him around the chest with one muscular arm. "Don't make this harder on yourself," he said.

The guard hurried Freddy into Arabella's car and climbed into the backseat with him. Arabella rushed out of the house with a pistol in her hand. Uncle held one, too, as he stood in the doorway, but he didn't shoot. He was shouting to whomever was behind him. Arabella took the driver's seat.

The car was pulling away now. Freddy was sweating, even in the brisk autumn air. He bit back an urge to curse, knowing he shouldn't anger Arabella now, but he'd been so close to escaping.

"Marcus, I'm sure the Valkenraths will be finding every guard they can spare to go after me," Arabella said. "Give me two hours with this boy, and then inform the others."

"What do you plan to do?" Freddy asked, trying to keep his voice even.

She smiled back at him, as if they were just out for a Sunday drive. "What a striking color your hair is. Do you know the saying about silver hair?"

"No."

"All the old wisdom is lost these days. Each strand is a spell worked 'too strong or all wrong.' You work magic every day of your life, don't you? And you do it at their bidding. But then, we shall talk about that more when I've gotten you home."

"I don't know that we'll have much time to talk before Uncle's men catch up with us."

"Rory Valkenrath isn't stupid. We're the same age, you know. I've danced more than a few waltzes with that man. I'm a woman of society and the face of a revolutionary movement with thousands of members. If he kills me in my own house, there will be a lot of angry people leading the investigation."

"I don't know. Apparently, he's pretty good at getting rid of people. And I *wanted* to escape him. But if we're going to work together, we should talk now."

"We aren't going to work together," Arabella said. "I'm going to tell you what must be done, and you can make your choice from there. I've been waiting too long to find you. I heard talk of a silver-haired boy at the Telephone Club. I asked around there, and what do you know? I heard the boy was always accompanied by Gerik Valkenrath. The gossip in this city can be a beautiful thing. And here we are." As she spoke, her words curled into anger. "And if Rory really wants to send his goons after me, I shall use you as my shield."

She had pulled down an attractive street. These were not the staid gray mansions of Gerik's and Uncle's, which had seen several emperors come and go. The houses here were fashionable, scaled-down versions of country villas—whimsical stone and pointed towers, glass greenhouses built on roofs, flowers spilling from window boxes. She pulled up to one of them. "Lead him into the house," she told Marcus, trading her grip on the steering wheel for the pistol she kept under her coat.

Marcus muscled Freddy along the stone path to the front

door. A nervous-looking young housemaid greeted them and took their coats.

Arabella took Freddy's arm now, pressing the barrel of her gun into his back. "Marcus, I thank you for your part. Make yourself scarce."

"Are you sure I should leave you?"

"Oh, yes. I know what I'm doing, and I want to do it alone. This way, Freddy." Arabella waved him up the stairs. Through open doors along the upstairs hall, he caught glimpses of half-finished paintings and empty canvases, sheets and splatter and unglazed pottery. She brought him into a study adorned with a stuffed, spiral-horned gazelle, a tiger rug, and a variety of birds preserved in midflight around a painting of her as a young woman, with her long hair spilling free, twined with flowers.

She was dressed modestly now, in a plain cream suit and pearls, but over her desk hung photographs of her youthful self—in pith helmet and sporting linen, posed with elephant tusks, or with only a draped cloth to cover her, exposing a white length of back. There was just one photograph of another young woman. Compared to Arabella, she looked innocent, though impish. "Do you remember when you brought her back?" Arabella asked, indicating the young woman's picture.

He nodded. "She came to slowly. Like she'd been dreaming. I don't think she said anything to me."

"She was my daughter, Sigi."

"Sigi?" The same name Nan had mentioned.

"Yes." Arabella's tone was bitter. She shut the door behind them. "You must listen to me closely and understand well. This magic of yours is causing thousands of people to

197

suffer—including you. If you bring someone back from the dead, it is your responsibility to release the person again, but if you don't do it, if you keep working more and more spells, it will take its toll on you, as it clearly has."

"I know," he said.

"If you know, then you would have already let them go."

"I can't let them go without touching them."

She scoffed. "Of course you can!" She paced quickly to the window and back. "Have you heard the stories of Queen Sofie's witches?"

"No . . ." He wasn't sure he wanted to hear them, either.

"A hundred and thirty-five years ago, this paranoid queen employed curse-workers to cast spells upon her enemies. These witches she demanded so much of withered away into nothing. The first sign was always the hair. Every strand of their hair turned silver, and their faces grew thin, just like yours. Have you noticed yourself tiring when you run or take too many stairs?"

"A little . . ."

"And I'll bet you are always quite hungry, and you never seem to get enough sleep."

He shrugged, although it was true. He didn't want to admit any weakness to her.

"It will grow worse. Soon, walking will begin to seem like an effort. But of course, I'm sure Queen Sofie liked it that way. Bedridden witches can't escape. They said she had a room of them, and servants to feed them and clean them and keep them alive as long as their magic didn't kill them first. It is said that at the end they were nothing but skin and bones, and their hair had fallen out."

She took a step closer, her long skirt rustling softly. "That will be you, Freddy. And Rory and Gerik know it, even if they haven't told you. Day by day, they are leading you into an adulthood of complete helplessness—pure magic, neatly trapped for them in the withered shell of a boy. You might have ten or fifteen more years of this. Another several thousand people. And then one day you will die, and they will all go with you, because in the end they need their connection to you to survive."

No, Freddy had not expected a story like that. But it made sense.

The pressure to have an heir. This was the explanation he'd wanted from them, because none of their reasons justified their urgency.

Gerik really didn't care about him.

He knew Uncle didn't; the man didn't seem to care about anyone. But Gerik, for all his irritating gregariousness and chauvinistic views, had been indulgent and even kind. Whereas Uncle would have worked him to the bone, Gerik would limit the number of revivals he could do. He made sure Freddy always got plenty to eat. He insisted Freddy needed to see his parents at holidays. Gerik had let him keep Amsel, even though the cat sprayed on the curtains sometimes.

He couldn't imagine how awful it would be to be trapped in bed, with dead people placed under his skeletal hands. His rooms already felt like a prison, but at least he could walk the little garden, work on clocks, read a book. Maybe Gerik wanted him to have a child to save him from the fate of Queen Sofie's witches. But if he really cared about Freddy, he would have told him it was time to stop.

"You see, don't you?" Arabella said. "You need to let them all go this moment."

"What about Sigi?"

"I wanted to see her one last time. For so long, our plan was to get all of the dead out of the underground. But I never expected to find you. This might be my only chance to end all of this. If I kill you, they will all die, and I would still rather have put Sigi out of her misery than let this abuse continue. As I told you, I don't have time to be nice. The Valkenraths will be here before long."

"But I heard . . . she's being held in a cage."

Arabella's hand twitched. "A cage? Have you seen her?"

"No. But I overheard." It seemed like too much to explain Nan.

He could see that Arabella was rattled, but it wasn't enough to make her reconsider her plans. "Well, all the more reason to put her out of her misery," she said, her voice low. "And then I will make the Valkenraths suffer for what they did. But I don't blame you, Freddy. I understand you are a victim, too. You will not suffer—as long as you can end this magic."

"Wait—just listen. This isn't the way. We have to get them out of the underground. There's an entrance in Vogelsburg."

"I know there are entrances," she said. "But there are also dozens of reasons why we might be stopped before we could possibly get them out. Viktor and the rest, they were always talking of these plots and logistics, how nothing could be done unless it was all done properly and peacefully. Well, I'm tired of waiting. Look within and feel it, feel those threads connecting you to all the people you've ever revived, and cut them loose. If you can't do it, then the only way to undo it is to kill *you*. But I know you can." She walked to the door. "Try to figure it out. I'll give you ten minutes."

THIRTY-TWO

As soon as she left, Freddy went to the window. Prickly shrubs below and the gate beyond seemed to mock the very suggestion of escape.

Arabella wanted him to destroy his life's work and end thousands of lives in ten minutes. Maybe she was right that it needed to be done. But not at this moment. Not on her terms.

He turned back to the study, which had an air of stifled adventure, with all the pictures of Arabella in linen pantsuits and the taxidermy on every wall. The gazelle seemed almost to stare at him with its glass eyes.

Dead animals everywhere . . .

A wild thought shot through his mind. Did these count as dead animals anymore, after having been skinned and reconstructed? He'd revived people with gaping holes in their vital organs, but Valkenrath had never brought him parts or pieces. Still, dead was dead. He brought life to things that shouldn't function.

He touched the wing of a pheasant frozen in mock flight.

At first there was nothing—he might as well have touched the desk. But deep down, he felt the telltale tingle, a sweet strength rising to his command. It didn't flow freely, the way it had when he brought back fresh bodies, but it was there to be coaxed.

The pheasant's wings suddenly flapped, stirring dust. Its head moved stiffly, the beak opened, and a wheezing sound emerged while the wings continued to flap, faster now. It was like some doll brought to life, testing alien limbs.

He had never known he had this kind of power inside him. Gerik and Uncle brought bodies to him and he revived them; it had always been that way, but he had never tested himself like this.

The pheasant thrashed, and he could feel its panic the way he had felt Amsel's hunger. *Very soon, I will let you go*, he thought, hoping maybe the animal would sense him, too. *But I need your help.*

The pheasant's wings settled into a restless flutter. He tugged it free from the base. Wires ripped from its feet, but the bird didn't seem bothered. It half-flew, half-crashed to the ground, where it limped a few steps, head turning from side to side. It seemed to be blind and silent. All the better. He could revive every animal in this room before Arabella returned.

Now he knew to free the birds from their bases first and revive them afterward—two ducks with rounded black crests, a white egret with long plumes, a fierce owl, all brought to life, making attempts to fly, crashing into walls. He watched them for a moment, the initial rush of bringing them to life fading as, again and again, a brief ruckus of wings ended in a thump against the wall.

He scooped up one of the ducks. Tucked under his arm, it stopped struggling. *Just one more . . .*

He turned to the gazelle. It was only about two feet tall, but the horns were fierce enough to skewer someone.

He pushed magic from his fingers, imagining it coursing down the gazelle's legs like running water. The head creaked sideways. It moved even more stiffly than the birds did, its limbs making squeaks and groans, but when he tried to urge it toward the door, it wheezed and attempted to run, smacking pell-mell into the side of the fireplace.

"It's all right," he said, stroking the animal's back. The fur was thin in places. "I won't keep you long." The gazelle calmed.

He remembered feeling Amsel's fear when the cat went without serum. Seeing the way the animals responded to his touch, he wondered if the transfer of thought could go the opposite way. Maybe he could keep them calm, influence their movements.

He shouted, "Mrs. von Kaspar! Get back in here!"

She pushed through the door, her mouth opening to speak and then hanging silent as she took in the birds flapping madly around the room. Her face drained of color. *Keep moving!* He tried to push his thoughts toward them. *This way!* The egret knocked against her hip, and the key in her hand clattered to the floor. He had meant to simply run, but this was even better. He snatched up the key.

"Oh, no, you don't." Arabella kicked him in the head, scraping his cheek. He shoved his elbow into her, trying to knock her down, but she held her ground.

"Don't move." She pointed the pistol at him. "Drop the key."

He went still, but he kept the key.

"What have you done?" she growled. "What kind of grotesque magic is this?"

"I'm done with doing magic at someone else's orders. I'll let the dead go—after I've freed them."

"You're only making it worse, Freddy. You're a monster just like the men who've kept you."

"You call me a monster? You're giving up on your own daughter!"

Arabella's gaze darkened even further. "Of course I don't want to give up on Sigi. You don't know how badly I want to tell her I'm sorry. But I have no other choice. I—" She broke off as the gazelle struck her with its horns. It moved too awkwardly to do more than throw her off balance, but this was his chance. He flew to the door, slamming it shut behind him, thrusting the key into the lock.

"Stop!" she shouted. A bullet punched a hole in the door. He moved sideways.

He turned the key, tried the handle to see that it was secure, and bolted down the stairs and toward the front door.

Arabella was screaming to be let out, and he heard servants behind him saying, "What's going on?" and "It's that boy! Stop him!" But the maid at the door looked somewhere between surprised and bewildered as he rushed past her and flung the door open.

He didn't stop. He didn't let himself think about the stitch rapidly developing in his side. He veered down a side street.

When he hit the busier street ahead, with congested traffic and shops, he finally slowed, his breath coming sharp and desperate. He ducked into a stationery shop, knowing he must look half mad.

"May I help you, sir?" asked the man at the desk, but Freddy was too breathless to speak. "Is someone chasing you? Perhaps you should move along if you have no need of stationery."

"I'm fine," Freddy gasped. "Just . . . give me a second."

He turned his mind back to the animals. He had promised them he would let them go, but he had never released his magic from a distance. This was his test, feeling the threads of magic, even from afar.

He closed his eyes a moment, looking inward. There—

The magic shimmered like memories of dreams upon waking. He felt the sparks of their lives—the birds, the gazelle.

Thank you, he thought before letting them go.

THIRTY-THREE

Was Nan dead or dreaming?

A new memory floated into her mind easily, painful though it was.

Sigi was dead.

Arabella told her amid the lively clamor of the club, clutching her drink and her cigarette holder, her eyes dry but seeing nothing around her.

"She's dead," she repeated. "And they took her."

*

The whole account didn't tumble out until Arabella had Nan back in the privacy of her home. She clutched the edge of her desk as she spoke, as if the news had left her dizzy and she needed something solid to hold on to. Photographs Sigi had taken were scattered in piles everywhere, all those faces and their untold stories.

Sigi's roommate had found her dead in the apartment, with pills and a suicide note. The girl called the authorities, and no one told Arabella for days.

"They took her to frighten me," Arabella said, speaking slowly as if she had to let herself absorb her own words. "They know I'm working against them." She stretched her fingers toward Nan but then drew back, apparently remembering that Nan did not like to be touched. Arabella gripped the desk again.

"I should have checked on her," she said. "I was—relieved—she had moved out."

"What did the suicide note say?" Nan asked, still trying to grasp that Sigi could be dead.

"'Don't blame yourselves.' But of course I do. I should. Sigi was usually a happy child, but when she got into a mood, it was a very low mood. I never knew how to talk to her, even when she was younger. She looked just like her father, dark and stocky. My fault for marrying an ugly man with money, I suppose. But Sigi never even seemed to care if she was pretty or if anything around her was pretty. I always liked pretty things, myself. That desire to capture beauty was what made me into an artist when I was young."

"Her photographs aren't beautiful, maybe," Nan said, reaching for one of a workman with large ears and gnarled hands. "But they are . . ." She smiled wryly. "There's something about them."

"I—I also got all her diaries, her papers," Arabella said. "She wouldn't want me to read them, I know. She tears me apart in them. But I understand her, for the first time, when I read them. All her compassion and her pain . . . I wanted her to be like me. I've failed her."

"And you think they've sent her underground?"

"I know they have."

Nan realized then that a pile of papers next to her chair was

Sigi's, too, the top sheet a turbulently scribbled poem. Why did Nan feel so strange, looking at Sigi's photographs and papers? She had barely known her. Sigi seemed to be everything Nan was not. Full of feelings, so many they had overwhelmed her. They had spilled into art, and now her art was all that was left of her.

Only, no. She was underground, where she certainly wouldn't have a camera, probably wouldn't even have paper.

"What can we do?" she asked Arabella. "If there's no way to get to the underground . . ."

"There is one way, of course," Arabella said, toying with one of her earrings.

"To die," Nan said. "But you think I'm an immortal guardian of fate."

"I never said—"

"I found your book," Nan said. "You'd scribbled a note in the margin."

Arabella's expression shifted slightly, almost to irritation, as if Nan had broken the rules of the game. "Well," she said, "you fit the description."

Nan felt something unfold within her. It should have been fear, but it wasn't. She wasn't like other people. She had always felt like there was something she must fight. Something she must do.

And now she was here.

"I could do it," she said. "I could die."

"No one ever comes out of the underground," Arabella said, with a note of caution. But Nan could see that she was hopeful. Nan didn't care; she wasn't doing this for Arabella. Maybe a little bit for Sigi. But mostly it was for herself. Maybe this was how other people felt when they fell in love, a sense that fate was working as it should.

"I will," Nan said. "If there's any way, I'll find it."

Arabella nodded slowly. "Yes . . . yes . . . When they bring you back, Nan, you will see the one who is causing all this. You have to try to stop him. Do whatever you have to do."

"But if I kill the person who is doing this, won't Sigi die with him?"

"Sigi has died," Arabella said, sweeping up the photographs. "She chose death. That moment when you are brought back might be our only chance to save her, at least, from a worse fate."

"I see," Nan said. "I don't think they would let me have a weapon on me when they bring me back."

"I'm sure you're right. But you must see if you can find a way." The eagerness in her tone suddenly dropped away. "You really are prepared to do this, my dear? Death is—"

"I know what death is," Nan said, feeling her first small tremor of fear. She forced it down.

*

Nan couldn't do it at home. She had to go somewhere where her body would just be another poor anonymous soul, perhaps with radical ideas, because those were the people who disappeared.

She went to the club, to see Thea one last time. If her resolve faltered, it was renewed when Thea apologized for not seeing much of Nan anymore. Her mother's bound-sickness kept getting worse. Nan was doing this for her, too—to set her mother free.

In the wee hours of the morning, she walked to Frederstrasse with nothing in her pockets but a copy of the Worker's Paper and the small glass vial of amber poison Arabella had given her.

She ducked into an alley next to one of the coffee shops and fished out the bottle.

Thea's worried face sprang to mind. She would be hurt that Nan had left without an explanation, but she would never understand. Thea would never let Nan do it.

Nan drank.

Her heart began beating faster. Her stomach felt very warm. She tried to cough. It was harder to breathe. She collapsed, thrashing and writhing on the packed dirt of the alley. Her eyes fluttered.

She could hear the familiar thrum of music in her mind, growing louder and louder.

Nan saw nothing anymore. She clawed at the ground with her last bit of strength. Pain roiled through her stomach. Her body betrayed her. It had always been strong, and now it was helpless and suffering, and she wanted to cry out but could only gurgle and gasp.

This was death—

The familiar, comforting music swelled through her, and suddenly she was free. She was one with that sound that was more than sound, the music of life itself, and it was more beautiful than it had ever been.

*

She became aware of her body all at once, a physical world of ceiling lights blaring in her eyes, clinical smells, and a cold surface beneath her.

Nan woke as if from a dream and looked into the face of an unfamiliar boy.

"Where am I?" she asked, blinking. All her senses seemed heightened.

Something was wrong, and she ought to know what, but she couldn't. "Who are you?" she asked.

And then she remembered. Arabella. Sigi. The underground.

But it was already too late.

THIRTY-FOUR

Nan woke with a cry.

What had happened? Her feet were bound, but not her hands.

Right. Freddy. Freddy had been here. And then she had dreamed of the first time she died. This time, the second, was far worse. She let out a breath. It didn't hurt quite as much now, and the pain that remained was not unwelcome. The air dragging through her lungs, the piercing ache in her chest, the bruises—and the trees out her window. They looked different. A different kind of gray, almost like . . . green.

The green of a kiss.

No, that didn't make sense. The trees were gray to her, now and always, because they were of this world, and she was not.

The door opened with a creak. "You are one stubborn little cuss, aren't you?" She shut her eyes, still too exhausted to speak, but she heard Valkenrath's footsteps approach.

His cold hand touched her cheek. Her eyes flew open once more.

He drew his hand back. "Warm. How did you get your hands free?"

"I don't know," Nan said, not wanting to mention Freddy, but she was having trouble thinking quickly. She let out a weary sound, not quite a sob, and then coiled her emotions back up. She couldn't let Valkenrath see her weakness.

"How much do you remember?" he asked.

"Everything. I remember everything." Arabella and Thea; Sigi who kissed her, and Sigi the monster in the dark, and Sigi the girl with a camera and a suitcase.

"Good," he said. His face was impassive, craggy with exhaustion. "You've died twice now. And yet here you are as if nothing ever happened. How did you do it?"

"I'm not human," she said. "I'm a guardian of fate. I came here to stop you. You have to listen to me."

"I think you're delirious."

"No. I'm not. You know I came back from the dead. Isn't that enough that you should believe what I say?"

"I don't have proof of *how* you came back from the dead."

A part of Nan wanted to say, *All I know right now is that my chest hurts and I'm tired and I don't have a clue what to do next.* But she did actually know one thing. This man was the core of everything. The magic was Freddy's, but the plan was his, and if she wanted to fulfill her purpose, she must do something with him.

"I know why you are unable to explain," he said. "You're in cahoots with Arabella von Kaspar. She gave you something. Some kind of spell to feign death, or—or you have your own source of serum." He grabbed her arm, jarring her poor broken body so that she almost wished to return to that dreamy world between life and death. "Tell me everything she said to you, and I won't hurt you."

"Arabella didn't tell me much. She found accounts of people like me, and I believe them, because I know what happened. I killed myself to get to the underground, and although you took my memories from me, I quickly realized I didn't need your serum."

She wasn't sure what was angering him: her calm, or the answers that he clearly didn't want to believe or understand. She knew it had always bothered him that she didn't fear him as the other workers did, and now his eyes suddenly flared with fury. He hauled her out of bed arm-first, and she sucked in air, squeezing her eyes shut, trying not to give him the satisfaction of her crying out.

"You aren't invincible," he said. "You are hurt."

"I'm healing," she said. But right now she felt torn up inside.

"Here is how I see it, Miss Davies. There are a few possibilities. One is that Arabella von Kaspar has given you something to keep you alive and made you swear not to tell. If that is the case, then it is my job to make you tell. The other possibility is that you're telling the truth. You are here to stop me. You are, as you say, a guardian of fate. But there are so many questions. How are you expected to guard anything if you have no power? Unless you're keeping it from me." He shook her shoulders so rapidly she wanted to retch, but her stomach was empty.

Tears trailed down her cheeks. She remembered telling Sigi she never cried, and it was true, but they were coming now, and thinking of Sigi made it worse. Nan had promised Sigi the sunshine, promised that she would not die in the tunnels, and now Nan had nothing. She had no strength, no answers—just this man looming over her who didn't care about anything.

When she looked at him, she could only seem to imagine him withering like the workers he controlled. Did he love, did he feel, did he see beauty, any more than she did? She didn't think so, and of course, he didn't have her inner music, her inner purpose. He might as well have been that man in the tunnels—shambling along, ugly and hungry.

"I pity you," she said softly.

His eyes narrowed. "I pity no one."

"I know. You're dead inside."

"You don't know anything about me."

"I do. For so long I've felt that something was wrong, and now I know what it is. You're the imbalance. You created all of this, not Freddy. He's just a boy. And you're just a man. But I am—*immortal.*" With the word, she summoned all the strength left within her and kicked him. She grabbed his hands. She didn't quite know what she was doing, but all along she had been able to see the emptiness in his heart. Maybe she could fill it with something. Maybe she could make him see. Or *hear.*

If she had powers, she didn't know how to use them. But one thing had always been with her—the thrum of ethereal music inside her.

He tried to yank his arms from her, and she pulled him closer to her, and she listened for her song. If he could hear the music of fate, he would have to understand. She wanted him to understand. Understanding was so much more beautiful than killing him—and that might be the only alternative.

She caught the strains, and it grew louder, and she moved her lips as though she might almost be able to join in as she tried to open it up to his ears.

He cringed and looked around him. "What is that sound?"

"It's beautiful," she said. "It's the sound of balance. It's the song of the other world."

"It's—horrid." His eyes widened. "You're filling my head with this. You are magic. I knew—" He pulled his hands away from her and covered his ears, but he still seemed to hear the music after breaking away from her. It was inside him now, just as it was inside her, but she breathed in the beauty of the slow notes that swirled around her and filled her up. This was her magic, her mission, and for the first time she didn't feel awkward and lost, but extraordinary.

Valkenrath had backed up against the wall, bending over, gripping his head. He was breathing hard. Something in him seemed loosened, as if thoughts he had previously blocked from his mind were forcing their way through the cracks. A clock on the wall ticked slow seconds in the sudden silence, and he didn't say anything.

Now someone knocked on the door. The spell broke. Valkenrath turned sharply on his heel, finally tearing away from her, and opened the door.

"Rory?" Gerik said. "What's going on?" He looked at Nan.

"I'm trying to find out what she is," said Valkenrath—*no, Rory,* she thought, as if knowing his given name gave her more power. He sounded ragged. "But she's done something to me." When Gerik started to walk into the room, Rory put a hand on his chest. "Don't touch her."

Gerik halted. "Freddy's gone," he said. "Arabella is at the door, and she says he ran off. I don't really know what she wants, why she's come back, but I don't trust her, and I'm worried about the lad." He frowned at Nan, seeming uncertain. "What did she do to you? You look awful. But so does she."

"I don't—quite know." Rory looked reluctant to even attempt an explanation. "Why don't you try to find Freddy. I'll deal with Arabella." He glanced at Nan. "You come with me."

THIRTY-FIVE

Nan caught a split second of Arabella's usual composed expression before she noticed Nan was there. "Nan? Dear god . . ." Her eyes swept over the bloody work suit. There was still a hole in it right over Nan's heart. "What happened?"

Arabella stood in the entrance room, late afternoon sun flooding the space behind her from a row of windows that faced west.

Rory was a storm cloud darkening the room, glowering and troubled. Although Nan's spell had been interrupted, he seemed rattled, gesturing and raising his voice when he was usually so controlled. "You took Freddy," he said, "and then you *lost* him?"

"Quite a trick he pulled on me," she said. "He brought my hunting mounts to life."

"What about your guard-spy?"

"He'll be informing the rest of my associates of what is happening."

"You know this girl," he said, grabbing Nan's arm and jostling her forward. "What is she?"

"I don't *know* much." Arabella straightened her stance, as if prepping for a duel. "But I believe she is something special. Not quite human. I thought she might be brave enough to destroy you and this world you've built. But it seems you've broken her instead."

"I'm not broken," Nan said.

"Well, you haven't killed Freddy, you haven't stopped Valkenrath, and you haven't freed my daughter. It's all right, Nan. I suppose you haven't come into your powers. I can only trust myself, in the end."

Nan let the words go. Arabella was not her goal, and she didn't really care what the woman thought.

"Since we've reached this point," Arabella said, "I want to see my daughter, who I believe is trapped down in your hellhole."

"Your daughter couldn't possibly be down there," Rory said. "We don't revive upper-class citizens."

"She wasn't exactly living like an upper-class citizen. She ran away from home to live in a sad little flat."

"I certainly will not take you underground. You're asking me to destroy everything I've built. If I call the chancellor, he'll have both you and Miss Davies imprisoned on some charge until we can decide what to do with you."

"If Freddy wants to let the dead go," Nan said, "there is nothing you can do except prepare." She looked at him, and he avoided her eyes—covertly, but she had begun to make him believe her. "Would you rather release the dead yourself, or have him make the choice for you?"

"What you ask cannot—should not—be done quickly," he said carefully. "The dead help to run the city."

"Then . . . let us help you replace them carefully," Nan said. She didn't really have the authority to say this. That magic belonged to Freddy. But right now she just had to keep Rory calm. Open. She had given him a taste of her power. That was a start. And, hopefully, enough. "Let's just start with Sigi. If we get Sigi out of the underground, Arabella, will you cooperate with Rory to help the other workers?"

"I suppose. If he truly does what we need him to do."

Nan turned to Rory. "Let us see Sigi."

"I don't even know for sure if Sigi is there," he said.

"Well, I do." Nan added pointedly, "She's the girl who got caught carrying a flashlight."

He raised an eyebrow, realizing now the state Sigi would be in when Arabella saw her—something Nan was trying very much not to think of. "I see."

"Freddy told me she's being kept in a cage," Arabella said.

"She tried to escape," he said. His tone was cool and unrevealing now. "Come with me."

He led them down a hall and opened a door with stairs to the cellar. It was like any other cellar, cool and cobwebby. A steel door leading to the underground was tucked behind a supporting beam of the house. Now Nan remembered these doors and passages—the room where Freddy revived her, the hall through which the guards had dragged her.

"You built all this down here?" Arabella asked.

"I didn't build it to begin with. Years ago, this house

connected to a network of rooms beneath the royal palace."

"It's vaster than I expected," Arabella murmured a moment later, seeing halls shooting off to the sides. "I must say, I'm impressed you were able to keep your prisoners from escaping."

Of course, Nan knew the way he had kept them from escaping. But Rory didn't say anything about the serum to Arabella.

When Rory opened the next door, Nan heard something scream. No, someone. Sigi. Nan hadn't realized they'd reached a side entrance to the cafeteria.

Nan lowered her eyes and remained in the doorway while Rory moved forward, Arabella behind him, more reluctant. Nan didn't want to see Sigi like that again, but she couldn't block out the sound of her, moaning and scrabbling in the cage.

"What is that?" Arabella asked.

"That is your daughter," Rory said.

Arabella's scream drowned out Sigi's moans. Nan looked up. She couldn't seem to stop herself. Sigi was withered almost beyond recognition, her eyes too wide in shriveled eyelids. She didn't recognize her mother or Nan. She thrust her nose between the bars, smelling the life of them, reaching with shriveled fingers.

"Help." She spoke hoarsely. "I need blood . . . blood. . . ."

Rory was impassive to Arabella's despair. He took a vial from his pocket, removed the stopper, and handed it to Sigi. "Drink this now."

Nan took a deep breath. *It will be all right,* she thought. She clutched at the buttons of her work suit.

Nan's eyes were riveted on Sigi, so she didn't even notice Arabella take the gun out.

Until the shot went off, echoing sharply in the wide space.

Rory's eyes widened, his hand clutching his chest while a stain spread on the back of his jacket.

Arabella pulled the trigger a second time, and his knees gave out. He died quickly, right at Nan's feet, with a look of surprise on his face that Nan was sure echoed her own.

"He was doing what we asked!" Nan said, just those few words short of speechlessness.

Arabella's face was streaked with tears. "Look at my daughter. Didn't you die so that you could stop all this?"

"Yes, but . . . shooting a man in the back?"

"It isn't on your conscience, Nan. Don't worry about it."

"He was starting to understand. I know he was. I took his hands and—" She broke off, looking at Sigi again. Maybe Arabella was right. But it didn't *feel* right.

One of the guards rushed through the door, halting in his tracks when Arabella pointed her gun at him. "Stop right there! Put your hands over your head. I'm a *damn* fine shot, as you can see."

A second guard had come in behind the first one.

"Madam, there are a lot more of us than there are of you."

"I will take out as many of you as I can before I go down," she said. "I don't care. I've done what I came to do. And that is my daughter in there." With her free hand she pointed at Sigi, whose moaning had grown subdued after drinking the serum. She was crouched on the floor of the cage. "He did this to my *daughter*. I just want to see her before I go. So leave this room if you don't want to join *him*."

The guards looked at each other. The first one nodded.

They slowly backed out and shut the door behind them. Nan doubted they went any farther than that; they were only biding their time. She hoped they didn't think her an accomplice. She didn't know how many times she could handle dying in one day.

"Arabella," Nan said, speaking as carefully as she could. "Please. Sigi will be all right once the serum takes effect."

"Sigi is going to die," Arabella shouted back. She was still holding the gun, not quite pointed at Nan, but close. If she shot now, it might nick Nan's arm. "I don't know if I can describe how it feels to lose your daughter and feel like you were the one who had driven her to her death."

"You're in pain from seeing Sigi like this." Nan spoke haltingly. What else might Arabella do in her grief? "But she isn't gone yet. You can still say what you want to say. It's not too late."

Arabella's cheeks were flushed, anger and hurt mingling in her red-rimmed eyes.

But she lowered the gun.

"Sigi!" Nan turned to Sigi, who was still huddled in the corner of the cage. Even her curls were listless as they spilled over her face. "Talk to me. Is the serum working?"

Nan's heart was beating faster. She grabbed the cage, and her suddenly sweaty hands squeaked on the bars. "Sigi, I want to get you out, like I promised. Please."

She turned to Arabella again, feeling an alarming desperation. "I don't know how quickly the serum reverses. I told her I'd make sure she saw the sunshine before she died."

"Was there something between you and my daughter?" Arabella said.

Nan didn't answer. She took a deep breath. *Sigi is going to die.*

Sigi is going to die.

And she had to let it happen. She had to make sure Freddy accomplished his mission, and see that he got out safely so his magic couldn't be abused again. She had forgotten the guards outside the door, but they were there, and they wouldn't stand idle for long.

Sure enough, she heard Gerik's voice booming, and he burst in the door, a furious figure brandishing a gun of his own, brisk steps in expensive polished shoes. His eyes alighted on the fallen body of his brother. "Who did this?" he demanded. "Which one of you killed him?"

"I did," Arabella said. She spoke without anger or arrogance; in fact, she sounded subdued. "My daughter is a living corpse crying for *blood*. You can't scare me with your weapons. I don't care if I die."

Gerik was hurrying to Rory's side. "Where is Freddy? Damn it, this is all your fault. You took the boy and now my brother."

"Did you hear a word I said? I don't care one whit about your brother. He started this. And if I see Freddy, I'll kill him, too."

This seemed to jar Gerik. He had crouched beside Rory and taken his hand, but now he turned. "Arabella, please. I am sorry that your daughter somehow ended up in the rabble. That was surely a mistake. We don't keep people with noble blood."

"What does it matter how noble her blood was?" Arabella said. "No one deserves this! But I know it's too late for Sigi.

Maybe it isn't too late for you. I want you to give an order for all of your workers to evacuate aboveground."

"I—I cannot do such a thing! We'll have blackouts and shortages, and without serum they'll turn into . . ." He waved at Sigi. "What would I tell the chancellor?"

"I *want* blackouts," Arabella said. "I *want* shortages. I want the people to know how you've betrayed them."

Nan approached Gerik very slowly. "I could have helped your brother understand, if I'd had more time." Now she was almost standing face-to-face with him. "You can't keep the workers, and—" She was conscious of Arabella's impatience. "I think it has to happen now, even if it does mean blackouts. Freddy can't let them go one by one, and we can't tell the people one by one. They deserve to know what's happened."

"Rory's the one who made all these decisions." Gerik didn't seem to want to look at her. "I really didn't have all that much to do with it. The chancellor—"

"So now you will blame it all on Rory and the chancellor?" Arabella sneered. "You knew what was going on just as well as they did."

"I did, but"—Gerik clutched his forehead—"I never came down here. I never saw any of this."

Nan didn't want Arabella to gain too much control over the conversation. "So, you couldn't find Freddy?" she asked Gerik.

"No." He was looking at Rory again. "No, I didn't. I—"

"Please . . . you must . . . listen to Nan," Sigi groaned from behind them. She crawled to the bars and pulled herself up, hand over hand, on shaky knees. "I've always known . . . down here . . . that . . . I shouldn't be here. That I chose to kill myself, and I'm sorry now, but this wasn't right. . . . I wasn't supposed to keep living like this. Please . . . let us die."

Gerik looked at his brother instead of at Sigi. As if Rory's still form would rise from the pool of blood and offer his opinion.

Sigi is going to die.

Sigi is going to die, and I will hold her while she does.

THIRTY-SIX

Thea heard the pounding footsteps before the knock. She rose from the table and wiped her hands on a napkin, her thoughts turning abruptly from hunger to panic.

"It's Freddy. Please open the door!"

He practically fell in the door when she opened it. "There's a cab waiting. We have to go now."

"What? Where?"

"Nan told me to go to Vogelsburg, so that's what we'll do."

"Nan!?"

"Just trust me. Gerik, Uncle, Arabella—everyone will be looking for me. I'll explain when we get there."

Thea snatched up the purse with Father Gruneman's gun and hurried down the stairs with Freddy. She heard Miss Mueller's door opening behind her and the old woman asking about "all the ruckus," but Thea didn't pay attention. Yesterday had been Sunday, her day off, and she had spent it in a state of painful indecision, wondering where to turn next. With Father Gruneman dead, she didn't know if she ought to go back to the Café Rouge tonight. She would not hesitate now.

But why Vogelsburg? It had suffered heavy damage during the war, and no one lived there now. The cabdriver apparently wondered the same thing, because he glanced back at them and said, "You're sure you want to stop in Vogelsburg? There's nothing much there except squatters. It's dangerous for a couple of kids."

"We're sure," Freddy said. "Drop us off where the subway used to be."

"What are you doing there, anyway?"

"None of your business, mister," Thea said, with her best Telephone Club sass. "We're paying you, aren't we?"

"It's not a good place for a rendezvous, I'm telling you."

"And I told you to mind your own business."

"That's why I need you along, Trouble," Freddy said, smiling a little even through the panic in his eyes. She couldn't ask him what he'd already been through today, not until they had privacy.

"I hope I'm the worst of the troubles we'll be dealing with," she said, trying to tease back, but the words were forced.

As the city she knew was replaced by the war-torn outskirts, the only shops seemed to sell liquor, with rough-looking men hanging around outside. Drab five-story apartment buildings had gone up, but there were still vacant lots and burned-out husks of buildings.

A couple of blocks later, the apartments gave way to complete rubble, piles of bricks that had been moved off the street but not off the sidewalk. Some of the buildings clearly used to be quite elegant, with arched windows or attractive towers that still stood while the rest of the buildings were skeletal wrecks.

The bright but broken pieces of a street organ rested on the corner, and the occasional book or shoe rotted in the gutter, but the only sign of recent inhabitance was some laundry hanging between windows. The cab slowed.

"Is this it?" Thea asked.

"This is it," the cabdriver agreed. "Used to be a nice old neighborhood, but there just isn't the manpower to rebuild it." He turned a corner. A gaunt, tanned woman was tossing the contents of a chamber pot out the window of a house that looked half-destroyed. The poorest people still lived in the remnants of buildings, but there appeared to be only a handful of them.

The driver stopped the car in front of the subway entrance, which was still perfectly intact, at least from the outside. "There you are."

Freddy paid up and they climbed out. The cab drove away, and Thea shivered, more from fear than cold. She hadn't had time to really wonder what she was getting into. The woman with the chamber pot looked at them out her window. "Hello," she called, but her tone said something more like, *Who the hell are you?*

"Hello," Freddy called back. "Do you own a flashlight?"

"You going down there?" She pointed at the subway stop, as if there could be doubt. "It's dangerous. Convicts hide down there sometimes."

"Terrific," Thea muttered.

"We're looking for her father," Freddy said. "We think he went down there and got lost."

It wasn't exactly a lie, Thea supposed.

"Why would he go down there?" the woman asked.

"He's a newspaper reporter," Thea said. "He heard there was something going on underground."

This answer didn't seem to surprise her. "I have a lantern. I'll sell it to you."

Freddy offered her a few bills, twice what a lantern probably cost, and held them up so the woman could see. The woman nodded and turned back into her house. Freddy and Thea walked up to her window. A moment later she handed out a lantern and what might have been a curtain rod, or something like it, once upon a time.

"You'll want something to beat off the rats and the crazies," she said, grinning. Thea could smell her rank breath and unwashed body from where she stood. "Good luck finding your father."

"Thanks," Thea said. Her voice came out strangled.

They walked to the subway entrance. Their footsteps seemed too loud. No, it wasn't their footsteps that were too loud; it was this place that was too quiet, without voices or automobiles. Grass pushed between the cracks of the subway steps.

It was even quieter underground. In the dim light, they could see that the station was still intact, eerie with the whispers of prewar life, details in stained glass and signs in fonts no one used now. The turnstiles with slots for tokens still stood—well, one, anyway. The other had been busted out. A chair remained in the empty ticket booth. It was warmer here, with air that smelled moist and earthy. "What are we doing, Freddy?" she asked. "Tell me what happened. You saw Nan?"

"She was . . . dead. Again. After I revived her, I tried to take her with me, but she was too weak, so she told me to come here if I wanted to find the people underground."

"What will we do when we get down there?"

"We have to try to get the workers out, like Father Gruneman wanted. And we can find your father."

I don't want to find him.

The horrid thought skirted past her mind.

Of course she did. She did.

But not here.

Not this way.

Her last memories of him were good ones. He was young and healthy, optimistic that the war would end quickly and life would be better for it. She remembered saying good-bye to him at the train station. She'd been crying, but he didn't seem scared. He'd told her to take care of her mother, and her mother had laughed and said, "For goodness' sake, Henry, she's got her hands full taking care of her dolls." He'd laughed, too, and said, "Take care of your dolls, then."

They were both so normal, that last time she ever saw him.

"And then what?" she asked Freddy.

He said nothing.

A huge lump sat in Thea's throat. She didn't want to acknowledge it. "And then you will let them all go."

He shook his head. "I just keep wondering if—could it hurt to save one person?"

"But if people found out my father or Nan was allowed to live when everyone else had to die, that would be terrible. I don't want to lose them, but you have to make things right. And right doesn't always mean happy." Gently, she straightened out his lapels; they weren't resting correctly. "And you can save my mother. Cure her bound-sickness."

He lowered his eyes. "Yes . . ."

It was so dim and damp here in the tunnels that, even standing close to him, she felt the loneliness all around them. Everything down here was forgotten. She was still holding his lapels, and now she leaned against him and put her arms around him, unsure which seemed more important: feeling his arms fold around her in return, or letting him know that he wasn't alone in what he had to do.

She was so sad as she held him, knowing they couldn't put off descending into the darkness much longer. But like the last tiny ember glowing in a dying fire, she realized one bright thing had come of all of this: she had met Freddy. She thought, when all was said and done, she might like for him to take her to the Hornbeam again, just the two of them, listening to music born from the forests where their bloodlines had sprung.

It will happen, she told herself, and then she pulled back a bit. For a moment, his arms didn't seem to want to let her go.

She frowned. "So—how do we do this, anyway?"

"Arabella had a man working on the inside," Freddy said. "She sent him away when we got to her house and told him to get her people ready. So if we can find the revolutionaries when we start getting the workers out, I think they'll help us. We just have to persuade the workers to follow us out. I think we should tell them we're with the revolutionaries, too. We don't want them to know who I really am. They might panic."

"So . . . we're not going to tell the workers they're going to die?"

"I don't see how we could."

Thea suddenly realized she would have to choose between lying to her father and telling him he was about to die. "Should I tell my father?"

She would see him soon. She'd have to decide then. She didn't know what state he'd be in. And would she be able to get him to the asylum, to see Mother? His death should cure her bound-sickness, but it would be much better if she could get well by seeing him one last time. He should be allowed to die in her arms.

Thinking of that, she knew she would have to tell him.

When they'd received word that her father was likely dead, she wished she had been able to say good-bye. But not like this. How would it help? He knew she loved him. She was going to see him, and she prayed he would still be like the father she remembered, but maybe he'd be broken from the years, and that would be her new memory, and she was afraid of that.

She had to see him one last time. And he would want to see her. And so she would come.

But it hurt. It was like a thousand tiny cuts on her heart.

THIRTY-SEVEN

Freddy lit the lantern and led the way to the tracks. A train was parked on them, but the windows were coated in grime. "Do you know where to go from here?" she asked him.

"Yes. I didn't used to be able to feel the presence of the people I've revived, but now I can sense them ahead."

"So do you think it's true, what Father Gruneman said, that you don't have to touch them, or even see them, to release the magic?"

"Yes. When he said that, I didn't think it was possible. But since then I've been trying to use my magic in different ways. I'm more aware now."

They climbed down, and it seemed to take only moments for the tunnel to swallow them up. Grates some two stories up cast patterns of light and shadow at first, but as they continued deeper, the lantern became their only light.

The track was on a gentle downgrade. The exit was no longer close enough to sprint to if something emerged from the darkness ahead. Eerie shadows wobbled on the gray walls beyond the lantern's glow.

A bit later, the track joined with a second. Now two tracks ran side by side, with puddles between them, so Thea walked carefully. She heard something skitter in the dark. Freddy trained the lantern on a scruffy brown rat just before it scurried back into the darkness.

"I suppose we should be glad that's the first one we've seen," he said. "We haven't had to fend them off with a curtain rod yet."

"It's the darkness that's so awful. There could be a thousand of them just out of sight somewhere."

But rats weren't the worst of what they could encounter.

They came to a door placed in the left wall. Freddy opened it, revealing a staircase descending another story—at least.

"Oh, *no*," Thea said. "Where on earth are we, anyway?"

"The city has miles of underground rails and old tunnels, I've heard Uncle say." Freddy started down the stairs. At least the steps were dry and clean, but as they neared the bottom, she caught a whiff of something like smoke and . . . food.

"Do you smell that?" Freddy whispered.

"Yes. Could we be getting close to the revived people?"

"It's not that."

A prickle ran down her spine. "Then what is it?"

"Hopefully, not a convict." He stepped off the stairs, into a narrow ridge hemmed in by solid wall on one side and crumbling wall on the other. "It seems to open up ahead." He extended the lantern outward.

It looked like a natural cavern ahead, or maybe part of the old catacombs. She didn't see any bodies, but there were shadowed niches in the walls that she didn't care to look at too closely.

And the remains of a campfire.

Freddy swept the lantern over obvious signs of habitation. A blanket was crumpled beside a cup and a bowl, a wooden box, and a pile of small animal bones picked clean of meat. Rat bones, maybe. A few empty liquor bottles lay on their sides.

"Who's there?" a deep voice barreled from the depths of shadow. A man sprang out from a niche in the wall, growling in his throat like an angry dog. Thea stumbled in the dim light, trying to get away as he launched himself at them. He was tall, with large hands, a matted dark beard, and steely, wild eyes.

Freddy held the curtain rod like a weapon. "We just want to pass peacefully."

"It's dangerous down here, boy," the man said. "You need to get out and go right back where you came from, or I'll eat you for dinner."

Thea remembered Father Gruneman's gun and opened her purse, and the man's attention snapped to her . . .

And suddenly shot past her. At first, Thea didn't see or hear a thing.

Then, shuffling footsteps. They moved faster as they grew closer.

"It's him," the man hissed. He suddenly shoved Freddy away, turned, and ran.

Thea didn't really want to know what would scare a man like that. She took out the weapon. It was cold and heavy in her trembling hands.

"Where did you get that?" Freddy asked.

"Father Gruneman."

"Put it away," he said. "I know him." He was looking into the darkness. Boots came into the circle of the lantern light, and then legs in tattered, bloody clothes, and then emaciated arms, the skin a withered brown, mottled, ending in filthy fingernails.

Thea dropped her eyes before she could see the face. She didn't want to see the face. Her heart stampeded through her chest.

She heard a sniff, and then a whisper. "Living . . . flesh . . ."

"It's the first man I ever revived," Freddy said, his voice coming out choked, as if someone had hands around his throat. "Our neighbor. The day before the Valkenraths took me away."

"You never knew what happened to him?" Thea asked. "How old were you?"

"I was three. And no—I never knew."

"You," the dead voice said. He was inching closer, and Thea knew she had to turn around and face it with Freddy.

The fear—surely the fear was as bad as anything. *Seeing something can't hurt you. It won't touch you. You won't let it touch you.*

She turned.

Her stomach roiled and yet—she was surprised to feel as much pity as terror. The dead thing lurching toward them in the shadows looked desperate.

Could my father be . . . like this?

"Mr. Schiffer . . ." Freddy said.

The dead man breathed raggedly. "Mr. Schiffer . . ." it repeated. "So long since I have heard . . . my name." He took a step closer. "It's you . . . little Frederick Linden . . . all grown up . . . look like your mother . . ."

Freddy clutched Thea's arm. "Why are you here?" he shouted. "How did you, of all people, get down here?"

The sunken eyes bulged a bit. Thea dropped her eyes to the ground again. "They took me," he said. "Years and years of *tests* . . . potions and needles and trances and treatments to keep me alive. But I got free. I showed them, yes. . . . Find yourself a new guinea pig. They have so many now." He reached for Freddy with fingers that were hardly more than bones and nails. "Where were *you*, Freddy? You're the one who called me back."

Slowly, slowly, Freddy let go of Thea. "I'm here now. I only ask one thing of you, Mr. Schiffer. Do you know the way to the underground?"

"Yesss . . ."

"Show us there. Please."

"I don't want to eat the girl," the man—she couldn't think of him as Mr. Schiffer—said.

"You won't," Freddy said very firmly.

The man started to move, and Freddy followed. Thea ran prayers through her head because she didn't know what to do anymore. She didn't want to see her father like this. She didn't want to follow the dead thing. She didn't want him to even think of eating her. She was unnerved by how calm Freddy was.

But she forced her feet forward, to stay with Freddy.

The dead man led them deeper and deeper into the tunnels,

and as they walked it seemed that all she heard was the painful shuffle of his boots and his ragged breath. Freddy never took his eyes off the man. Thea mostly kept her eyes on Freddy. The man led them down another set of stairs, and there Thea imagined she was in the very belly of the earth, far from the sun or the sky or any open space.

A single light shone ahead. Thea had never known how comforting one weak lightbulb in the darkness could be.

"Are we getting close?" Freddy asked.

"Yesss . . ." The man stepped into the electric light, which was stronger than the glow of the lantern. "I want . . . flesh. I want to live again. Please help me." He reached for the edge of Freddy's jacket, and Freddy stepped back.

"Mr. Schiffer, I have to let you go. You need to go on to the next world."

The dead man shook his head. One of the greasy tangles of his remaining hair fell into his eyes. "All these years of this, and all I get is *death*? You owe me something, boy. I deserve to go home." His eyes slid to Thea. They seemed to strain in their sockets, trying to get a good look at her. "Just a good taste, how much better I'd feel . . ."

Suddenly his hand snatched out and grabbed Thea's arm. She would rather have a dozen rats crawl over her than one touch from him, his awful, withered flesh. She tried to pull away, tried to kick him—tried not to *feel* how his fingers gripped her. Freddy hit him across the chest with the curtain rod, and he screamed like a wounded animal, but he yanked on her harder.

"Freddy!"

Freddy grabbed Mr. Schiffer's arm, and abruptly his hand went limp, falling away from her, his body crumpling to the ground.

"Is he—?"

Freddy was breathing hard. "He's dead."

THIRTY-EIGHT

Freddy raked his hand through his hair as though trying to wipe away the feel of Mr. Schiffer's skin. "He was a carpenter. He had a daughter—or maybe even two—I can't remember anymore." His expression hardened as he stared at the body. "The Valkenraths must have used him to figure out the serum."

"Poor man." Thea never would have thought her heart could break over something she found so horrifying. She lowered her head and whispered a prayer for him. It was a lonely place to die.

"If only I'd known he was here," Freddy said.

She squeezed his shoulder, and he started moving forward again.

Knowing they were drawing close, they quickened their pace, and soon they reached another abandoned—but lit—subway station.

"Ahead," Freddy said. "I can sense them."

Upstairs, hallways branched left and right, with regularly spaced doors. Everything here was ordered and lifeless, drained of color and personality. Thea heard a few doors opening, and some low voices.

"It sounds like they're awake," she said.

"I wonder if the Valkenraths got here before us." Freddy looked grim. He started creeping rather than walking. It was hard for Thea to keep her shoes from clicking on the floors.

". . . maybe I should see what's going on," a man was saying.

"Do you think something's happened with those two girls who were in the cage?" another man answered.

"Why would I have heard a gunshot?"

Thea glanced at Freddy, and he nodded and turned the corner, revealing himself to the men standing there. There were actually a good half dozen of them, although only two had been speaking, and they all looked stunned.

"Who are you?" one of the men asked. "You look familiar." He was the tallest among them, and perhaps the oldest as well, with a large bald spot. But all the men looked very similar: gray faces in gray clothes, tired faces that didn't really look any different from those of the workers who poured off the trains in the morning to work in the city.

"We're revolutionaries," Freddy said. "We're going to lead you out of here."

"No way out," one of the men said, so promptly that Thea sensed he'd said it a hundred times.

"But then how did they get in?" a younger man asked, looking excited. "Where did you come from?"

She shot Freddy a quick glance, realizing she wasn't sure she could find her way back; it wasn't as if they'd had bread crumbs to drop. "The Vogelsburg subway station," she said.

"Something's already going on," the balding man said. "Thomas heard shots in the cafeteria."

"Guards are massing around there," said a younger man, who looked excited. He was just joining the conversation, having come down the hall as they talked.

"Please listen to me," Freddy said, raising his voice above their conversation. "All of you need to get out of here. You're very close to the outside world, and there are people aboveground ready to help you. Wake everyone up and gather out here in the halls. I'll lead the way."

They were all looking at Freddy with confusion and almost a touch of awe.

"Who are you?" the man with the bald spot asked again. "I know you."

"*Hurry,*" Freddy said. "We don't have much time. Get moving—make sure everyone's up."

"But where are we going?" one of the men asked. "What's aboveground? This is all we know."

Thea remembered Arabella saying at the meeting that the workers might have no memories. But being confronted with it—it was worse than Thea had expected. Would her father even know her face when she found him?

"What's aboveground? Your families." Freddy stepped up onto the concrete ledge beside a stairwell so he could be seen by the increasing crowd—a few women were trickling in at the back now. "You might not remember them—but they remember you. They miss you. They think you are all dead and gone. All of you, in your old lives, you were parents, and children, soldiers and laborers and writers—every kind of person, and they took that from you, to force you into slavery down here. But it can all end tonight. You can be free, and when your families see you, they will know of your imprisonment, and this can never happen again."

Thea could see that the people believed him. Maybe they didn't remember, but they knew there was more to their lives; some of them had tears in their eyes.

She could hardly bear to see their hope, knowing that Freddy had to lead them with a lie. He could promise them freedom, but not for long.

"Now, go, gather everyone here. I know there are more of you." He spread his arms, and the people began to disperse, even as more bleary, pajama-clad workers were wandering in.

Freddy stepped down off the ledge and rubbed his head. "I hope this works."

"It looks like they're listening to you, at least." Some of the people were ducking back into their rooms and grabbing things—clothes, sticks, even a tobacco tin. "But I need to find my father."

"I'm sure we'll see him."

"I don't know—what if he just pushes his way out through the crowd and we never cross paths? Can you sense him?"

"I'm not sure. There are so many people here. Maybe if I take your hand."

She had not touched his hand again, all this time, since the first two visions. Now she offered her hand, and when their fingers met, the vision of her father flashed through her mind once more.

"Come on," Freddy said, keeping hold of her hand. "I think I can find him, but we need to hurry. I don't want to abandon the crowd for long."

They stuck to the walls, slipping by against the tide as workers poured out of starkly lit halls and flowed down stairs.

"Here," Freddy said, gesturing to an empty hall. "Up ahead. He's here somewhere."

Thea heard male voices, speaking low behind one of the doors, and a familiar head peered out when their footsteps drew nearer. "Who—who are you?" Familiar brows furrowed, and her heart almost stopped.

"It's me, it's me, Thea! I'm your daughter, Thea!"

"Thea . . ."

She could not imagine a longer moment than this one, when she saw her father after eight years of hoping for him, convincing herself he was gone forever, missing him, seeing him every time she touched her mother . . . and now, having him look at her like this. His face searched hers. Hopeful—but unsure.

The forgetting—it must have saved him from bound-sickness. But she hardly knew which was worse.

"My daughter," he said. "Thea. That's your name."

"Thea!" she repeated. "Please . . . remember." She reached for him, and he took her hand. This seemed to spark recognition in his eyes.

"I've been trying to remember for so long . . . Thea." He threw his arms around her. "Thea, Thea." He kept saying her name and looking her over, as if trying to join two pieces of a puzzle.

Her eyes ran over every detail of his face, every line and crease. He didn't look as if he'd aged from the last photographs that were taken. His hair was the same shade as hers. They both had the faintest of freckles on their noses. He was hers, hers. *Don't take him away. . . .*

"So many times I almost remembered you," he said, tears trailing from his eyes. "It was maddening. Just little pieces. But—yes—yes, I'm starting to remember. You've grown so much." He put his hands to her cheeks now. Her hands, grubby from her travels, had left smears of dirt on his shoulders and face.

"You're here, you're alive." The word slipped out, and just as quickly she thought, *No—*

She could feel Freddy's eyes on her, and when she glanced back at him, he turned away.

She was only making this harder for him. But she needed this moment.

She put her head against her father, clinging to him. She was somewhere beyond joy or grief, simply swamped with every emotion until she felt drowned by her feelings, until she could hardly imagine she had ever been laughing with Nan or working at the Telephone Club. This moment was all there was or had ever been.

"Thea," her father said. "That boy you came with . . ." He paused heavily. "Who is he?"

"He—" How could she talk about this now?

"I'm starting to remember him, too." He paused and frowned. "I was injured, and he . . . was there when I woke up. He was younger, though. About your age. I mean, when I last saw you. He had blond hair streaked with silver then. I'd never seen anything like it."

"He . . . has magic," she said. She struggled for words to explain.

"The men in my dorms, we've been here for many years, and we've long thought"—he held her shoulders gently—"that we're dead, only we've been kept in some unnatural half-life."

"Yes," she whispered. "But I don't want to be the one to tell you. . . ."

"This life isn't natural," he said, clutching her shoulders a little tighter. "All of us veterans feel we've accepted that. If he's here to undo the magic . . . then . . . that's what we want."

She nodded, swallowing her sadness—the danger of this situation felt too close to lose herself in sorrow. "Do you think other people are going to remember Freddy, too?"

"Possibly."

"That isn't good. We don't want a panic. We have to get everyone moving out of here. There isn't time." She caught Freddy's eyes.

"We'll just have to move as quickly as we can," he said.

"Yes." She drew closer to Freddy as they hurried back to the gathering crowd, but she held her father's hand. She was never going to forget how his hand felt—warm and comforting and perfectly fatherlike. It seemed smaller than it used to be, but only because she had grown. He still felt strong.

Freddy had just stepped onto the ledge again when a worker came running from one of the halls, shouting, "Valkenrath's dead!" His footsteps stopped just long enough for him to shout it again, then moved on. She heard him slow again and pound on doors, still screaming the message, and now the conversation in the room rose to a din. Some of the people moved out to see what was going on.

Freddy shot Thea a glance of alarm. The workers were looking to him now.

"Well—good!" he said. "He won't be able to stop you. Follow me!"

The workers parted to let him move forward. Not long ago they'd found six men, and now there seemed to be people everywhere she looked, more than on the sidewalks of Lampenlight on Saturday night. As Freddy made his way down another hall, the crowd pressed in just behind them.

It wasn't difficult to figure out where to go. She heard shouting in the distance. As they drew closer, they crossed paths with a few workers who had gone ahead to see what was going on. "There's a strange woman in the cafeteria," one of them said. "She's the one who shot Valkenrath."

"Are there guards up there?" her father asked.

"Yes. Some."

Freddy pushed forward to a group of milling guards, all of a similar height and build, wearing what looked like police uniforms stripped of badges or markings. Their eyes alighted on Freddy with obvious recognition.

"Freddy," one of them said, with an undercurrent of relief running beneath his military bearing. "Gerik's asking for you."

"Is it true that Uncle is dead?"

"He's been shot. But what are you doing down here?"

"Let me see him," Freddy said.

The guards were giving the workers a hard look. One of

them outstretched a palm, indicating they should keep back, as they opened the doors for Freddy.

"Them too," Freddy said, indicating Thea and her father.

"But—that's—" The guards looked flustered. "You shouldn't be down here. We can't let them in."

"If you want me to revive Uncle, then I insist," Freddy said.

Some of the workers were clustering behind Thea and her father. Waiting to see what would happen. Their energy was beginning to shift; they were growing bolder. She felt it. But for now they kept a distance.

"All right," one of the guards said, stepping aside. "Quickly."

Thea and her father hurried into a large room with tables and chairs from one wall to another.

That was when she saw Nan.

Nan, her clothes bloody, her face grim and streaked with tears.

THIRTY-NINE

"Nan!" Thea flung her arms around her friend. "You're—you're *here*!" She pulled back, taking in the dried blood on Nan's clothes, skimming her fingers over the crusty, ragged bits of Nan's shirt. "What happened to you?"

"I was shot. But—but I'm all right."

"Shot?"

"I'm all right," Nan said insistently, as if she could force it into truth, and quickly she threw her arms around Thea, as if that could make it true, too.

They broke apart again as Gerik, a gun in his hand, muscled his way past a flood of workers to get to Freddy.

"Freddy!" he said, his empty hand flung toward his brother. "Don't just stand there! We need Rory. Everything's out of control."

"I won't revive him unless you call the guards off and let the workers go," Freddy said.

"I know *she's* gotten to you." It was obvious who "she" was, even though he didn't look at Arabella. "But there's no time for you to listen to some foolish radical! She doesn't know the first thing about running this city."

"She hasn't gotten to me," Freddy said. "It's you who lied to me my entire life. You told me my magic was saving people, when you've exploited them all along. And you were going to let me degenerate until I was an invalid, weren't you? That's why you wanted me to have children."

"Yes, to save you!"

"Save me," Freddy repeated, his voice dangerously low. "You know this is your chance to redeem yourself, Gerik. To tell me the truth. The only reason you wanted to save me was because you know that if I die, they all die."

Now Gerik shot a glare Arabella's way. "Lad, I don't know what—"

"Don't 'lad' me. I'm not your little boy. I'm the person who holds the fate of all the workers."

Gerik had barely begun to lift his arm in a direction Arabella apparently didn't like when she suddenly grabbed Freddy's arm and pressed the gun to his head. "Gerik, I think you're just stalling for time now. Listen to the boy, or I'll take him down with me. If he dies, all the workers will be gone in a blink."

Thea thought of the gun in her purse, but Arabella kept glancing back and forth, although she always returned to Gerik. She was watching for anyone to make a move. And Thea had never shot a gun before.

"He's going to kill the workers anyway," Gerik snapped.

"Gerik!" Freddy sounded briefly hurt. Then his eyes flicked to the corpse of Gerik's brother on the floor. "You and Uncle can see each other again in hell."

Thea couldn't imagine what Freddy must be feeling. Sometimes she had felt so alone, caring for Mother, but it must be far worse to be raised by someone who cared for your power instead of your own self.

Gerik looked as if he'd been struck. "Freddy, I cared for you like a son. I did. But I couldn't forget why you had come to me. And what do you think will happen when these workers go free? They all run to their families? They have no memories. And they need serum. You know about the serum. They already haven't had it since breakfast. By tomorrow night the city will be overrun by monsters—or corpses."

Arabella let Freddy go. "*You* started all of this, Gerik Valkenrath," she said.

Gerik made a brief motion of his hand, and then he suddenly snatched Thea's arm, while a guard rushed to grab Arabella before she could react. Now Thea had the cold barrel of a gun pressed to her own temple. Gerik's fingers were digging into the skin of her upper arm painfully, but she didn't dare move. Both her father and Nan were standing frozen, separated from her now by the eternal space between a gun and her head.

"Freddy, let's try this again," Gerik said. "If you kill all these people, you're killing the heart of the city. You need to revive my brother and come with me, then I will explain it all to you." Thea tried to keep still, tried not to think about the metal warming where it touched her.

"I have no reason to trust you anymore," Freddy said. "And this has nothing to do with Thea. Let her go."

"Tell me honestly," Gerik said. "Do you really want to stop using your magic? Can you, even? It's a gift. It's what you live for. You know it. You could never really be satisfied tinkering with clocks."

Freddy shifted his stance slightly, revealing that Gerik had hit upon some truth, but he said, "At least I'd be working with my real father."

Gerik's grip on Thea's arm tightened. He was afraid, too. He knew he was losing. Thea's eyes flicked to Nan. Thea had always admired Nan's bravery, but Nan had never looked bloody and broken like this. And Thea's father? He looked like he wanted to act, but there was a guard standing right behind him, glaring and obvious.

Thea sucked in a breath and threw her weight away from Gerik, twisting her arm against his grasp.

Freddy shoved a guard out of the way and lunged for Gerik's arm, trying to get the gun. Thea's father ran to her. "Are you all right, Thea?"

"Fine."

"Gerik, please," Freddy said, suddenly lifting his hands. Gerik still had the gun after their struggle. "Is this really how you want it to be? Threatening me? Pointing a gun at a girl who just wanted to know where her loved ones went?"

Gerik hissed a curse under his breath, but he sounded defeated. "Damn it, Freddy." Then he said, "Just let me talk to Rory one last time."

The workers had been massing around the door of the cafeteria, now barely contained by the guards.

"Tell the guards to leave the workers alone," Freddy told Gerik. "Then I'll revive, one last time."

"Fine," Gerik said. "You heard him. Let them go."

The guards lowered their weapons.

This was it now.

The beginning of the end.

FORTY

Thea turned to Nan. She didn't want to think about Nan wearing a bloody work suit, Nan doomed to death like everyone else. She had no words.

"I'm so sorry," she said, even though those words didn't feel right, either.

Nan drew back. She had an odd smile. "I'm not going to die," she said.

"You're . . . not?"

"I'll explain later," she said. She looked behind her at the girl in the cage.

"Who is that?" Thea asked.

"That's Arabella's daughter . . . Sigi." Nan swallowed, as if struggling to find words. "They didn't give her serum for a couple of days, to punish her, so she degenerated, and she's coming out of it. But she's still—she—she was my best friend down here, and maybe more."

"Nan . . ." This wasn't like Nan. She didn't seem empty anymore. "Oh, Nan . . ." Thea put her arms around her friend again. She didn't know what to say. Sigi was going to die, and maybe she wouldn't even be well enough to say good-bye. Thea could imagine nothing worse than seeing a loved one turn into a horror like the man in the tunnels.

Nan finally shoved her away gently. "I'll be all right. You should go with your father. I'll find you later."

Freddy had walked toward them as they talked, his face drawn. "Thea, you should take your father and go. I still have to revive Uncle and make sure they don't try to stop the escape. I know where you live. Wait for me at your apartment."

She searched his face, wondering if she'd ever see it again. But she understood that they each had a task, and neither one of them would have peace until it was done. She took one of his hands and one of Nan's. "Stay safe, both of you."

Nan forced a smile. "I will if you will."

Thea hurried back to Father's side, and they started to walk out together with the crowd. The way out was clear now; she didn't even see the guards around anymore. Maybe they were planning on skipping town before things got ugly for them, too. A few of the workers, talking to one another excitedly about seeing the sky, quickened their steps, but others were very quiet and solemn, and she wondered if they were the ones who guessed at the truth, the way her father had.

Father glanced at her. "So you're pretty close with that Freddy, aren't you?" He sounded like he was trying to cover concern with a teasing tone, and that was so like him that it hurt.

She looked down, making a feeble attempt to brush grime off her coat. "Sort of. We're only just getting to know each other, really, but it's been so intense." She hastily added, "I mean all of this. Rescuing you and everyone else. Not us. I haven't even kissed him yet. I mean, we're not—"

"Yet, eh?" He smiled. "You don't have to explain. I know we don't have enough time to say everything. I guess no one ever does. But you look well."

Well. It seemed such a weak word to describe anything. But it was true—there never was enough time or enough words to say everything.

As they walked, she tried to sum up the past eight years. Good things first. They still had the same apartment. Rationing had ended. They all missed him very much, but they managed. As she spoke, bad things wormed their way to the surface: Mother's illness and Thea's having to leave school . . . He was so familiar and so distant at once, and she felt like he ought to know it all already. When he started asking questions about his life with her and her mother, she didn't know how to answer.

"We're going to try to find her," Thea said. "I'm sure you'll remember her better when you see her."

"Sometimes I see her face in my dreams," he said. "I can't wait to remember the woman it belongs to."

They emerged into what appeared to be a cellar. She heard shouting somewhere above her head, and footsteps thumping on the floor. So many workers were trying to escape up this single staircase that everyone was backing up into the cellar like herded cattle.

People were still cramming in behind her, faster than they could move ahead. She was pressed against the wall. The room was quite stuffy, but there wasn't enough space for her to get her coat off.

Her father called down, "Wait! There's no room!"

"What's going on?" called one of the men halfway up the stairs. "We all want to get out of here! There are still more coming!"

"Please, stay calm!" Thea said, feeling the mounting panic in the narrow space. "There will be help coming outside. Break the windows!" she shouted upstairs. "Get out of the house any way you can, as quickly as you can!"

Just above her head, the lights flickered as the bottleneck on the stairs began to ease.

She clutched her father's hand tighter and pushed her way forward.

FORTY-ONE

Nan watched the workers flow past her, to see the sky, to breathe fresh air.

Sigi was curled up in the cage, face to the wall, breathing raggedly. Arabella had the door open and was trying to coax her out. "Sigi, darling? Please. It's all right. Please look at me."

Sigi didn't respond. Nan remembered when Helma was in the cage and Sigi told her not to look. *I'd hate being looked at if—*

Freddy was crouching, placing his hands on Rory. The older man stirred to life. He seemed angry at Freddy, but Gerik said, loud enough for Nan to hear, "I begged him to! I wanted a chance to say good-bye to you, damn it!"

A moment later, Freddy left them alone. He glanced around, saw Nan looking at him, and smiled faintly, awkwardly.

"You do have a gift, you know," she said.

"Huh." He looked skeptical.

"You allow people to say good-bye."

Freddy glanced back at Gerik and Rory. Now they appeared to be arguing, in a quiet way. "For what it's worth."

"It's worth a lot." Her eyes wandered, almost against her will, back to Arabella, keeping watch over Sigi.

"Your friend?" Freddy asked more gently.

"Something like that. . . ." Nan's mouth twisted briefly. "I don't have much to go home to."

"Thea's missed you terribly," he said. "She talked about you all the time." He raised his eyebrows. "But I know exactly what you mean. For what that's worth."

"That's worth a lot, too." She chewed her lip. Thea would need her. It helped, to tell herself that someone would need her and love her.

"Mother?" Sigi's bleary voice jolted Nan's attention. Sigi's curls stirred on the floor, and then she drew herself into a sitting position. Her face looked drawn but Sigi-like once again.

"Sigi?" Arabella reached to smooth her daughter's wayward hair.

Sigi's eyes darted to Nan and then away again, and she shuddered. "Mother—"

"Please listen, Sigi. I know we've never gotten along, but I need to say good-bye to you," Arabella said. "I wasn't a very good mother. I know. I've always been so obsessed with the resistance. But when you disappeared, it became—more meaningful. The least I could do, in the end, was to have vengeance for you."

"Oh, *Mother*," Sigi whispered. She drew herself into a hunched position, letting her hair hide her face.

"When you were gone, my dearest girl, oh—forgive me, but I read all your diaries and papers, and I realized how much we have in common that I never knew. How bright you are—"

"My diaries!" Sigi moaned. "Please stop. I don't want to remember. Those were—they weren't for you to see."

"But I was grateful for those diaries, Sigi. I needed to understand you. The things you'd never told me. The things you cared about. The reasons you took your own life. We're more alike than I ever realized. I know I've made such awful mistakes. How can I make you understand how much I love you?"

"You could have cared more when I was actually alive." Sigi grabbed her mother's arm. "Mother, I do love you. Of course I do. But you never really listened to me. You wanted me to be someone I never was. Even now you're telling me I'm more like you than you ever thought? That was the problem. You only loved me when I was *like* you. You didn't want a daughter who was stocky and didn't care about fashion. Who liked sad poetry and slapstick comedy. Who could be horribly shy and hated having a fuss made over her. And why would I want you to have vengeance for me? If you read my diaries, you'd know that I'm a pacifist!"

"Well, I—" Arabella faltered.

"She wasn't all wrong, Sigi," Nan said. "Something had to be done to save all of us, and your mother did it. She was wrong about some things, but not that."

Sigi finally looked at Nan again. "Nan . . . I'm sorry about everything. I must have been . . . so awful. I remember it, even though it seemed like it wasn't me at all."

Nan took a step closer to her. "It wasn't you." She crouched in front of Sigi and took her hand. "We don't have much time, so I just want you to know . . ." All the things she felt weighed upon her, and Arabella's and Freddy's presence froze her words.

262

She would never have the time alone with Sigi that she wished for, so she just had to say something. "Your kiss is the color green. When I was lying there, half dead, I thought of you, and I saw it. It was familiar . . . and beautiful."

"Is it really true?" Sigi whispered. "You really can't see colors?"

"Only that one. But I'll never forget it. I'll never forget you." Now the memory of green was like the feeling of sadness. A single color in her vision, a single emotion in her heart.

"Oh, Nan . . ." Sigi slowly looked around, as if she had a sudden new awareness of her surroundings. "I'm going to die down here without seeing the sunrise, aren't I?"

"No. We'll get you out of here." Nan looked behind her. An endless stream of workers moved slowly down the hall.

Sigi shook her head. "It's all right. I don't want to fight my way through that. You could get hurt." She wiped her nose. "You'll stay with me, won't you?"

"Of course."

"No!" Arabella suddenly whirled on Freddy. "I won't let you take her." She grabbed his arm. "You can't take her!"

"Mother, stop that! For heaven's sake, he isn't the Grim Reaper!"

"No! This isn't right. I'm your mother. My life is already past its prime. I've done everything I ever wanted to do, and then some, and I don't even know what I'm good for anymore. You're so young. You have so much to do, so much to experience." She shook Freddy again. "Take me. Take me in her place."

"I can't defy death," Freddy said. "You certainly agreed on that point up until now."

"This is different," Arabella said. "I know a soul must go to its death. I know there has to be a sacrifice. That's why I'm willing to make it. Maybe I wasn't a very good mother in life, but I can be one now. Freddy . . . you can do it. I know you can. You can bring *taxidermy* to life. What can't you do, when it comes to the business of death?"

"Freddy . . . you can't—can you?" Nan's voice was shaking. She didn't want to let herself hope for more time with Sigi. A life with Thea and Freddy and *Sigi*. They had all been through so much, and they could all be together.

She briefly shut her eyes. It wasn't right to ask any more of Freddy.

"I don't know how difficult the spell will be," Freddy said. "But I'm willing to try."

"You don't even know me," Sigi said. "I can't ask you to do something like that!"

"But I want Thea to be happy. And Thea cares for Nan. And Nan clearly cares for you. So I almost know you." He turned to Arabella. "Are you sure?"

"I am."

"Mother, you can't do this." Sigi finally got to her feet.

"Go see thousands of sunrises, Sigi," Arabella said.

ꓷORTY-TꟼO

reddy took Sigi's hand, and then Arabella's. Sigi's was cold, but her face was almost back to normal now, her eyes bright and strong.

In theory, he knew precisely what to do. He needed to take the thread connecting him to Sigi and connect it to Arabella. He thought he could use the threads as a conduit, trading her life for Sigi's fated death. Then he would sever both threads. If he was able to do this, he would no longer be just a reviver. He might find other ways to save lives in the future, use his magic in ways Gerik and Uncle never imagined—redeem himself for all his unintentional sins.

"Have you said your good-byes?" he asked Arabella.

"Are you sure this will work?" Sigi grabbed Nan's arm.

"Yes," he said, even if it wasn't quite true.

Arabella lay on the floor and shut her eyes. "I don't want to *fall* when I die," she said. She reached for Sigi's other hand. "I'm ready."

"Oh, Mother, stop," Sigi said, starting to cry. "I can't stand it."

Arabella almost—*almost*—looked pleased, as if all she had wanted in life was to hear Sigi cry on her deathbed.

He let the magic flow. Warmth spread to him from Arabella and then into Sigi, much more vibrant than the magic he felt when he revived the dead. He had always given life, and now he was taking it first. His body felt as pliable as jelly, his senses fuzzy, his connection to the ground weak. But none of this was bad.

This was the strongest magic he had ever felt.

And now the threads. He severed them, breaking the spell. Arabella was gone. Sigi was still here. He had done it.

His head was still full of the dizzying magic, and he reached for the ground. Where was it? This was as bad as when he brought Nan back. No . . . worse. His stomach convulsed, his eyes blurred.

"No," he spat out. It was always this—the thing he loved, the thing he was best at, was also his undoing. He loved his magic, and yet it was killing him. The room spun worse than ever. "I need to—"

He felt an arm—probably Nan's, thin as it was—support his shoulders.

"Freddy," she said firmly. "You look like you want to faint."

"I won't," he insisted, but she was right. He was so very weak. "I'm . . . fine," he managed, and she helped him find the floor.

FORTY-THREE

"He's out." Nan was holding him up.

"Well, I can't blame him." Sigi was staring at her mother. "He did it." She bowed her head. "I—I can't believe—"

"We have to get Freddy out of here." Nan spoke softly to Sigi, but she looked at the Valkenraths. "Just wait here a moment."

Nan stalked over to Rory. He was sitting on the ground—something she doubted he'd done in a while—with his hands crossed over his knees. He was profoundly quiet while Gerik kept going on about "that time when" and "remember how Father . . ." He sounded apologetic and distressed, but when Nan approached them, he broke off and looked angry.

"If you hadn't started all of this . . ." he said. "I don't know what I'm supposed to do now. Everything's going to hell. And you "

Nan was standing, patient and strangely calm.

"Stop looking at me like that," Gerik snapped. "You won't be so pleased when you see what you've unleashed—when we're dealing with civil war and more starvation. Oh, the people will certainly appreciate what you've done then."

Behind Gerik, Rory slowly stood and put a hand on his brother's shoulder, quieting him. "You said I was dead inside, Nan Davies." Rory always said her last name, softly, almost mockingly. "But I saw the glittering world of my youth disappear when the empire fell. I fought for what I believed in then. I saw men die in front of my eyes. I saw arms and legs blown off. This war I opposed, because I already knew what war could do. You would have been a little girl. You might recall the starving children in the streets, the people peeling bark off trees to make soup. I was willing to do whatever it took to help the city prosper, and I don't regret dying with that choice on my head. I hope your revolution has a plan, or you will see it all happen again."

"I wouldn't have shot you," she said. "I was willing to work with you. But this magic had to stop. And I think you understand that."

"I believe what you have told me. I just hope your powers will carry you past this point, because all you've created tonight is chaos." He turned away. "I won't be here to find out. Freddy needs to let me go."

"Not yet," Gerik said. "What do I do about all this mess?"

Rory looked at him. "You're resilient, Ger. Just run like hell and lie low. The people aren't going to be kind to you when they find out what's happened."

Gerik made a grumbling sound and glanced back. "Freddy . . ." he said, tugging the tip of his mustache. Freddy was coming to, Sigi offering a hand to get him to his feet.

Rory walked over, with Gerik just behind him.

"Finish the job, Freddy," Rory said. "I don't want to watch all this break down." He noticed the prone remains of Arabella a short distance away, her face frozen in what was almost a smile, and he frowned.

"Just—like that?" Freddy asked. The pain of this responsibility was plain on his face.

"Just like that. I want to die standing."

"It's easier"—he held out a hand—"if I can touch."

Rory looked at Gerik one last time. He shook his brother's hand. Gerik looked crumpled, his face quite red. Then Rory touched Freddy's fingers. Freddy's breath caught, and the life seemed to be drawn out of Rory, deadening his eyes and loosening his stance. Gerik caught him as he fell.

"Lad, I— I'm sorry—" Gerik began.

"Don't try to turn around and apologize now. There's nothing you can say to me."

"I'm going straight to your parents' house," Gerik said. "I'll make sure they get out safely. They might need protection until the dust settles."

Freddy nodded curtly. "They'd better be safe. None of this was their fault."

"You stay safe, too," Gerik said.

"We all need to go," Nan said, taking Freddy by one rigid shoulder. "Freddy, come with us."

FORTY-FOUR

Thea and her father made it to the top of the stairs, the people behind them shoving Thea in their rush to escape. The workers were pouring out of every door and window, and Thea saw people in plain clothes stopping them as they emerged, gently questioning some, directing others. She recognized the man with the mustache from the Café Rouge.

The revolutionaries *were* here. Thank heavens. But what were they doing? A man was standing on the hood of a car, shouting, "This is your one chance to fight back! Everyone in uniform is your enemy!" A delivery truck pulled up, and a man hopped out and opened the back to reveal piles of bats and sticks. He began pressing them into every empty hand. Some of the revolutionaries themselves had pistols and shotguns in plain sight. Thea covered her grubby purse with her hand, conscious of the unused gun she carried.

Her father had stopped in his tracks when he came out into the open air. The sky was scattered with clouds that broke just to reveal half a moon, and he was staring upward.

"Father, we have to hurry. We have to find Mother, and it's dangerous here."

"We are . . . we are," he said. He kept looking up as she tugged him forward.

"I remember this," he murmured. "The city—the sky—" He wiped his eyes. "Your mother . . . I can almost feel her."

"She's just a few miles away," Thea said. "We'll see her soon."

A siren howled in the distance.

She ran for the front gate, which was flung open to the street. The asylum was a few miles away, but if they could just get away from the crowds and keep moving, they'd be all right.

Thea kept expecting that they'd soon reach the city streets she knew, the lonely streets where the only sounds were distant, the windows were dark, and dew clung to the occasional patches of grass. But these streets never seemed to appear. The revolutionaries were everywhere, forming loose barriers of humanity, and the workers were joining them to fight. It was more mob than army, but some of them held serious firepower, and she saw a girl forming balls of light from thin air. Thea had never seen anyone work magic out on the street before, and it seemed to promise more to come.

She heard an increasing amount of distant noise—shouting and gunfire. Flustered, she turned east when she meant west, and they had to backtrack a block.

The noises seemed to be getting closer quickly, and then she heard gunfire ahead, on Kline Street.

"Oh no," she said, turning back around the way they'd

just come. "Maybe we can go around. The asylum is near the hospital, and it should be safe there."

They hadn't gotten far when they heard a disconcerting rumbling behind them, like an automobile but deeper and slower, and a group of workers came running, one clutching his chest with a bloody hand, another with blood trickling down his head. Thea had barely registered this when her father suddenly shoved her to the ground. She stayed down, scraped up and gasping, as he knocked a trash can in front of her. The rumbling was very close, and a volley of shots sounded all around her.

I'm going to die, I'm going to die—

The shots rang in her ears, and her mind was empty of everything but the thought that it could all end, any second, one bullet to her head or her heart—

Then the shots ceased, and the rumbling moved on.

She peered out beyond the trash can. Her father was on the ground. She let out a cry, checked behind her to be sure it was really safe, and ran to his side. He was flat on his back, a big bloody hole punched in his chest, close to his heart. He was still moving and conscious.

An ugly sound of fear came out of her throat. It wasn't just that he'd been hurt. It was seeing it—seeing him live through this. Seeing him move his arms and sit up and clutch his chest. That wound would have killed anyone—unless he was already dead.

For all the explanations she'd heard of how her father was dead, for all that she'd told Freddy she understood she must let him go, a part of her had still brushed aside the truth of it.

Seeing him live through this told her more clearly than words could have that he was truly, truly dead. She was alive and he was dead, even though both of them were moving and speaking.

He was clutching his chest, his breathing rough.

"Does it hurt?" She didn't know what to ask. "Should I do something?"

"No, I—" His voice sounded like something blocked it, and he cleared his throat and coughed blood into his sleeve. "I'll manage. It's not much longer—is it?"

She bit her lip hard and shook her head. She helped him to his feet.

He wasn't the same anymore, though. He didn't speak now; it seemed to take all his concentration to keep moving. He didn't appear to be bleeding as much as a living person would, but he still kept his hand covering the wound. He put his other arm around her.

"I love you, Thea," he said. "I'm so sorry . . . all those years growing up without me—all the things we won't have time—"

"No—don't say those things! Father—"

"I need to rest," he said.

"But Mother *must* see you! She's the one who is sick because of you; she's the one who knew you were alive. . . ." Thea buried her face in her hands.

"I can't—" The words came painfully, and she didn't want to cause him pain, but she also needed him to speak; she wouldn't be denied his voice so close to the end. "I can't die this way, but I can be hurt. And I am hurt. I need time to knit back together. . . . I know I don't have that time. I don't know what awaits me on the other side, but I know there will always be love between you and me and your mother. And sometimes . . . we just have to accept the way things are. We have to accept that I'm leaving you. And we have to accept that maybe . . . we can't get to your mother."

"It's not far," she insisted, trying not to choke on her words. "It's not far now. I—I could bring her to you. But I don't want to leave you."

He walked into a narrow alley and sat down heavily. "I'd like that," he said, his eyes glazed. "How I'd like to see her. I can just rest a moment."

"Okay," she said. "Okay. Stay here." She quickly kissed his head. "I love you, too, Father. I'll be back very soon."

FORTY-FIVE

"Phonographs and marzipan and fall leaves," Sigi murmured beside Nan, closing her eyes as they pushed their way out with the rest of the workers. She opened them again when the entire stairwell shook so that dust and bits of plaster sprinkled on their heads.

"All that trouble to save me, and I'm going to die anyway!" Sigi cried.

Nan grabbed her hand, and so did Freddy.

"We're not going to die," he said. "I insist."

The lights flickered again, and then—gone.

"Come on," Nan said. "We can push our way out while everyone's panicked." Standing at the doors and windows of Rory's house were men she thought must belong to the resistance— their clothes were shabby and bohemian. They were moving the workers through. "This way, come on." One young man noticed their group.

"Aren't you—Sigismunda von Kaspar? And the silver-haired boy. I'd better get Yann."

The world aboveground had gone to hell. Houses and cars set on fire, people unconscious or hunched on the ground bleeding, running and fighting and shouting everywhere: revolutionaries, workers, policemen, even servants from the grand houses. Nan stayed close to the young man, who was talking to another man with silver in his hair. He noticed them and urgently waved them forward.

"What's going on?" Nan asked the man with the silver hair, whom she assumed was Yann. "Who started all the fires?"

"We did," he said, running as he spoke. "The more chaos, the better. Where is Arabella?"

"She's . . . dead," Sigi said.

He pulled off his cap. "Oh, no. . . . I'm so sorry, Miss Sigi. We've never met, but I heard a lot about you."

Sigi looked a bit appalled.

"Arabella gave her life for Sigi's," Nan said. "We need to get out of here. All of you should."

"I'll get you to safety," he said. He put his cap back on.

"We need to meet up with Thea," Freddy said.

"Don't worry—we won't forget Thea," Nan assured him.

They ran down the street after Yann. The streets were so busy it might have been a holiday, only with celebration replaced by tension. An old couple in ragged clothes ran around shouting for someone named Torsten, and Nan realized that word must have spread that the missing dead were wandering lost, and so their relatives had gone looking for them. Sirens howled nearby. She heard a gunshot. Sigi was shivering, covering her ears.

Nan put an arm around her.

"This is horrible," Sigi said. "Is this what we wanted to happen?"

"It isn't what we wanted," Nan said. "But it's a consequence."

Rory was probably right—more people would be hurt and die. That wasn't what she wanted. Of course not. But for so many years, she had carried that feeling of imbalance and wrongness inside her, and she had to let that be her compass, even if the immediate repercussions were violent.

Yann's car was old enough to need a crank. "Get in," he said while he worked at it. "She'll go in a minute."

"Where are we going?" Nan asked.

"Our base of operations, in the old factory district."

Nan wondered how far they could get in a car, but at least the windows would give them some protection.

Yann was aggressive, honking the horn liberally and driving on whichever side of the road suited him. The power was out for several blocks. People ran through the darkness, and two men carried a dead or injured person wrapped in a bloody sheet. Hundreds of stories raced by in those blocks, and none of them appeared to be happy ones.

"Don't worry," Yann said. "This is war. It's unpleasant business. But we've been preparing for it. The reign of suppression and terror will be over soon enough, and all of this paves the way for a new regime a government for the people."

"Who will lead?" Freddy asked.

"I had hoped it would be Arabella," Yann said. "But we have some different factions in our ranks. That will all shake out as we go. All I know is, we have to band together to keep anything like this from happening again. Of course, I hope you'll be right there with us, Freddy. To have you will be invaluable."

Freddy scoffed. "That certainly isn't what Arabella said. She was happy enough to kill me."

"She was . . . impulsive at times."

"Is that really a quality you want in a leader?" Freddy asked. "If I ever use my magic for anyone else again, it will have to be someone who can make good decisions."

"I'm sure the right leader will . . ." Yann trailed off as they turned the corner to an appalling sight. Half a dozen workers lay writhing in the street, conscious but shot to pieces: holes in their chests, a hand blown off. Freddy stiffened, leaning forward to get a better look.

Sigi covered her mouth. "The army must have come through," she choked, "and they can't die! They can't die unless you let them go, Freddy!"

"Stop the car!" Freddy shouted at Yann, who had slowed to maneuver around the bodies but wasn't stopping.

"We can't. We have to get you to a safe place."

"Stop the damn car!" Freddy grabbed the steering wheel, and the car jerked toward a lamppost.

FORTY-SIX

Thea had never run so fast, for so long, in her life. She was glad the night hours were hers; she was accustomed to the darkness, although she wasn't accustomed to sharing the streets with so many people at these hours, or this awful smoky smell, or the ever-present air of confusion and fear.

The asylum was a foreboding building by day, a terrifying one by night, the gothic towers looming over stone walls in the darkness. She hadn't considered how she'd get in, but even as she approached the gates, she could see a number of workers crowded at them, and then she could hear an awful sound on the wind: women shouting and moaning.

Bound-sick women.

She hadn't even thought of it, but they might sense their husbands were free. And the spell must have tugged these workers here as well, even if they didn't remember their wives enough to be sick.

A man who appeared to be a night watchman was on the other side of the gate, trying to reason with the men. "I'm afraid I can't let you in! These women are being treated for illnesses."

"But that's my wife in there!"

"What's her name?"

"I don't know. I just think she's in there. . . ."

"If none of you can tell me who you're looking for, why should I let you in?"

"Please," Thea said, making her way alongside the men to press against the metal bars. "I'm looking for Mrs. Henry Holder. She's my mother. But you'd better let all of them in. The wives will be cured of bound-sickness if they can just see their husbands."

"I—I don't know about all that. Where did they come from?"

Thea didn't have time for this! "They've been trapped underground! Brought back from the dead and robbed of their memories, and all they want is to see their wives. My father is bleeding in an alley somewhere, and if he doesn't see my mother, I'll—" She didn't know what she'd do, though. "Please!"

The night watchman looked flustered but unconvinced. "I'm under strict orders."

"Her name might be Alice," one of the men ventured. "Is there anyone named Alice?"

"I'm sorry," the night watchman said.

Thea saw that he had a gun. And she had a gun. So she might point hers at him, but she knew she couldn't shoot a man who was just trying to do his job. And would he shoot her? If there was any justice in the world, he should see all these desperate men, any of whom could have been her father, and let them in.

But he wasn't going to. Her father was dying, her mother was behind the gate, and Father Gruneman had given her the gun.

She took a deep breath and slipped her hand in her purse. Her hands were cold in the night air, and the gun cold in her grasp as she drew it out. "*Please.* Do you know what I've gone through tonight?"

He put a hand on his own weapon. "All right, miss. Calm down. Put that away."

"Let me *in*."

He removed his pistol from the holster. "Calm down," he repeated.

Her hands were sweating through the cold now. "I've had a living, walking corpse try to *eat* me. I was in the abandoned subway tunnels, searching for good men like these, trying to free them so they could see their families just one last time. Can you imagine having rotting, withering flesh trying to claw at you? Whispering for blood? Can you imagine the eyes of something dead still . . . *looking* at you?"

"I cannot," he said, sounding unsure.

"Well, in a few hours, that's what these men will become, if—if they don't see their wives!" She invented the last bit, but it burst out of her mouth as if true, because she so wanted to believe it. She wanted to think her mother's touch might heal her father, save him, keep him close forever. . . .

It was at that moment that one of the women screaming out the windows of the asylum building, across the wide green lawn, jumped out, plunging four stories. She didn't get up again.

Thea's breath caught painfully in her chest. It was too far to see if it could be her mother.

This seemed to be the last scrap of evidence the guard needed that matters had gotten beyond his control. He opened the gate.

All the men started running, and Thea with them, still holding the gun carefully. The men were faster, and they stormed the doors for her. The staff already seemed to be in an uproar, trying to corral the women. Their screams echoed through the lobby, a heartbreaking din of "Where—?" and "Let me go!" and the names of lost husbands.

Thea grabbed the first woman she saw, a young one in a nurse's dress. "Where is my mother, Mrs. Henry Holder?"

Father Gruneman had told her that hopefully she would only need to point the gun at people, and it seemed to be true. She felt like a different person with a deadly weapon in hand, the woman looking at the gun in terror. "I—I think I just saw her. I'm not sure."

Thea let the woman go, spotting her mother standing against the wall, clutching her head as if trying, amid the shouting and sobbing, to sense the magic that bound her to Thea's father.

Thea ran to her side. "Mother!"

Her mother's tense expression turned to relief. She was already dressed to move. "Your father," she said. "I know your father is close. You've seen him. You've seen Henry. Where is he?"

"He's—he's hurt. And he's going to die soon. Mother—" Her voice faltered.

"We'll get to him." Her mother grabbed Thea's arm. "We just have to hurry."

FORTY-SEVEN

The car crumpled against the post, throwing Freddy and Yann forward. They hadn't been going fast. Freddy glanced back just long enough to see Nan and Sigi blinking back at him, and then threw open the door.

He had brought these men back from the dead. Brought them back to slave away, to lose their memories—to die in agony. He ran to each of them, touching their heads or hands, severing their threads as quickly as he could. After the first two, after they realized, they started begging him, thanking him, as they died.

As if he'd done them any kind of favor. They ought to be using their last breath to curse him.

It was getting easier to feel them slip away.

Yann got out of the car. "We don't have time for this! We can't let anyone find you! Look, maybe it's time. Just let them all go. Enough of them have gotten out; we can take it from here."

Freddy turned on Yann. "This isn't your magic. I'll decide

how and when to do it. I'm not working for you, and I don't want your protection."

How long would it be before the revolutionaries wanted to keep someone important alive? He couldn't trust anyone, he realized. And Yann was already talking as though Freddy belonged to them.

"You *need* our protection," Yann said. "You know that every person aware of your existence will be looking for you, and the word will spread." He reached for Freddy. Like he was going to grab him. Drag him back into a world where his power wasn't his own.

Never again would he allow someone else to be the keeper of his magic.

"If you don't come with me, the chancellor's men will find you," Yann said.

"No." He shoved Yann and punched him in the jaw. Yann staggered back, and Freddy punched him again before he could recover.

He heard two pairs of boots behind him and saw Nan and Sigi, and this spurred him on. He wasn't alone.

Maybe Yann was right about one thing: if the workers were suffering, maybe it was time to try to let them go. But at this very moment, Thea might be rushing her father across the threshold of the asylum. He had to see her first.

They kept running until they were sure Yann wasn't following anymore. They had taken a few turns, and he wasn't in view. The power was out here, too, the streets dark and busy.

"We have to get out of these work suits," Sigi said, her voice tremulous. "If the police or the army shot those workers, they might shoot us, too, if they see us. They won't know we're alive."

"If we can just get to Thea's apartment," Freddy said, "we can figure it out from there. We're not far."

As they moved from a largely residential district to Thea's neighborhood, where shops and apartments mixed, they saw that some of the shops had been looted. Shards of window glass glinted on the sidewalk, and people were running off with cans of food.

"What is this?" Sigi said. "Are people going insane?"

"They're panicked," Nan said. "You come from a good family, so maybe you weren't fully aware of what the war years were like, but most of us had to get ration books and stand in breadlines, and sometimes the food ran out. We would stand for hours and get nothing. That wasn't really so long ago. At the first gasp of anarchy, people just want all the stuff they can stockpile."

"I knew it was bad," Sigi said. "But I guess I don't remember *how* bad."

"Well, maybe we should join in," Nan said, pointing to a raided dress shop. "We do need to get out of these work clothes."

"I think we're a little late," Sigi said. The mannequins in the window were stripped naked.

"There are still some things left," Nan said, picking her way over the glass. "What size do you wear?"

Sigi groaned and said, "I'm coming."

Freddy stood guard at the window while they quickly exchanged their work suits for dresses. Even he could tell they weren't very flattering, but neither of them complained.

Thea's street was one of the quietest they had yet seen, and they reached it as the sky was beginning to pale in the east. Just seeing a familiar place gave him renewed strength, and he charged up the stairs.

The building was silent. As if everyone was still asleep.

Thea's door was shut, and when he tried the knob, it was locked. He knocked, and there was no answer.

"She hasn't gotten here yet." Nan stated the obvious.

"What do we do?" Sigi asked.

"I hope she isn't hurt . . . or running into trouble," Freddy said.

Nan sat down against the door with a sigh. "There's no way of knowing, really. I guess we can wait for a bit. But, Freddy . . . when are you going to let the workers go, if Thea doesn't come back soon?"

"How long before they'll start to . . . turn?" Freddy asked.

Sigi's brow darkened. "Another day, I think."

"You can't wait another day," Nan said. "They're suffering. The army is shooting them to pieces. You saw what happened. And it might take Thea a long time to find her way back here."

He sat down on the stoop and closed his eyes. Nan was right. But when he imagined Thea racing to bring her father to her mother, he couldn't stand to think of ripping that chance out of her hands. He closed his eyes, trying to find the individual thread that belonged to her father. Maybe he could sense Thea through it. Maybe he could find out.

Before, he had sensed Henry through Thea's touch. Now it was not so easy. He searched through the fog of confusion and pain, and—there—

Henry was hurt. Freddy's stomach twisted. His own heart skipped as he sensed Henry's ripped insides, organs too destroyed to function, a life clinging by a thread. A thread that led back to Freddy.

He couldn't see Thea. He didn't know if she was there. He could only feel Henry's trembling life, and he knew he would have to break his promise to Thea. He would have to hope she and her mother were with him.

"The sun is rising," Sigi said softly. "I'd like to see it. Freddy, do you think you could wait for the sunrise before you let them go? Because all of us were always talking about the sun, and how we missed it."

Thinking of Henry's pain, he wanted to say no, but he might want to suffer through it and see the sunrise, too. Freddy didn't want to decide for him. "Yes, I can wait until sunrise," he told Sigi.

They found a stairwell to the roof and climbed onto its flat surface. The sky was turning a faint orange now, and then the colors began to deepen and change, blooming into different shades, transcending the drab apartments.

"Oh," Sigi said. "It's so beautiful. I forgot just how beautiful. It looks so new, like it couldn't possibly happen every day."

"Just like I promised," Nan said.

"You did," Sigi said. "But I hardly dared to believe you."

Nan took Sigi's hand, and Sigi turned as pink as the sunrise. Freddy crossed to the other side of the roof, looking not to the sun now but to the edge of darkness.

I promised you something, too, Thea. But there's no way for me to know. You'll forgive me for doing what's right, I know.

He had never before realized how quickly the sun rose. It seemed almost as if at one moment the western sky was still deep blue with a few determined stars shining in it, and in the next moment the whole world was full of all the light and hope of morning.

He closed his eyes and turned inward. Thousands of threads, years and years of spellwork . . .

In one moment it was undone.

FORTY-EIGHT

The sun was rising as they found their way back to the alley where Thea had left her father. He was still sitting there, still alert. When her mother saw him, she burst into tears, and then she flew to his side. She took his hand. He stroked her hair.

"Henry, I knew," she whispered.

"Oh, I missed you," he said. "I couldn't even remember you, and yet I missed you like a piece of my own soul. I still *knew* you."

Thea crouched alongside them, and each put an arm around her. Her tears were falling now, and she didn't stop them. She let them blind her.

"I love you both so much," her father said. "And I don't want you to be sad. It hasn't all been bad . . . only being away from my family, and knowing—knowing you were out there somewhere and I couldn't remember. It's all right now because"—he suddenly clutched his chest—"you're here."

"Father!" Now the light in his eyes was fading, and his arm was falling away from her. Her mother still clutched his hand.

He looked happy. Peaceful. Far away.

Thea nudged him, trying not to lose herself as she lost him. "It's too soon!"

Her mother pulled Thea against her, folded her arms around her, and held her against her chest. "It's all right, my love," she said, her voice cracking with tears. "I'm back. I'm free. Your father's at peace. It was enough."

"It wasn't enough."

"No. It never is, really. My other half . . . has gone . . . but we have each other again." Her mother started to cry again in earnest; they were both sobbing and holding each other, not caring that they were in some awful alley.

But even through her tears, Thea couldn't forget how much was still to be done.

"I have to get home," she said softly. "I told my friends, and—it's very important."

"I don't want to leave your father here," her mother said.

Thea didn't, either. They tried to carry him, but he was heavy. Maybe if they had a stretcher. No, even then it was so far to get him home. And what would they do with his body? Father Gruneman was dead, anyway. She didn't want anyone else to hold a funeral service. There were other bodies sprawled on the street.

They had to leave Father there. Thea covered him with her coat. It was so dirty, she would have to get a new one anyway, and she didn't feel the cold.

They both said a last good-bye, and Thea wondered what the point was, really. All these good-byes. It was awful. He was dead already. Hopefully, he was talking to Father Gruneman in the next world. She tried to cling to that thought even though it felt too pat, too perfect, like a fairy tale, but then . . . Father Gruneman loved those.

She remembered the empty feeling that everything seemed to have when Father went to war, and how it was worse when she and Mother heard he wasn't coming back. Here it was again. Like she was alone, even though her mother was there. Like nothing really mattered. Colors dulled, foods tasteless, nights sleepless. And that was why, in some ways, she hated that she had to see him again, go through it all again.

But it was also worth it.

A military truck drove by, loaded with grim-looking troops, and she remembered that the city was still dangerous. The peril was driven home even further as they reached their neighborhood and saw that many of the shops had been looted.

"I hope we'll be able to get food," her mother said. They both remembered the years of hunger. Thea wouldn't let herself think that far ahead.

And then, when she climbed the stairs, they were all there waiting for her. Nan and Sigi, and Freddy. She couldn't imagine how he must be feeling, holding all that power in his hands and letting it go—ending thousands of lives that should have ended long ago. When he saw her, he scrambled to his feet and rushed to her, searching her face.

"Thea . . . did he . . . ?"

"He died in my mother's arms," she said. She didn't need to tell him how brief it had been. Maybe one day she would tell him about that moment, one day when they were far away from this time and place.

"Thank god." He clutched her against him.

Then he released her, and she took his hand, and for the first time she could hold his hand without seeing that terrible vision. She met his eyes.

And then she kissed him.

It certainly wasn't like her parents' first kiss, on a sleigh ride in the snow, with the comfort of a simple age all around them—the kiss her mother always murmured about in the throes of bound-sickness. This was a kiss that said, *Life is short, and sometimes awful, but we've made it through what we must today, and we'll do it again tomorrow—together.*

ACKNOWLEDGMENTS

Just the other day, I found an email from 2008 where I described some of my current writing projects. One of them was this:

"The plot is based very loosely on the silent film *Metropolis*; the setting just as loosely based on Weimar Berlin. Thea is a shapeshifting teenage actress who is hiding the fact that her mother is going mad to protect her from an institution. When she is asked to impersonate the ailing queen, she uncovers a plot to exploit the city's dead as undead labor beneath the city streets."

I didn't properly begin *Dark Metropolis* until 2010, and the story obviously changed a lot! But it's amazing to think back on everything and everyone that brings a book into being. As always, I must first and foremost thank my partner, Dade. It is embarrassing to admit how much he helped to plot this story. I literally came to him like, "Tell me how to make this ending exciting and accomplish X, Y, and Z," and he rattled off a scene-by-scene plan immediately. Without him, my characters would probably still be trying to escape.

I started writing this book as I nursed my beloved cat, Tacy, through the final months of her life. It was the first story I had written from a place of grief rather than a place of joy, and while I was writing it I found out my friend Lisa Madigan, a fellow client of my agent, Jennifer Laughran, had terminal cancer. Sometimes funny thoughts come out of rough times, and in this case I had some vague idea that I would write this book to cheer Jenn up because I figured she would love it and could sell it. Amazingly this plan worked, although filling the hole left by Lisa's death is something no story could do. Lisa, you will always be missed.

I must also give hearty thanks to the Hyperion team, who have impressed me with their care and attention to detail, from cover design to copy edits, and to Tracey Keevan for making what can be an author's nightmare—your editor leaving the house—entirely painless. But especially to my editor for this book, Catherine Onder. I learned so much from working with her that I will carry with me into other books, and she also made this book a whole lot better!

While doing edits on this book I was also buying a house and moving from Florida to Maryland, the timing of which I don't recommend unless you enjoy heaps of stress, so I'm grateful to everyone who helped: my parents for support of many kinds, my sister Kate for lots of bubble wrap, my grandparents for surprise financial aid, my aunt Heidi for making a long drive to help me unpack, my awesome real estate agent Diane Derr and her team, and anyone else I might have forgotten because that entire year was a huge blur. Now I have a proper writer's dwelling, a house with stories of its own.

And, last but never least, to everyone who reads my books.